SHADOW PLAY

BOOK ONE: KIM & JESSIE

SHAWN C. BAKER

Cover art and layout by Jonathan Grimm Art.

Also by Shawn C. Baker:

A Collection of Desires: 7 Tales of Modern Horror

To Kirsten. For Everything

To my friends and family, too many to name. I love you all
for your support

To M83 for the inspiration

The black shape moved through seven-year-old Patagonia Barker's line of sight and disappeared into the darkness of the corridor to her left. It happened so fast that Patagonia - Patty for short - wasn't sure what she had seen, except that it was definitely not her older sister Kim or their friend Cassie, whose family lived in the house they were visiting. The image, firmly entrenched in that ambiguous state between a child's imagination and their burgeoning understanding of the world around them, stayed with her, and Patty sat perfectly still for several minutes, her eyes trained on the darkened corridor before her, watching for a recurrence.

There was none.

The corridor in question led to Cassie's kitchen, where just a few moments before Patty had witnessed the two older girls arguing. Patty had meant to ask for a glass of water, but seeing the basement door open, she ran back to the den without saying a word.

Cassie's basement was scary.

Alone, Patty tried to return to her dolls but could not, the image of the open door burned into her mind, a harbinger of something awful. She wanted to leave, but their parents had left Kim in charge, and as long as she was here, that's where Patty had to stay too.

Lately, Kim had taken to teasing Cassie about her fear of the basement. This even though all three of the girls believed it to be haunted. Why else would Cassie's dad forbid them to go down there, or secure the door with three large, rusted locks? Beginning just last week though, Kim had started goading her friend to find the keys for those locks. She said she had dreamt about Cassie's basement, that there was something down there calling to her. This worried Patty, as she suspected it wasn't so much the basement that Cassie was afraid of, but her father. Cassie's dad was not the kind of man you disobeyed. He had a stern face and a quick temper, and Patty knew he had hit Cassie on more than one occasion.

A scream shattered the silence of the house and Patagonia's breath caught in her throat. The voice sounded like Kim, and when it came again it seemed far away, as though it had come from…

"The basement," she said through a sob of terror.

Your sister is ours now…

Patagonia ignored the voice in her head - louder these past few days - and walked toward the kitchen, darkness swelling as the sun in the windows behind her sank below the trees that lined the property.

"Kim, is that you? Cassie?"

No answer. Bracing herself, Patty slipped through the gloom of the open doorway and emerged into the kitchen only to find the basement still wide open, and neither her sister nor Cassie anywhere to be seen.

"Don'tbeinthebasementpleasedon'tbeinthebasementpleasedon'tbeinthebasement," Patty's mantra as she picked her sister's phone up off the counter and approached the edge of the stairs that descended beneath the house. A single, exposed bulb hanged just inside the door, illuminating the first few rickety steps. Holding the phone's flashlight before her, Patty saw a brief glint far below. She sucked in a large breath, braced herself and walked straight down the stairs to the cold concrete floor, the light from the phone opening a small circle of light. Patty jumped when another girl appeared before her. She would have screamed if her common sense hadn't played its hand quick and told her what she should have inherently understood right off the bat. The girl was her. She was looking at a mirror.

Relieved, Patty let out the breath she had ransomed and turned casually in a circle. She was surrounded by mirrors. A lot of mirrors.

A noise from the stairs made her jump, and when she looked there was nothing but her own shadow, thrown by the bulb against the wall to her left. Shaken but feeling stronger for it, Patty turned back to the mirror just in time to see hands reach out of the darkness. She did not even have time to scream before she was gone.

PART I

CHAPTER 1

SATURDAY, AUGUST 24TH

The house was a behemoth. Standing in front of it, fifteen-year-old Jessie Roberts was instantly reminded of all of the haunted house movies he'd ever seen.

Well, the scary ones anyway.

"So what d'ya think, hon?"

"I think… I think it's insane mom."

"I know. But honestly, most of the houses out here are. The entire area used to be forest preserve."

"Now, that's not exactly true," WJ, Jessie's mother's co-worker chided from behind them. A world-renowned Sociology Professor, WJ had made it his mission to help Talia Roberts - one of the most sought-after Palaeoanthropologists in the nation - secure a house after accepting a teaching position at nearby Knight University. WJ had recently settled into tenure at Knight, and since meeting Talia had been nearly inseparable from her. So much so that Jessie had begun to suspect his mother's interest in WJ reached well beyond the professional.

"The forest was not legally 'preserved' until after the

houses began going up. Local lore says an eccentric billionaire moved in at the start of the twentieth century, bulldozed the few bootlegger shacks that peppered the area, and brought in a foreign architect to help establish a 'community among the trees.' They were able to build about a dozen houses before the state stepped in."

Jessie rolled his eyes. "Wikipedia much" is what he felt like saying, but out of courtesy to his mother he kept his mouth shut. WJ Wasn't a bad guy, but he always sounded like a museum tour guide. An especially annoying tour guide, truth be told. Jessie winced at the idea of having him live so close or - shriek - eventually move in with them.

"However, your mother is right about one thing, Jessie."

"Many things," Talia countered with a playful elbow to WJ's ribs, "I am right about many things."

'Yep' Jessie thought, 'boyfriend for sure. Why doesn't she just tell me?'

"Haha, okay, well in this particular instance one thing. As you can see, most of the homes here are very old and very... ornate. A lot of the architecture in this area is experimental, to say the least."

"Whoah! Hey, wait a minute, this is a Cruchetti isn't it?"

WJ's face erupted in a smile and Talia swatted him with her purse.

"You never told me that, Wendell! Cruchetti designed some of these?"

"All of them. He was the foreign architect, and Gallows Hill was his biggest project, as well as his last."

"Great," Talia said shaking her head in mock frustration, "I really don't want to get lost every time I need to find the bathroom."

"Talia, you're exaggerating."

The conversation had thus far proved distracting - and

traumatic - enough that they hadn't even made it inside yet. His mom and WJ's voices droned into the background as Jessie mounted the concrete steps that led to his new front door, a double-sided work of almost medieval craftsmanship carved from what looked like a majestic example of Cherry. Jessie grasped the doorknob, a strange, serpentine-shaped metal complete with ancient patina, and slowly pulled the door open. He peered into the darkness on the other side, the smell of abandonment filling his nostrils. In that darkness, he thought he heard something, a tiny voice in the distance:

"Cassie?"

The sound of the mover's truck pulling into the driveway behind him broke the moment, and Jessie rejoined his mother, the voice quickly dismissed as fancy.

"...all I'm saying is I agree the man was a genius, I just don't know how I feel about having to live in one of his creations. What's the theme of this one? The last one I read about was designed around Venus' orbital resonance with Earth. The breakfast nook smack dab in the center of the pentacle. How's that for your bagels and coffee?"

His mother laughed, and Jessie remembered why he tolerated WJ.

"Jessie, what do you think? I don't know if you're familiar with Cruchetti, but even if you're not, you must see that your mother is overreacting."

"Looks haunted to me."

Thankfully, the sound of Talia's cellphone ended the Cruchetti discussion. "Talia Roberts..." she said and excused herself, leaving Jessie awkwardly paired with WJ, who tended to use any time alone with Talia's son to try and force bonding.

It wasn't that Jessie had anxiety over someone replacing his father, because he barely remembered the man. What

Jessie didn't like about WJ was his self-appointed role as the 'know-it-all.'

"Well Jessie, I can certainly see why you'd say it looks haunted, but I assure you, that's not the case."

"No shit, Sherlock,"

"What was that, Jessie?"

"Nothing."

They stood in silence for a few moments, watching the movers begin to unload the truck. There were three of them, all long-haired and tattooed. Jessie smiled when he sensed this made WJ uneasy.

"Now, if they can just manage to not damage anything."

"What's to damage Wendell?" Talia rejoined them, "All we have is a couch, a desk, and a couple of lamps."

"Yeah, well, you didn't exactly hire the cream of the crop when it comes to–"

Again with the flirty elbow.

"Could you knock it off, please? If they hear you, they're liable to chuck my computer out the window."

"Sorry… GREAT JOB BOYS!" Wendell's exaggerated praise for the movers was the last straw; if his mother and WJ were going to act like love-struck teenagers, Jessie was out.

"Ah, I'm going to go explore a bit, okay guys?"

"Sure honey, just be back in time to eat. Oh god, I haven't even had time to think about that. What should we do for dinner?"

"Don't worry. You like pizza, don't you Jessie?" Wendell called after him as Jessie flipped up his hoodie and skulked away. "Of course I like pizza, you ask me that like once a week."

"What's that Jessie?"

"Yo-kay! Pizza it is guys! Be back around seven latest."

With his back to them, Jessie raised his hand above his

head and waved as he walked away, then switched it to a one-finger salute after he'd lowered it again. He didn't want to give his mom a hard time, which meant he didn't want to be overtly mean to WJ, but enough…

"…is enough."

CHAPTER 2

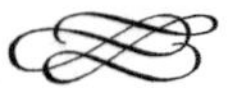

Coming out of the drive, Jessie headed left, surveying the land around him. His mother and Wendell were right about one thing: what houses he saw were huge. The one directly next to theirs was something out of a Victorian novel. Staring at its dark, wooden façade, Jessie traced the long driveway's twists and turns back at least a quarter of a mile. The entire route was lined with imitation British gas lamps, and terminated at another massive front door, this one complete with demon-faced knockers.

"Dracula's place," he said to himself.

"Naw, he lives one over. This one's empty," the voice from behind him startled Jessie, and when he spun around, he found himself face-to-face with a tall, pretty girl roughly his own age. She had long, fiery-red hair and deep, impossibly black, pupil-less eyes.

"Something wrong?"

"Your… your eyes?"

"They're contacts."

Jessie laughed. He felt his posture relax, noticed the girl did the same.

"You scared the hell outta me!"

"I do that sometimes."

She was striking, her eyes accentuated by gothic make-up the likes of which Jessie had only ever seen in music videos or weird movies. No one he'd met in real life had ever made such a commitment. But call him crazy – on this particular girl, it worked.

Boy did it work.

"So, you're moving into the old Tenorio place, huh?"

"Uh, I guess, although I don't know who they are. I'm Jessie."

"Kim. Kim Corduroy. Like the pants."

"Ha. Jessie Roberts, like… ah, like Julia Roberts."

"Who?"

"Old movie star? Never mind." Now that the introductions were dispensed with, his adrenaline seeped away, replaced instead by something else. Nerves. The more he looked at her, the more he realized this girl was gorgeous!

"So, ah… you live around here, I guess?"

"Only on the weekends. My dad lives over there," Kim turned and pointed across the property opposite, to a house that sat so far back on a wooded hill it looked like the emerging moon was balanced on its uppermost spire. The house, like all the others he'd seen thus far, looked fortified and mysterious.

"Wow, people around here sure like their privacy, huh?"

"I guess. My dad says it's because a lot of bootleggers and gangsters used to live around here. Personally, I just think this town attracts weirdoes. Are you a weirdo?"

"Ah…" Jessie fumbled at being put on the spot.

"I guess you wouldn't tell me if you were."

They began to walk.

"Where'd you come from Jessie Roberts?"

"All over. We move around a lot."

"Cool. You ever been out of the country?"

"Yeah, but not since I was too young to remember anything, just vague images of deserts and forests and stuff."

"That's weird. Not cities?"

"Not so much. My mom's an anthropologist, so we usually live by digs."

"What's she digging for here?"

"No. I mean, nothing. She's teaching at the University this semester, hoping to settle there."

Kim thought for a moment and then nodded in something Jessie hopelessly tried to peg as either understanding or approval.

They were nearing the end of Jessie's street, and the last house on the block had a mailbox that looked like a large, old boat. He stopped to study it for a moment.

"Who lives here, Captain Ahab?"

"*This* is Dracula, goes by Old Man Freighter 'round these parts."

"Freighter? Really? So one of my new neighbors is Corduroy and the other's Freighter."

Jessie was floored when Kim lashed out and gave him a hearty push with both her hands. His feet almost skidded out from under him in the loose gravel before the mailbox.

"What of it?"

"Whoah! Nothing, I'm just starting to feel like my last name is pretty freakin' lame is all."

There was a tense moment where it seemed as though Kim might be sizing up whether or not he was making a joke at her expense, then she smiled and gave him another, more good-natured push.

"You're pretty tough. So, if you only stay with your dad on the weekends, where do you live the rest of the time?"

"With my mom silly. My mom and little sister."

"Oh. Do they live nearby?"

Kim didn't answer, and Jessie got the impression he was calling upon things he shouldn't, so he let it drop. As they moved past Freighter's, the street forked and dead-ended in forest and rubble.

"Whoah! What's this?"

Before them, a leaning street sign identified the disappearing road as Caliper Lane. A few steps beyond that, the blacktop crumbled into wasted gravel, and the woods swelled to consume it entirely. A little further on Jessie could see the remains of a house.

"This? It's a doorway. To another world."

"Yeah, right."

"Seriously. Sometimes I see lights out here, and hear voices."

"Lights?"

"Yeah. Like in windows. Spooo-keeeey!"

With his new friend goading him, Jessie took two steps toward the ruins. His eyes trained back into the darkness, where random swells of wreckage rose from a tide of vegetation.

"A ghost house! Awesome. What happened?"

"It burned down. Real mysterious stuff. When I was younger, I heard old man Freighter tell my dad it had something to do with magic.

"Come on."

"Yeah, well Freighter's had more than one mental breakdown, so you know."

"Like, he went crazy?"

Kim nodded, "After his wife died. Local legend says her spirit haunts his property. More spooky crap. Lotta that in Gallows Hill. Just wait Jessie, you're close, so it won't be long until you hear him outside at night, bottles clanking around, stuff breaking. Some nights, no lie, he howls at the moon."

A chill ran the length of Jessie's spine.

"Wow. Interesting neighborhood. Does this... howling... happen often?"

"You'll see. Okay, look, I've gotta get back, but it was nice to meet you, Jessie Roberts."

"Wait, ah, tomorrow's only Sunday, right? So you'll still be here? You want to show me around some more? New guy in town and all..."

"Can't. Dad's taking me shopping in Woodsville, maybe to a movie after. I'll be around though. Summer break and mom's out of town."

"Okay, cool."

"Bye."

As she walked away, Jessie followed Kim with his eyes, then turned back to the dark corridor before him. In the distance, past the burnt stone and shattered walls of the long-dead house, Jessie thought he saw something move...

"Boo!"

Jessie jumped - literally jumped - several inches into the air and came down only to find Kim standing before him smiling.

"Sorry, couldn't help myself. See ya around," she walked away again and after a moment wherein his heart worked its way back down out of his mouth, Jessie began to laugh. Once more he watched her go, all smiles.

"Welcome to the neighborhood I guess, eh?"

CHAPTER 3

Jessie set out to continue a brief circuit of the neighborhood but stopped when he realized it was nearly dark and there wasn't a single street light in the area. He ventured a little further up the other side of the fork from where Kim had left him, what his phone's compass told him was Northwest. It was six-thirty and the encroaching night was crisp, charged with energies that, while enticing, also felt dangerous. He couldn't stop thinking about living next to a lunatic. A literal 'lunatic,' as in a man who howled at the moon! Uneasy, tired and more than a little hungry, Jessie turned back the way he had come, intending to call it a night. Only when he reached Caliper Lane again, something in the woods caught his eye.

He stopped and walked to the edge of the derelict road. Staring into the darkened trees, Jessie saw that the moon cast its rays onto the ruins Kim had shown him, the place she had called a doorway to another world.

Don't you wonder what it's like inside?

And yes, as if the question had come from some outside agency, Jessie found that he did wonder what mysteries this dead place might hold. He felt the darkness reach out to him; the longer he stared, the more Jessie thought he could see other houses, deep in the woods. Sinister gables, dormers, and spires poking through the thick canopies of mammoth red oak, spruce, and hackberry trees, beckoning him in.

Just a few steps, just enough to get a look inside...

Without realizing it, Jessie lifted his foot from the gravel at the end of Caliper Lane and planted it firmly into the underbrush, crushing down blades of thigh-high grass. The vista opened a little more; he thought he could see lights in far off windows...

He was several steps into the woods now. In his head he pictured Kim standing alongside him, but he was only vaguely aware that it was not her voice that spurred him on.

It wasn't his either.

Secrets herein. Secrets the likes of which you could never imagine...

Past the first visible chunk of blacktop now and in the distance the darkness became clearer. As he approached the forested corridor's threshold, his eyes balanced to the lack of light. Buried beneath the ground cover, just a few feet before him was the jagged remains of a mailbox. He moved closer to it, saw the letters SHIN on its side.

Just a little closer...

HONK!!!

The sound snapped Jessie out of his trance. He spun only to see headlights bearing down on him. Frozen, he braced for impact, then realized the car had stopped directly in front of him, sizing him up, leering...

HONK HONK!

Relieved, Jessie realized it was WJ in his dark blue Mercedes.

"Jessie! What're you doing? You were supposed to be home ten minutes ago. Pizza's on man, get it while it's hot!"

WJ Honked the horn again, needlessly, but Jessie was glad he did. Supposed to be home ten minutes ago? He pulled out his phone and saw that the time was indeed ten past seven; he'd been standing here staring for close to forty minutes.

"C'mon, hop in dude."

Very tired and a little freaked out, for once Jessie did exactly as his domestic nemesis suggested.

~

Jessie grasped the serpent-shaped handle and opened the door to his new home, held it for WJ and the pizzas. There was a flicker, and a light came on. The darkness retreated, weakened by sconces placed intermittently down the long corridor before them.

"Wow, looks like a tunnel or something," he observed.

"Don't worry, it's not as severe as it looks," the voice came from his right, and Jessie turned to see his mother emerge from the subtle bend of a grand staircase. He'd not seen this at first; the stairs were laid into the wall in a manner that made them almost impossible to see until you were looking directly at them. It was a funny trick of the eye, and unlike anything he'd ever seen before. His curiosity activated, Jessie turned to the left and noticed a similar effect there, where an open-framed doorway was hidden between two slightly askew walls on either side of it.

"This is so cool! You guys weren't kidding about this Caravetti guy!"

"Cruchetti dear, and no way! You explore later, I'm starving!" Talia playfully scolded, snagging the pizzas from WJ and heading into the corridor before them.

"Okay, but this place is really weird."

Jessie followed his mother through the corridor, the path snaking a bit, moving first away from and then back towards the center of the structure. They finally came to an open doorway and emerged into a foyer complete with an armoire, coat rack and a large, hand-made mirror that hung on the wall.

"Looks like he misplaced the foyer, eh?" Talia said in a husky, nineteen-fifties gumshoe voice. Jessie's love of movies came from his mother, her tastes, however, skewed more toward the Noir classics of the '30s and '40s.

"It's one of Cruchetti's trademarks," WJ said, "He calls this the "Midway" and that space just inside the door the "Zero Point.""

Jessie laughed; he didn't know what was funnier - the ridiculous names or the fact that WJ knew such things.

"Yeah, ahh… shouldn't this have been just inside the front door? I mean, why do these hallways curve so much? It's like all the rooms are cut off from one another."

"You'd drive yourself mad trying to understand it, Jessie. Trust me, there is no practical reason for any of this. It's Cruchetti's flair."

"Appropriate choice of words, considering the man himself went mad at some point and, what? Disappeared?" Talia asked.

"Something like that. They called him, 'The Mad Architect' in some circles. Of course, he'd be long dead by now, but no one saw him after Gallows Hill was completed. No one today even knows what he looked like. There are no pictures, no identifying documents. Nothing but his architectural legacy."

To illustrate his point, WJ made a sweeping gesture in deference to the room around them, what Jessie had already dubbed the "out of place foyer" in his head. It was large, slightly ovular in shape and, besides the corridor they passed through now, featured twelve other openings set into the walls and an area where it looked like another had been patched over.

"Most of them are locked. Your mother's looking for a key," WJ said as Jessie tried several of the doors.

"Okay, that's super weird."

"What's even weirder is I don't remember any of these being here when I originally looked at the place for you guys. Guess I'm going senile."

"Do not joke about that in my presence, please," Talia said.

From his vantage point, Jessie could see a much larger room just through one of the open jambs. He detoured for a moment to steal a peek, and found himself inside a cavernous room with a western wall made entirely of floor-to-ceiling windows. Talia peeked her head in behind him, "Ah, the den. This was what you sent me pictures of, wasn't it, Wendall? Look at that view of the woods - one of the selling points."

"It's like staring into a fairy tale."

Behind them, WJ laughed, "Wow. Well said."

Talia turned to him, "So, how well do you know this house?"

"Well, obviously I scoped it out before I suggested it, but other than that not at all. There's very little available in this area, Knight's Side or Gallows Hill."

WJ moved into the new room and turned three-sixty with his arms outstretched to both sides. For a moment, Jessie thought he could see this man as he had been when he was a little boy.

"A lot of the houses in Gallows Hill have this exact room. Another of Cruchetti's signatures."

"Whatever. Again, Stah-ving!" Talia turned, and both Jessie and WJ followed quickly, ducking back into the foyer and taking the corridor straight on from the entrance. More sconces lighted the way to the kitchen. Dinner awaited.

CHAPTER 4

"So just what the heck were you doing in the woods Jessie?"

Talia stopped eating and trained a speculative eye on her son, waiting to hear the answer to WJ's question.

"It's not the woods. Well, now it is, but it didn't used to be. It's an old, dead road. There's the remains of a house out there. I was just exploring."

"Property? There's property out there? Isn't that trespassing, then?"

"Jessie, I don't think your mother wants any bad blood with the neighbors."

"Lord no," Talia paused as she fought a losing battle against a long, stringy bite of mozzarella, "Especially not the first day we move in."

"It's abandoned," Jessie answered, struggling with his own slice. Across from where the movers had set up the modest table, he eyed the door to the basement. It was the only one of the three apertures in the kitchen that actually had a door - a thick walnut number with rusted hinges and a series of locks on its face that were damaged beyond repair. Something about the look of that door made Jessie nervous. It looked like it was designed to keep people out at all costs.

Or to keep something in…

"How do you know that already?"

"I met somebody."

"A neighborhood kid? Coooool. What's his name?"

"Kim."

"Nice!" WJ raised his hand in an embarrassing ploy for a high-five and Jessie just shook his head.

"Where does she live?"

"I'm not exactly sure. She comes here to stay with her dad on weekends."

"Oh. Broken home. That sucks," WJ said, lowering his hand.

"Wendell! She's not an after school special. Really, 'broken home'?" His mother's scolds made Jessie smile. Everyone fell silent, and the resulting friction between the two of them made Jessie feel bad, so he played a tune of kinship for the sake of the meal.

"No, he's right, but she seems pretty well-adjusted," he said and instantly regretted his tactics when he saw WJ smile, no doubt at the idea of Jessie lending him aid, "Anyway, she showed me around, gave me some history. Kim said the guy who lives two houses down told her dad that house in the woods burned down under like, mysterious circumstances or something."

"Well, someone still owns the property, and that definitely makes it trespassing."

"Talia, if there's no house on the lot, what harm can a little exploring do?" Jessie smiled, as now it was WJ coming to his aid. Were adults even remotely aware how easy it was to manipulate them?

This tit-for-tat wasn't lost on Jessie's mother though, and she didn't seem to care for it.

"Well, maybe we should call the police and ask them whether there needs to be a house for it to be considered trespassing, hmm?"

"Talia… I just mean… Jessie, there wasn't a no trespassing sign, was there?"

Talia's chair made a loud screech as she stood up suddenly.

"Wendell, honestly!" she snapped, and walked curtly from the room, her heels echoing off the walls of the long corridor. Jessie held back a snicker at WJ, whose piece of pizza remained held aloft, mid-bite. He gathered three more slices onto his plate, grabbed his glass and followed after his mother out of the room.

WJ looked further defeated by Jessie's tug on the ripcord. "Jessie?"

"Sorry, ahhh, homework," he was off toward the upstairs. He'd not even seen his bedroom yet.

WJ held his pose for another moment and then dropped his piece of pizza back into the grease-stained white cardboard box from which it came.

"School hasn't even started yet," he said to the empty room.

CHAPTER 5

After he finished eating, Jessie plugged in his hotspot, fired up his laptop and set out looking for any information on Caliper Lane and the house that once existed on it.

He found nothing.

After a while, the day's events caught up to him, and Jessie decided to call it a night. The movers had brought his bed up earlier, but he hadn't unpacked anything yet, so when he turned his attention to the boxes and realized they were all marked "Upstairs," the problem became apparent: his room in the last house was in the basement.

"Therefore, it is a logical conclusion that these are marked from where they originated, not where they were bound for," he did his best British accent, talking aloud to himself as he shuffled into his slippers and headed out into the hall. The second-floor corridor was exposed, looking out over the den and its massive windows, and Jessie was treated to a full view of the three-quarters moon as it drifted out from behind a dense bank of clouds. It looked like an enormous eye opening in slow motion across the sky.

Jessie heard WJ leave shortly after he'd abandoned him at the table. Talia had let him out, their intense but muffled voices an indication they made up. Did they kiss goodnight?

Jessie tried to tell himself he didn't care.

He crept toward the stairs, making sure the coast was clear. His mother's room was at the far end, second to the last from the South side of the house. No light from under the door because at this hour she was more than likely asleep.

"So that's me alone," it was a Scottish accent this time, his vocalizations unconscious tactics to break the tension he felt walking through an unfamiliar house. An unfamiliar house in the middle of the woods, designed by a madman. By himself. At night. Heading into the basement no less.

"Cleee-shay-ay," he sing-songed aloud, doubling back for a moment and grabbing a small screwdriver from off his desk and putting it in his pocket.

Just in case.

In addition to his and his mother's rooms, there were three others upstairs: two bedrooms and one Talia had referred to as a parlor, whatever that meant. Jessie checked the bedrooms first. When he didn't find his sheets there, he turned to the parlor but found it locked just like the rooms downstairs. Curious as to the location of the keys, Jessie relented and headed downstairs. He marveled at the intricate carvings that adorned the deteriorating balustrade. Strange glyph-like symbols ran the length of what appeared to be one incredibly long, solid piece of wood. He followed the stairs in a quarter-circle curve until they ended at the front door.

As he'd noticed earlier, the walls hid the passage to the left of the door by a trick of perception, standing slightly askew from one another. Even as he looked at it, Jessie found he couldn't understand what principle of geometry was at work, and frustrated, entered anyway. He was in the den again, swallowed by its opulence, those enormous windows running the room's entire magnificent length, opening the house to the scrutiny of the night. Stepping around piles of boxes and half-unpacked possessions, he took his time, this view his favorite part of the house thus far. When, at last he reached the other end, Jessie stepped through another open doorway directly into the kitchen.

The basement door stood wide open.

"That's weird," he muttered, no accent this time as he stepped up to the threshold. A draft of cold air hit him in the face. Jessie ran his hand across the unfinished surface of the wall just inside the door but could not locate a light switch.

"Oh come on," he said aloud, trying to force his eyes to acclimate to the darkness. It took a couple of minutes, but eventually, he could just barely make out the top two stairs. Frustrated and groggy, for one moment Jessie attempted to extend his foot down to the first stair but quickly realized he'd be asking for it to try and ghost step his way down. Thankful for his caution, he retreated back to safety at the top. As he did, something caught his eye.

A glint of light dangled in the darkness before him; it took a moment before he recognized it for what it was: the pull-chain on a light bulb. Reaching out, Jessie grabbed and caught it on his third try. One pull and Lo and Behold, there was light. Not a lot of it, but enough that he could see several of the mover's professionally packed boxes at the bottom of the stairs.

A noise behind him caused Jessie to turn; there was nothing but his own shadow thrown by the bulb against the wall to his left. He'd started for nothing and felt silly. Because of this, and because he thought it absurd he should be afraid of a basement, Jessie picked his right foot up and planted it on the first stair.

CREAK

"Well now, that's to be expected. Let's just hope they're not too old to support my weight."

Nonsense, he chastised himself; the movers had carried dozens of boxes down the steps, so there should be no doubt they would hold for him.

Bearing this in mind, he descended to the next step, paused and waited for further evidence of stress. There was none. Taking a deep breath, he descended the remaining stairs at a quickened, no-nonsense pace.

The basement was extremely dark, and outside the immediate circumference of the bulb's light, the space fell away into cold, unexplored creepiness. From what Jessie could see of them, the walls were unfinished concrete, various degrees of degradation claiming pieces here and there, leaving examples of twisted wire mesh exposed, often clotted with soft Earth and chunks of roots. The floor gave off a coolness that, while the slippers protected his feet, he could feel creep through the air around him, searching for entrance to his bones. The texture of his steps was gritty, dirt clinging to the rubber soles, marking his passage. Directly across from the stairs stood an old mirror on a swivel base. Its design was gorgeous, worn with age but of a craftsmanship that struck Jessie as belonging to another time. He approached, and its glass caught his reflection. Shivers shot up Jessie's spine as he studied himself; there was something about his face he didn't recognize.

A noise behind him broke his reverie, and Jessie turned only to come face to face with himself! His blood ran cold for a moment before he realized it was the mirror again, the mirror that was originally over there –?

Reality wobbled until Jessie saw his mistake: it wasn't the same mirror.

Now that he looked around, there were a lot of mirrors, at least half a dozen, all almost exactly like the first. They were positioned at the outskirts of his little circumference of light, also arranged in a circular pattern. Jessie watched his reflection as he turned from one mirror to the next, beginning a full three-sixty sweep and watching the iterations that followed.

He began to turn faster, spinning in place and watching the reflections speed by, an impromptu game that lightened his mood. His laughter perpetuated itself, until out of the corner of his eye he thought he saw one of his reflections standing perfectly still. Their eyes met, and something left him then; a part of Jessie crossed an invisible threshold and seemed to animate the boy in the mirror before him.

"Happy birthday," he thought he heard it say, and then he tripped over his own feet and fell to the floor, knocking the mirror over, the glass splitting in a jagged crack that ran its full length. From all around him, the sound of a great engine filled the room. It sounded like a semi truck had pulled up out front.

"Jessie, are you down there?" It was his mother's voice, tired.

"Uh, yeah mom. Sorry if I woke you."

Talia descended the steps halfway and stood perplexed by her son, still dressed in his jeans and t-shirt, slippers the only sign he was aware that it was the middle of the night.

"What the heck are you doing kid-O? It's like three in the morning, haven't you gone to sleep yet?"

"Ah, no. No, but I was about to, and then I realized I never unpacked my pillows and stuff, and the movers put the boxes in the wrong place and–"

Talia came closer and saw the boxes marked basement. A light bulb went on over her head.

"Oh crap, that's my fault. I must have labeled these what room they were coming from, not where they were going. Sorry, Jessie."

Talia came the rest of the way down the stairs. Jessie moved closer to his mom, and she put her hand on top of his head and did that scruffy kid-thing with his slightly-too-long, blondish-brown hair.

"It's okay."

The sound grew louder, but Talia showed no sign she heard it.

"Wow, look at all these mirrors."

"I know, right? What do you think they're all here for?"

"I don't know, I'll have to ask WJ. Maybe the people that lived here before made them or something."

"Ah, hadn't thought of that. I thought it was something creepy."

"Of course you did, that's because I let you watch all those horror movies growing up that your Aunt Cathy thought I was crazy for letting you watch."

Mother and son shared a laugh and then looked at one another.

"It is creepy though, isn't it?" Talia admitted.

"Very. Mom, do you hear that?"

"Do I hear what, dear?"

"Sounds like an engine? A big one?"

"Okay, you clearly need some sleep, now you're hearing things. Tell you what, let's find your stuff so we can both go upstairs and leave the Kingdom of Mirrors for another time."

"Okay, mom. Sounds good to me."

Three in the morning, and while Jessie and his mother searched for bedclothes, Kim sat alone in her bedroom staring at a picture of a girl several years younger than her. She sang:

"As shadow to cast
And mirror to light
As right is to left
And day is to night

Fold a space
And tuck some time
Lift your hands
Recite this rhyme

The door will show
The path within
Now through the glass
To Widdershins"

Kim stopped singing when the floor beneath her feet began to faintly vibrate. An electrical hum swelled like a passing airplane, and the walls started to shake, giving birth to a low-end rumble that sounded as though it would tear her and everything around her apart.

Then the rumble stopped. The hum remained though, and beneath it, something else. It was the sound of someone crying.

"Patty? Patagonia!?"

"Kim? Is that you?"

Kim pounced to her feet and ran around the room, attempting to ascertain where her long-lost sister's voice had come from.

"Keep talking honey. Keep talking so I can figure out where you are."

"I'm afraid. I don't know where I am…"

She had it! There was a mirror leaning against the far wall, its surface painted over with thick, sloppy strokes of black so that only a few slivers of the glass underneath could be seen. Kim put her eye to the glass. Inside she saw something… she couldn't quite tell what it was, but it didn't look like her sister.

"Patty? Are you hurt? Talk to me."

"They don't want me to."

"Who's they?"

"They don't like you. They said you're a coward and a… some other word I don't know. They want to hurt you like they hurt me."

A tear stung Kim's eye; they'd hurt her. Bastards.

"Don't worry, Patty. I'll find you. Just tell me what it looks like there."

"There's a big door, but it won't let me out."

"What kind of door, sweetie?"

"I have to go now. They're coming."

"Patty no! No!"

Kim was left with an empty silence. Where was she? Where had Patagonia been hidden for the last five years? Kim had a pretty good idea where to start, and who to ask for help.

CHAPTER 6

SUNDAY, AUGUST 25TH

That first morning in the new house Jessie slept until twelve. When he woke, he did so from a vibrant dream: he was inside a house whose rooms continually changed position. In the dream, he stood encased in a mirror that sat on a shelf in a room made of wood. His view expanded to reveal more shelves lined with small glass orbs, people trapped inside each and every one, exactly like him. Inside one orb, a girl of about eight reached out her hand and said:

"You shouldn'a come here. You weren't a'posed to return."

He woke, and the image of the girl lingered, as did the hum from last night.

"What the hell is that?" he said and spent some time surfing the internet on his phone looking for possible explanations.

No dice.

When he finally crawled from bed, Jessie did so lethargically. He ate breakfast by himself, his mother no doubt out running errands. By the time he was finished though, the hum had become too much to take, and he left the house, expecting it to disappear with distance.

It did not.

"It's like it's following me."

Jessie followed Derleth Avenue to where it dead-ended at Rune Road. The hum was with him the entire time. He pushed it to the back of his mind as he stoked his natural curiosity about his new town. A left from here would take him back to the Turnpike, so he went right. He walked this way for about twenty minutes, a few more houses sporadically appearing in dark enclaves of trees, until he came to a street that branched right. A faded sign identified this as the unpronounceable Eeryx Way. Ahead of him, Rune appeared to go on indefinitely, so Jessie turned and took this new road Southeast until, as he suspected, he arrived at the fork from the night before. The wreckage of Kim's doorway to another world looked clearer in the daylight, and Jessie fought the urge to set out directly into the woods to explore. It was pragmatism that won him over; it had rained during the night, and he could see the ground beyond Caliper was soft, sloppy mud. He took one look at the holes in his sneakers and decided to postpone the exploration until he could return with better footwear.

As he started home, Jessie came to the house with the nautical mailbox and paused. Beyond the street this property was deep and sinister; a dense copse of trees formed a kind of canopy over its facade that approximated the darkness of night. Jessie stood at the mailbox for several long moments before he realized someone was watching him from an upstairs window. Seeing this, he became self-conscious and resumed walking back home. He could feel the eyes on him the entire way to his door, the hum growing louder as he walked.

He made it back to the house just as the sun began to sink and saw his mother was still out. Frustrated, Jessie tried to pass some time reading. This proved difficult, as his attention was stretched and he couldn't find any of his books among the various boxes that lay with their contents partially unpacked. Looking through these half-planted markers of his territory, he discovered a tattered old copy of Peter Pan that he'd not seen in forever. The book had belonged to his father, a first edition from the year of its original publication, 1911. According to Talia, dad had read the fairytale to Jessie countless times when he was a toddler, and as such, he had always felt a particular bond with it. It was one of the only links he still had to his father, and the realization that he hadn't held it in ages seemed a tragedy.

Settling in, Jessie read voraciously, making it to the part where Peter's shadow reveals itself to him as a conscious entity before being interrupted by the doorbell. Unless his mother had forgotten her keys, this had to be a neighbor introducing themselves. When he opened the door, Jessie was pleasantly surprised.

"Hey," it was Kim, looking particularly fetching in a yellow spring dress and combat boots.

"Hey. Wow, wasn't expecting you."

"Jessie, um, can I ask for your help?"

"Of course," he said, elated at the prospect. He waved Kim inside and shut the door.

"Do you hear that?" he asked.

"Hear what?"

"Never mind."

Kim looked at him queerly for a moment then placed a hand on his shoulder.

"Look, I know we don't know each other yet, but I need help and it's, well, it's kinda dangerous."

Yet. She said yet.

"Wow. Sounds serious, but that's cool. Talk to me; are you okay?"

Kim looked from side to side over her shoulders before continuing, "My sister's missing, and I'm afraid something might have happened to her."

"Missing? How long?"

"Long enough for me to think someone might have kidnapped her."

"Jesus, did your parents call the police?"

"No. I mean, I... I think Old Man Freighter has something to do with it. I need to break into his house and look around."

"Break into his house? Kim, if you think Freighter had something to do with your sister being kidnapped, tell the cops. You don't want to-"

"Yes! Jessie, I have to! I promised I would keep her safe and... and..."

Kim started to cry, and Jessie naturally embraced her. The sensation of her body wrapped in his arms made him feel like he was about to melt, and when Kim looked up and their eyes met, a charge pulsed through him. Almost an impossibility, he released the beautiful girl and went back to the situation at hand, as it felt dire.

"I can get my mom to talk to your dad. Or..."

"No! No parents."

"Why?"

"Look, the thing is, I don't really live with my dad. I don't live with anyone. It's just me."

"Kim, this is insane."

"It is, and I really hope you believe me, Jessie Roberts,

because I'm about to tell you a bunch of shit most people would definitely not believe."

"You can tell me anything."

"Okay, but do you mind if I have something to eat while we talk? I... I'm really really hungry."

She'd started to laugh and Jessie couldn't help but wonder how that was possible.

"What's so funny?"

"I'm hungry. I'm actually hungry!"

"So what? I'm always hungry."

"No, you don't understand. Jessie... never mind. Just feed me and I'll explain."

Jessie had a feeling if this was anyone but Kim he would be far less interested in humoring her. Be that as it may, this beautiful girl needed his help, and Jessie wasn't about to back out now.

They'd been in the kitchen for all of two minutes before the remainder of last night's pizza was digesting in Kim's stomach. Watching her eat and walk around, slipping in and out of the doorways, Jessie had a revelation.

"You knew the people that lived here before, didn't you?"

"What makes you say that?"

"Well, you certainly seem to know where everything is, and this isn't the easiest house to navigate."

"You're pretty slick. Yeah, I knew them. I played with their little girl Cassie when I was younger."

"Do you know what's behind all those doors? It's super weird that we moved into this house and can't find the keys to open most of the rooms."

"No idea. Cassie's dad was pretty strict. Most of the time we had to stay in the den or the kitchen or outside."

"So why do you think Old Man Freighter knows where your sister is?"

Kim undid her ponytail, set her purple hair tie on the counter. She shook out her hair with both hands as she spoke:

"Look, the thing is, my sister and I are, well, we're not normal. We kinda have powers."

"What?"

"Swear. That's why Freighter took her or helped someone else take her. He's got powers, too."

Her story made Jessie think of a friend he'd had when he was younger; Billy Blake liked to tell everyone at school how he had been to other worlds, had lunch with ghosts, all kinds of crazy stuff. Talia explained to Jessie that sometimes people told you things that you wanted to be true but knew were not. His mother said it was usually for attention.

"Prove it."

"Okay. Follow me."

Kim headed back into the corridor toward the Out of Place Foyer and Jessie followed. After only a few steps, Kim disappeared from right in front of him.

"Holy smokes!" Jessie jumped as she re-appeared behind him and for the second time since he'd met her yelled, "Boo!"

"How did you do that?"

"Specifics later. Right now, I need your help. You in?"

"Definitely."

Jessie stood spellbound. Kim was beautiful, and she was an adventure, all in one. He thought he might be in love.

"Okay, then, let's go!"

They ran the rest of the way through the corridor, out the front door and stopped cold when they heard the most bone-chilling sound ever. Outside, the large, red moon had crept into the sky. How was that possible? How long had they been talking? Where was his mom? The unreality of the time-loss combined with the sound sent shivers down Jessie's spine. Kim's words from yesterday came back to him:

"Some nights, no lie, he stands in his yard and howls at the moon."

"That's Freighter! C'mon, we have to go!"

Kim grabbed Jessie's hand and everything else fell away.

CHAPTER 7

Amped with fear, they double-timed it around the broken sidewalk that bordered the house.

Jessie could barely keep up.

They moved beneath the malevolent gaze of the moon, the windows of his den looming high above them as the land rolled down and away, followed by large sections of house he couldn't reconcile with what he knew of the interior: the locked rooms were, apparently, enormous.

His questions vanished as the horrible sound echoed again across the sky, tearing tiny holes in the fabric of his reality. They broke into an all-out run, turned a final corner, and the house was gone. For the first time, Jessie got a feel for the enormity of his new property. It sprawled before them like a massive field, dozens of ancient trees bordering the land in the distance, defining a rough edge to the leaf-saturated Kentucky bluegrass that lined the world in all directions, forest for as far as he could see.

"Kim? What-"

"Shh. Listen!"

She led them in a moment of intensely trained silence.

Their reward was the unmistakable sound of glass shatter-ing, followed by a barrage of garbled, profanity-riddled screaming that morphed into what sounded like a man, not a wolf, howling at the moon.

"Isn't it insane? Freighter's having one of his episodes and we've got a date front-and-center."

The word 'date' short-circuited Jessie's fear; he ran on with renewed vigor, Kim pulling him across the expanse of grass and straight on toward the trees at the edge of the lawn.

"Who is he?"

"A psycho."

"I mean what's wrong with him?"

Jessie's words were lost as they broke into the trees at the edge of the property line. Something dark and winged burst out of the branches above them, the leathery forms swarming the sky, outlined against the face of the moon for an endless Halloween moment.

Bats?

"AWRWWWAWWOOOOOOOOOR!"

Careening almost out of control, they raced deeper into the trees. Choking on darkness, Jessie hung on for dear life, dodging limbs, stumps, and thickets of branches that choked their path until, finally, they slowed. The howling had trailed off into a series of grunts that grew ever closer.

"This whole town used to be a forest, so property lines are mushy."

They came to the bottom of a slight rise. Kim put her finger to her lips and slowed, careful to make as little noise as possible. Jessie helped her brush aside scores of spindly, lacerating branches as they crept forward, stepping oh-so-carefully on layered carpets of ancient leaves, trying to lessen the crinkles and cracks that accompanied even their slightest movement. Jessie followed, Kim still holding his hand, one of her fingers playing tense circles across the face of his palm.

Fear be damned, her touch made his head swim.

They passed beneath an opening in the canopy of trees above their heads and the moon leered, smaller and brighter, and in a completely contradictory position to where it had been only moments ago. Jessie squinted, and something sank inside him when he realized it wasn't the moon he saw, it was a floodlight on the back of a house.

Old Man Freighter's house.

"ARWWWWAROOOOOO!"

This time, the sound came from almost on top of them, and when he heard it, Jessie's vision cleared quick. Freighter was maybe fifty feet in front of them, sheathed from sight by a thin circumference of trees. The floodlight clicked off and darkness swallowed them whole.

"Who's there? Show yerself!" the old man screamed, the gruff rasp in his voice evidence of a feral nature. They froze, but something of considerable size moved through the trees toward them. It wasn't Freighter.

"What the... *gasp*... what the hell was that...?"

Something grazed his left calf and Jessie freaked, lost his balance and fell into a puddle of leaves to their right. It was loud, there would be no disguising it, and sensing motion, the floodlight clicked back on.

Another howl and then Old Man Freighter was standing directly before them.

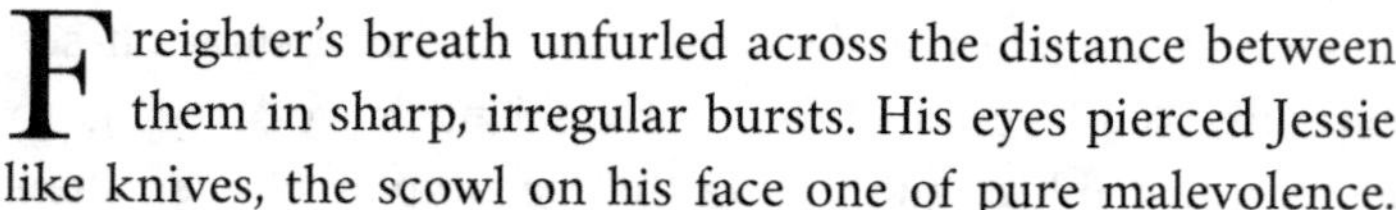

Freighter's breath unfurled across the distance between them in sharp, irregular bursts. His eyes pierced Jessie like knives, the scowl on his face one of pure malevolence.

They still had the fence between them, but it would take more than that to make Jessie feel safe.

"Who issit?" Who sent you?"

"Na-no one. We were... we were just..." Jessie turned to Kim for help and was horrified to find she was no longer by his side. In fact, after a quick scan of the trees, Kim was nowhere to be found.

"You were just what, trespassing on my property in the middle of the night? I ought'a tear ya ta pieces!"

"Okay, look, chill please. It's not even seven o'clock."

"You being smart boy?"

Jessie opened his mouth and then shut it again. There was no reasoning with this man, and Kim's disappearance had him rattled.

"What's a'matter with you, boy? You on drugs? What the hell'r you doing out here? Answer me gotdamnit!"

"I already told you! I wasn't trespassing! I'm not even on your land. I was just trying to find my friend, and..."

"You're in the woods on the other side of my fence spying on me in the night. I don't know what your definition of trespassing is, that fits into mine alright."

"Yeah, well you've got a pretty messed up definition of trespassing then."

The old man's anger erupted in another howl, this one up close and personal. Shadows raced from all corners, scurried over him in a way that made Freighter disappear for a moment. Was this the same thing Kim had done earlier? Jessie wondered if she was close by, using the shadows for cover. Involuntarily, he laughed at the thought of her sneaking up behind Freighter.

"Sumpthing funny, boy?" Freighter said as he reappeared.

Jessie didn't answer, and the old man's anger surged again. He grasped the fence and began shaking it violently, like he'd rather be wringing Jessie's neck. The previously vague figure became clear, all except for his face, which continued to boil in shadow. There was something about those shadows… something was wrong with them. The point where the old man's face should have been was… swimming, bubbling out toward the links of the fence and back again.

"You listen ta me and you listen good. This is my land, and what I do on it is none of your got-damned business, you got that? A man might need to do things on his land that he ain't proud of, things he doesn't want other people to see. Understand?"

"Yeah."

"Good. Now… RUN FER YER LIFE!" Freighter's voice escalated into a fearsome scream that tore straight through Jessie, and his feet were already moving before his brain could tell them to.

Behind and beside him, loud footfalls told Jessie Freighter was chasing, still separated by the fence but tracking to overtake him at whatever point in the immediate distance marked the end of the division. Jessie tried to veer into the woods on his right, but there was something there too, something beside him and low to the ground. He closed his eyes and braced to be overtaken, but it didn't happen.

So he ran. In his head, the hum that had followed him all day became a dull, crashing cacophony that perfectly accentuated the impending apocalypse hot on Jessie's heals. Hell, it seemed, had a soundtrack.

CHAPTER 8

With Freighter on his left and an invisible foil to his right, Jessie kept to the fence, leaping over pitfalls and fighting through thick tangles of branches that lashed his exposed flesh at every step. He knew he was racing toward a confrontation, but what else could he do? It was the sound of his pursuers' footsteps that drove him on relentless, exhausted, and terrified. A loud crack of thunder shook the sky and what began as a drizzle took only a moment to turn into a full-fledged downpour.

"You've got to be kidding," he screamed, his inner voice chanting death, destruction, dismemberment as the sound of the rain killed Jessie's only way to judge his position relative to his attackers. His visibility dwindling, his brain still rattled by the unending hum, Jessie came to a place where the fence had fallen inward. He leaped over it, fully aware his only path had robbed him of his shield and taken him directly into the old man's front yard.

The property was as overgrown in front as it was in the back. The driveway had disappeared long ago, the gravel that once defined it abandoned to snarling ground cover that grew more treacherous in the rain. Untamed foliage picked back up where the fence had left off and effectively trapped Jessie on the same side as his pursuer.

Jessie ran so hard his lungs felt like they were on fire and his heart throbbed, a barrage of explosions that shook his eyes, his teeth, his stomach. Despite this, or because of it, he did not slow a single step even as he dodged masses of trees, weeds and unkempt grass that rose from the earth and twisted together like barbed wire garrison.

Ahead and to the left, a light shimmered into view between the raindrops. A moment later the path brought him around the corner and into what looked like a room with walls of vegetation, something out of a movie about the jungle, complete with a junked car in the middle of the tableau. All the windows were shattered, the remaining glass panels jagged like the mouths of nightmares. He passed by the front entrance to Freighter's house, eye level with the large, rotted porch that enclosed the front of the building. Even in the rain, Jessie could tell it was identical to the porch on his own house, except on both sides of the door where stacks of old magazines and newspapers stood like makeshift columns, lashed together out of sheer spite and timeless dilapidation. The smell in the air was moldy and acidic, so much so that Jessie's eyes began to water.

Ahead, he saw lights through the trees and knew the street was near, maybe only a few hundred feet in front of him. Reinvigorated, Jessie began to zig-zag as he picked up speed. A moment later he burst into the street just as a blue Mercedes approached the mouth of the driveway. Unable to kill his momentum, Jessie took a nasty spill when a puddle of water slipped his legs out from under him. Headlights bearing down on him, Jessie drew in a breath and held it, braced for impact. It didn't happen; the car skidded to a stop in the grass to the right, missing Jessie by about five feet.

"Jesus Christ! Jessie, I almost... what the hell are you doing?"

Jessie was up and around to the passenger door just as Old Man Freighter emerged from the trees.

"Crap," he said under his breath, his eyes squinting beneath the sheath of the unending sonic assault that had taken root in his inner ear. What the hell was going on? It felt like the entire world was cracking in half.

Maybe it was.

"Jessie! Jessie, please, answer me! Are you okay? What's the matter with yo-"

"Just drive WJ. Please!"

An angry look split Freighter's grizzled mug into a Jack O'Lantern grimace. In the headlights, he resembled a hunchbacked monster skirting the tree line for shadow. He approached WJ's window, and despite Jessie's pleadings, WJ rolled it down.

"Can I help you, sir?" WJ shouted over the rain.

"That your kid?"

"Ah, no. Well, yes. I mean, I'm a friend of his mother's, and I'm watching him while-"

"Ain't doin' a very good job watchin' him," Freighter surprised them both when he stuck his head through the window and gnashed his teeth like a dog, "Ain't that right boy? Trespassing little bastard!"

"I wasn't on your property!"

"Now sir..."

"Shut yur mouth! That boy's gonna answer fer what he's done!"

Freighter's head - still wrapped in the oily black hood - made him resemble some mad, vampire monk. Was there something moving in there? Jessie looked at WJ and saw he was completely beside himself in fear.

And then he wasn't.

"Look," WJ grabbed the door handle and pushed, the door opened abruptly and caught Freighter off guard, sent him back-stepping with his head still inside the window. This did not set things off on the right foot between them, "With all due respect," WJ waited to continue until Freighter had regained his composure, "if you have some kind of a problem with Jessie there's a time and a place."

Freighter recovered his stance and stood breathing heavy in the rain. There was a moment where everything stood on the head of a pin. Then the old man raised his head to the sky and began to howl. Jessie watched in terror as the mouth of the hood, now aimed at the moon, issued forth half a dozen or so worm-like tendrils, squirming and snapping at the sky.

And then he turned and ran back toward his property. On all fours.

"Jessie. What the hell… what the hell was that?"

"Dracula."

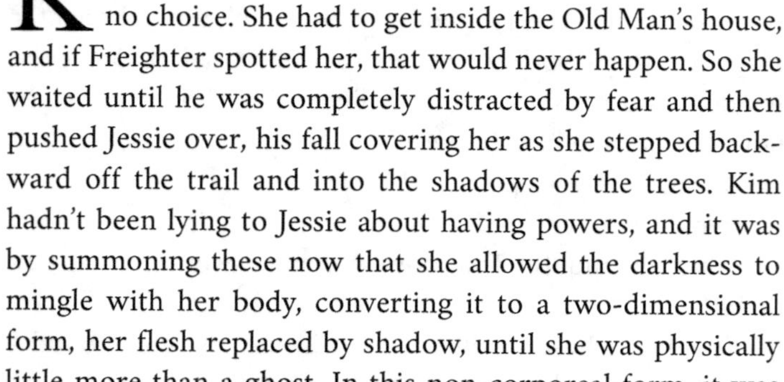

Kim hated to leave Jessie the way she did, but she had no choice. She had to get inside the Old Man's house, and if Freighter spotted her, that would never happen. So she waited until he was completely distracted by fear and then pushed Jessie over, his fall covering her as she stepped backward off the trail and into the shadows of the trees. Kim hadn't been lying to Jessie about having powers, and it was by summoning these now that she allowed the darkness to mingle with her body, converting it to a two-dimensional form, her flesh replaced by shadow, until she was physically little more than a ghost. In this non-corporeal form, it was easy for her to slip unnoticed to the outside wall; after that, the shadows gathered below a small second-floor balcony acted as her doorway, and merging with them, Kim passed directly into the house.

Inside, the room around her was a simple one: a frayed, orange-and-green rug lay askew over a worn hardwood floor; bookcases with dusty leather volumes lined all but the wall she had come through, and an open doorway before her revealed a staircase leading up.

She took the stairs two at a time, aware Freighter could return at any moment.

At the top was a wide corridor with wood walls and floor, lined with dozens of doors for as far as she could see.

"Where do I start?"

The first room she tried was a bedroom. Kim gave it a cursory look and exited, drifting from door to door down the seemingly endless halls, a ghost with the heart of a girl looking for a lost loved one. After half a dozen bedrooms she realized everything upstairs was living space, though not one of those rooms looked like they'd been slept in for years. The only one without a bed was one that had a small, green-upholstered chair, a globe, and a wall covered in dozens of keys, hung as if for decoration.

"Hmm; might be important," she said aloud, not realizing she was being observed.

From there she returned to the staircase - now in a completely different location - and descended once more to the ground floor. Here too, the layout had shifted in her absence. Richard had warned her this would be the case, but that didn't actually prepare her for the nauseous feeling that accompanied having the house move around with her inside.

Picking up her pace, it wasn't long before Kim found a door unlike any of the others: large and made of metal, with massive rivets across much of its face. Moving to pass through it, she was shocked to find that despite her immaterial form, the door rejected her. This made her remember her sister's words:

"There's a door, but it won't let me out."

The keys!

Kim studied the keyhole for a moment, turned back to the stairs and came face to face with a shimmering black shape that now blocked her way. Panicked, she tried to push through it, but an appendage shot out and caught her by the arm, snapped her forward so hard Kim went straight to the floor, her breath knocked clean from her lungs.

Kim's vision spun for a second, and when her breath finally returned, she screamed. The form was now that of a woman, with inky black shadows instead of hair; they floated out behind her like Medusa's tentacles. Kim lashed out with her own limbs; her two-dimensional form grew exponentially, expanded her arms so that she caught her attacker by the tentacle-hair and used the momentum to hurl her across the room. Then Kim turned and pushed as hard as she could toward the wall before her, hoping it was an outside one. Instead, she emerged into a foyer that looked identical to the one in Jessie's house. She picked up speed now, knowing full well that one of the doors here would open into Jessie's. It was exactly as Richard had explained to her previously: all the houses were linked by this foyer because all the houses were actually the *same house*. She didn't understand it, but there was a lot she didn't understand. Exhausted, she returned to her solid form and began trying doors. The third one on her right opened, and a moment later she was standing in Jessie's home, watching as he and an older man came in through the front door, Jessie soaked but unhurt, the older man talking nonstop about what she assumed was a confrontation with Freighter. Kim remained invisible in her shadow form, and Jessie did not see her even as he passed directly by her.

About an hour after she watched Jessie walk up his stairs with the man she learned was named WJ, Kim snuck up to the second floor of the house and through his bedroom door without opening it. She watched Jessie, asleep on his bed, his wet clothes hung over a plastic chair in the corner, his face peaceful and still from exhaustion. Staring at him and thinking of how he'd helped her, how after all this time things were starting to look up, Kim smiled. She stood there silently for some time, drawing her own peace from this wonderful boy, knowing she was on the verge of getting her sister back. When Kim finally went to leave, she saw Jessie stir slightly. She found a piece of paper and a pen on his desk and solidified her hand long enough to write a quick note, then slipped first from the room and then the house, certain she was on the verge of falling in love for the first time. She didn't even feel bad for involving Jessie in her nightmare, because the look in his eyes when she said helping her might be dangerous told her that Jessie wanted his world turned upside down as much as he wanted her.

Good. That was Kim's specialty.

Officer Chase Montgomery brought his Police Cruiser to rest off to the side of the roundabout that served as the driveway for the Knight's Side Sheriff Station. He was tired. Having tended bar at his sister's pub yesterday evening and come directly into the station afterward, fatigue was making it difficult to let go of the events of the last few hours. And if he hoped to catch any sleep before starting the cycle all over again, he was going to have to let it go.

For a little while, at least.

Once inside, Chase fired up the coffeemaker, plopped down behind his desk and closed his eyes. It was very early morning, still dark out, and while he waited for the bitter black imbibe that would grant him a second wind, he turned the thing over and over in his head without any luck of new perspective. Time slunk toward dawn and Chase nodded off for a moment, was startled awake when the coffeemaker began to belch and gurgle at the completion of its detail. Chase's eyes followed the machine's steam as it crawled up in lazy tendrils toward the open window three feet to the left. Along the way, the inconsistent cloud of vapor changed the colors of the wood-paneled walls from their customary faded rustic browns to variations of a sickly, jaundiced yellow, the unevenly spaced bookshelves growing hazy behind the apparition. Mesmerized, Chase snapped back to lucidity and shook himself to full attention. He looked at his computer. It was 5:00 A.M.; he'd be off in an hour, but he already knew there was no chance of sleep because tonight, the past had finally caught up to him.

When Wendell Briggington, a professor at the University in Knight's Side and a friend, called several hours ago to ask for a restraining order against local whack-job Bob Freighter, Chase knew all the bad stuff he had tried to pretend had ended five years ago was back.

And then he heard the voice mail from Dubois and Chase's world fell apart in a matter of minutes.

He'd been a cop in Knight's Side for nearly ten years. At the beginning, the town had behaved as he was pretty sure most small towns did. They had their problems, most of which consisted of breaking up parties around the University housing developments and closing up the occasional meth lab. Beside that, there would always be the low-level crime: shoplifting, bar fights and a fair amount of domestic disturbances. Once there'd even been a murder/suicide. But five years ago Chase had taken part in something he'd never forget, and even though he had spent the time since telling himself there was no chance of a repeat, Dubois's message proved that a naive hope:

Chase, this is Cuthbert Dubois. I will make this quick and appeal to you for your help using avenues other than myself. There has been an Event. Similar to what you saw five years ago, this recent activity was massive, and leads me to believe that Paolo has finally achieved his goal and The Hub has come on-line. I am reaching out to Richard, as well as our friends in South America, in the hopes that between all of us, we can deduce a method by which to stop him, lest what happened to that poor family happen to anyone else. Please call me as soon as you get this.

Chase set the phone down and cursed. The lies he'd repeated endlessly to absolve himself from having to explain what had happened five years ago were coming back on him now, and like anything else hidden and left to fester, things were going to be considerably worse this time around. Especially if what Cuthbert said was true.

To top it off, what about Freighter? Chase practically had to bite his tongue in half when WJ stopped at Gulliver's last month and asked if he knew whether the Tenorio house was on the market. Chase's gut demanded he tell Wendall to look elsewhere, but of course that would have meant he believed there was still something wrong with that house, so he'd balked.

And now? Part of Chase had always hoped the eccentric nature of the Tenorio home would be enough to drive new owners away. But it hadn't, and if the fabled Hub was real, and Cruchetti had managed to get it up and running, things could get bad fast. And indeed, things had been bad this evening: calls about strange lights in the woods, voices, lots of crazy shit. All signs pointed to Chase having to come to terms with what he feared most, so no, sleep was not an option.

The front door startled him when the relief detail walked in. Gil and Terry, the first a lifer on the force, milking a few extra years before social security, the second the very definition of 'wet behind the ears.' Knight's Side had long been both conservative and hopeful when it came to the budget for the Sheriff's department, and the Mayberry approach might have worked when Chase's brother-in-law had been Sheriff, but it wasn't going to cut it anymore. Fifty-seven year old Declan O'Rourke had been understaffed for most of his career, but that was a simpler time. When he was killed in a freak locomotive accident six years ago and Jim Rash took over as Sheriff, that was right before things began to change. The Sheriff station's role in the community became increasingly difficult, especially when it came to its unofficial jurisdiction in neighboring community Gallows Hill. And things were about to get even more complicated. Chase thought for a moment that he should level with his coworkers about what he thought was headed their way. But in that place where his common sense and intuition met, he knew they'd never believe him.

"We got it from here, Mr. Montgomery," Terry said as he sniffed the coffee pot. On the job six months, Terry still hadn't become comfortable enough to refer to the other officers by anything other than their pre-fixes.

"Alright kid." Chase started out, then stopped and turned to address Terry.

"Do me a favor, yeah? Anything weird comes in, something over say a five on the freak o' meter, give me a call. I got inventory with Nancy at the bar, so I'll be up."

"Sure thing Mr. Montgomery," Terry said, and Chase smiled.

Clocked out and in his cruiser, Chase stopped at the Big Tree Diner for a cup of coffee, then headed toward Gulliver's. On his way, he passed a work crew on the side of Kinghill Road, at the border between Knight's Side and Gallows Hill. A funny feeling told him to stop and say hi.

"Morning. You guys aren't state, what's the deal?"

One of the men, a tall, thin guy with a red beard and red hair sticking out from under a Steeler's cap gave Chase a salute and approached the window.

"Morning officer. No, we're with Wheeler's construction in Woodsville."

"Woodsville? What're you doing here?"

"Some rich guy hired us. Art installation or something. Not sure. My brother-in-law, Jim Wheeler's the foreman, he said the job was just to bury a couple of these boxes."

"Mind if I see one?"

"Not at all," Red Beard turned and picked up a small, glass box from out of a larger crate in the bed of the truck. Chase noticed worn lettering on the side of the vehicle that said Wheeler's in script. Red Beard returned with the box, offered it to Chase. As he took it, one of the other guys in the group waved at him.

"Chase Montgomery, that you?"

Chase strained his eyes until the other guy came closer. It was Reggie Lark; he'd been a local artist for years; a University drop-out who had started some online business and kept a gallery on the North end. Reggie used to pick up shifts at Gulliver's when he was still at school. Now, the way Chase heard it, kid did pretty good with his art.

"Reggie. Well, what're you doing out here?"

"Just picking up a little extra money. Have'ta buy plane tickets and a hotel in a few weeks, got a big gallery show coming up in Scotland."

"Well, congrats, kid. That's great. You know what this thing is?" Chase handed the box back to Red Beard.

"Ask me, it's a time capsule. I heard about some guy in Pittsburgh, does this weird show where he unearths time capsules with drawings of modern stuff in them, like world events? Tries to pass them off as prophecy, but it's all just been buried recently. Total scam. Still, whoever he is, he's paying us a thousand bucks a man for three, four hours work tops, so…"

Satisfied, Chase popped his truck back in gear, "Say no

more. He'd approached me, I'd be out here with ya. You boys have a good day."

"You too, Officer Montgomery. Good to see you."

Chase waved and pulled back onto the road. He'd been jumpy the last few days, no doubt about it. Nancy's monthly inventory would take a couple hours, but it might actually tire him out enough for some sleep before his shift later on.

"Here's hoping," Chase said, unconvinced.

CHAPTER 10

Jessie woke abruptly to find the sound louder than ever. He started to panic, then realized what he was hearing wasn't the enigmatic hum. No, this seemed more familiar, and it was coming from just outside his bedroom door!

Jessie's blood ran cold until his initial disorientation left him and he recognized the intrusion for what it was: a vacuum cleaner. He crawled from bed and saw a handwritten note on his dresser.

Got in and out okay. I can never thank you enough - for the first time in a long time I have answers. I'll tell you all about it later.

- Kim

"How the hell?" Jessie decided to drop his questions for now; he was just glad Kim was okay. He shuffled to the door. Outside, Talia plugged away at the hardwood floor with big, sweeping strokes of the machine, very noticeably irritated at its refusal to "Just do its job!" as she yelled at the last. When she saw Jessie watching her, she smiled, and something about that smile helped tuck the horrors of the previous night away beneath a soft, velvety sheet of reality.

"Sorry. Did I wake you?"

"It's okay, I was having a nightmare anyway," he smiled and motioned toward the vacuum, "You know those things don't work that good on wood floors, right?"

"You're fifteen, how do you know that?"

"Read it online."

"Good lord. You read about vacuuming online?"

WJ came up the stairs, "What's up guys? How's cleaning going?"

Talia smirked, "Ask Jessie."

"Huh?"

"Truly the internet will be the end of all things."

Talia clicked the vacuum back on, went after an errant dust bunny they'd all been trying not to acknowledge and managed only to push it further away with each thrust of the device.

"Ugh, this sucks!" she shrieked and clicked the machine back into its upright position, then reached down and gave the cord a nice big YANK that pulled it free of the wall socket down the hall.

"Hey, careful! You'll wear out your sockets," WJ said, throwing Jessie a look that told him he hadn't slept well either.

But he had slept here.

"Really, Mr. Handyman? Perhaps you would be so kind as to grab the broom and take over where I seem to be failing so miserably."

"I don't think we have a broom, Mom," Jessie said as he made his way past them and down the stairs.

"Great. Oh! Jessie? My schedule's changed again. I have to go to the University this afternoon. Will you guys be okay for lunch?"

You guys?

"Sure," he tried not to sound too freaked out, but his

encounter with Freighter hung heavy on his mood. Too much uncertainty.

The mention of lunch evoked an unexpected hunger. Clearly diving headfirst into the supernatural had not affected his appetite.

Fifteen minutes later, Jessie was full of coffee and cereal when WJ approached him.

"You okay?"

"I guess. I feel like, well, I'm glad you were there to see what happened because no one would believe me otherwise."

"Jessie, let's not tell your mom about this right away, okay? She's got a lot on her plate at the moment. You'll find out sooner than later, but apparently, the University's canceled her classes this semester."

"What? How the hell can they do that?"

"I don't know that they can. I promised her I would talk to the head of our department, but I have to play it cool. Meantime, she might have to pick up an expedition to qualify for insurance."

"Great. The whole point of moving here was so she didn't have to travel anymore."

"I know. Look, I talked to a friend on the Knight's Side Sheriff's Department and put in for a restraining order against that creep, so he shouldn't bother you anymore."

"Thanks. I hope you're right."

"If I'm not, I'll call... um..."

"What, an exorcist?"

"Ha. Look, I'm sure there's a rational explanation for... well, for everything."

Jessie could tell by the way WJ said this that he didn't really believe it; he was just saying it for Jessie's benefit.

Heels on the wooden floor:

"Wendell? Did you ask Jessie about the boxes yet?"

"On it," he said, and turned back to Jessie, "Your mom

asked me to help you bring up some of the boxes from downstairs? Said you guys went through a bunch of them at some point Saturday night or something?"

Jessie nodded and stood. When he opened the door to the basement a moment later, he felt the hum return louder than ever.

"You okay, Jessie?"

"Headache," he lied.

WJ nodded, and ran his hand over the wall just inside the door for a moment before Jessie slipped around him and snatched the chain. The bulb came on but made little difference. Even in the daytime, the basement was black as night.

They began their descent, and once they neared the bottom and WJ saw the mirrors, Jessie felt his excitement become palpable.

"Holy cow! What is this?" WJ picked up his pace down the stairs, and Jessie did the same as a sort of proximity response. Stepping onto the cold concrete floor, Jessie couldn't help smile watching the older man stalk between the mirrors, clearly fascinated at the prospect of the situation.

"Your mother said this was weird, but she didn't say how or why. My god, this is… this is weird with a capital 'W.' I mean Jessie," he turned and looked at Jessie with a massive, gaping smile that was half scholar, half child, "This has gotta be something, right? Something not like most things, if you catch my drift."

WJ winked on that one and Jessie fell into his orbit a little bit. There was something about WJ's fervor that Jessie found contagious, and it pushed that swelling tension further away. They stood in the middle of the mirrors, friends on an adventure, their reflections skipping back and forth around them, creating infinite hallways in some directions and crippling, haunted distortions in others.

"What did your mother say about this when you guys found it?"

"Well, I found it. It was like three in the morning when I realized all my bed stuff was down here."

"What were you still doing up at three in the morning?" The question was asked in surprise, not authority. Jessie answered it with a look that said, 'back off' laced with an underpinning of camaraderie.

"Mom mislabeled some of the boxes, and I needed my pillows and stuff."

"Sorry, not trying to say don't do that, just creeped out thinking about you coming down here at that time. Jeez, that had to be freaky."

Jessie lowered his defenses again.

"Yeah, my mind started to play tricks on me, I guess. Then mom came down and we just kinda switched to autopilot."

The two stood there surrounded by the mirrors for a moment, then looked at one another and smiled.

"C'mon dude, I'll bet this totally freaked you out when you came down here. It would me if it was the middle of the night in a new house, surrounded by the woods no less."

"Yeah."

"And it's really dark down here. I brought a couple of electric lanterns from home. Later on, maybe we can grab them and start exploring-"

From the top of the stairs, Talia called down to them.

"Wendell, you left your phone up here. There's a Chase Montgomery calling, you want me to answer it?"

"Crap! Be right back, gotta take this."

WJ turned and bolted in a lethargic, middle-aged run.

"ANSWER IT TALIA! I'll be right up!"

CHAPTER 11

"Jessie? Can I talk to you for a minute?" Talia's disembodied voice asked as he came up from the basement. Jessie wanted to follow WJ and hear his conversation, but he'd already made it outside, past Talia, who stood in the hall trying some of the doors with ornate keys on a large ring.

"Found this key ring, weird huh?"

"You have no idea."

"What?"

"Nothing. What's up, mom?"

"Look," she said, "Bad news. The University called earlier to tell me my classes this semester have been canceled.

"How is that even possible?" Jessie feigned surprise.

"Long story. Suffice it to say, that leaves us up a creek without a paddle.

"What are you going to do?"

"Well, here's the second half. I've been invited on a dig with one of the Professors. I don't want to go, but it's the only way to stay employed by the school until the first of the year."

"This is exactly what we were trying to get away from."

"I know. If you don't want me to go, I won't."

Jessie sighed. "I take it WJ will be watching me in your absence?"

"Would that be alright with you?"

"Are you two dating?"

Talia turned red, hung her head a bit, "I was going to tell you."

"It's okay. I mean, I've known for a while. I just wish you'd said something. All the sneaking around…"

"I wish I'd said something too, Jess. Look at it this way, at least you can use this for leverage against me once you get a little older."

He smiled, but Talia didn't think it was a real smile. She wasn't amusing him, she was condescending him because he was a kid and she spent all of her time in the 'grown-up' world of academia. In that moment Talia realized she'd forgotten how to talk to Jessie when it wasn't about his education or the shared experiences that made up their day-to-day world. She'd forgotten how to raise him because for so long he'd done such a good job raising himself in her absence.

"I guess I haven't exactly been the best mother."

"Don't say that. Don't ever say that. Mom, I love you, and I want you to be happy. I understand why you didn't tell me about you and WJ, I just need some time to deal with it in my own way. Okay?"

Talia hesitated for a moment and then smiled, "Yeah. That's not too much to ask. Sorry, I'm trying to overcompensate I guess."

Jessie smiled and nodded 'yes,' then hugged his mother. Talia had to fight a little tear from the corner of her eye.

"When I get back, I swear… well, how about we go somewhere special for Winter Break? Just you and me?"

"Mom, we're always going somewhere. How 'bout we just stay here and try to actually make this feel like home, instead of just another stop on the journey? I'm sick of moving around. I want to go to school, have friends. Maybe a girlfriend."

"Ah… does this have anything to do with your new friend from down the street?"

"Maybe," it thrilled him to speak aloud of the possibility.

WJ re-entered.

"What was that all about?" Talia asked.

"Nothing," WJ said and winked at Jessie.

~

Outside, a portly mailman came into view on the road beyond their driveway.

"Oh crap!" Talia began to panic, ran to the counter and shuffled a small nest of papers together into an envelope, "Jessie, I forgot to put our insurance papers in the mailbox. Could you run this out?"

"Sure mom."

Outside, the mail carrier had already passed their house, and Jessie had to run to catch him. As soon as he did, Jessie realized the hum had stopped.

"Hello? I have some mail."

"Greetings lad! You must be the new owner of the Tenorio house <Hurm>."

"Yes sir."

"Well, please inform me of your name lad, so that I can re-christen said house with a proper moniker instead of a past-tense, post-haste. Also, please inform one such as myself how a boy of, hmmm.." The man in the faded blue uniform sized Jessie up like a tailor would a particularly perplexing client, "Twenty mayhap? No...fifteen? Thirte- no, no (shaking his head). I never was very good with ages you know <Hurm>."

The sound the mail carrier kept making was something between a laugh and a throat-clearing exercise. Jessie found it made him smile.

"How does one such as yourself manage to buy a house such as this? Did you invest in the Google?"

"Ha, no. Ah, I live with my mother. She's a Professor at the University and we just moved here. My name's Jessie. Jessie Roberts. Mom is Talia."

"Then very well met we are, young Jessie Roberts! The Roberts' house it will henceforth be when spoken of from my tongue. For myself, Richard Penelope Fattingback, at your service. I know, I know, how could I ever have had a chance to be anything but my current circumference with a name such as that, yes? Perhaps my parents believed that since, in spite of my middle name being traditionally associated with the fairer sex, I had indeed remained a boy, that my surname would surely have no effect on my physical girth either. You can see they were quite mistaken, as despite my constant bipedal travels all over our fair Gallows Hill for the last twenty-odd revolutions of our lord the sun, I am, as is most often colloquially uttered, overweight or 'fat,' much like the prefix to my aforementioned name."

There was no fighting it by this point - Jessie wore an enormous smile and his eyes were wide as saucers. He was charmed but exhausted from the man's diatribe - he'd never heard anyone talk that much that fast - and the adults he interacted with most often were professors! Imagine! Almost afraid to speak after all that, Richard Penelope Fattingback recognized the effect he'd had on the boy and took it in good stride.

"But, my apologies young Jessie Roberts of the Roberts'

household! You appear to have an item of outgoing mail - a vital communique to a beautiful maiden perhaps - and here I stand filibustering your momentum when it is, in fact, my state-appointed career, nay obligation! to assist you in the delivery of said communication. If you would forgive a lonely postal courier his peccadilloes..."

Despite the relative insanity of this encounter, Jessie found that he liked this person very much.

"Thank you, Mr. Fat-"

"Bah! Call me Richard," then, in an aside Fattingback leaned in and whispered behind his cupped hand, "You most certainly cannot call me Rich, because in wealth and fashion, I regrettably do not currently reside." He snickered to let Jessie know it was okay to laugh and the two shared a moment of genuine hilarity. Jessie reached out to hand over the letter and that's when something strange came over him.

The light in the sky fell away, the hum returned louder than ever; one minute the sun looked normal, the next it turned black as sackcloth. Smiling, without moving his lips, Fattingback spoke again, only this time in a decidedly different voice.

"Lad, I risk my life to warn you, so listen good. The sound that has plagued you is that of a great machine that lies buried just beyond the walls of your house, of all the houses in Gallows Hill. You have awoken something, and because of that, they will come for you from both sides. Be prepared, and be careful who you trust."

When Jessie finally shook off the stupor, the sun had returned and Fattingback was already several yards away from him.

"Until we meet again young Master Roberts!" the Mailman called with a wave and a skip in his step.

"What the absolute hell was that?" Jessie asked aloud as

the hum returned, this time louder than ever. He had to see Kim, had to make sure she was okay, and have her help him figure out what was happening to him.

CHAPTER 12

Inventory at the bar went off without a hitch, but even after another three hours awake, bringing his current tally close to twenty-four, Chase could not sleep. It'd been like this five years ago, too. Right after it happened.

When the phone rang and Dubois asked Chase if he could meet, he was only too happy to oblige.

Part of him felt like wringing Cuthbert's neck. How long had Chase operated with the GHAS before he'd been told the truth, and then only out of necessity? When he'd originally hitched on, it was to pick up where his father had left off. The late Leviticus Montgomery had raised his children as a single father, and as kids, they'd watched him slowly unravel, caught up in what both Chase and his sister Nancy explained away as an elaborate fantasy brought on by their mom's death on her sixty-third birthday. Debra Montgomery had been considerably older than Leviticus, and a devout member of the Gallows Hill Antiquarian Society, the GHAS for short. What Leviticus learned after her passing was that the GHAS shared more DNA with historical organizations like the Secret Order of the Golden Dawn, or Aleister Crowley's Argentum Astrum than the Antique Roadshows of the word. Chase's father confronted Dubois, only to begin his own journey into the unknown. The outcome of this was Leviticus eventually spending the final year of his life in an asylum; during that time Chase tried to suss out the cause of it and thinking the GHAS villainous, he introduced himself to his father's former friend Cuthbert Dubois. He joined the group intent on infiltrating and exposing them. But much like his father, with Dubois, Chase began to see things he could not explain, and from there he was hooked.

Until that night.

Later, Chase realized that everything Cuthbert Dubois did came down to one thing and one thing alone: trumping his former business partner and lover, Paolo Cruchetti.

Exhaustion still in his peripheral, Chase left Nancy's and headed onto campus, where he met Dubois at the small cafe adjoined to the University. Dubois so loved the environment of Academia.

"Chase Montgomery, how good of you to meet with me."

Cuthbert stood as Chase approached, a tall man, lanky and beguiling in age. Visually, Dubois appeared to be at least seventy. His movements, however, were deceiving; when he stood, he did so flawlessly and with gusto, up in an instant, no creaking knees or sour joints. His face was angular, with sharp cheekbones and a pointed chin, the shape of which was accented by long, straight gray hair that perpetually slipped from its ponytail to swing in Dubois's face.

"Cuthbert. I hope you're wrong about this."

"Oh, I am not wrong. Do you hear it, Chase? The sound of the device activated at last."

Chase waited a moment, filtering out the background noise of the cafe.

"I don't hear anything."

"Surprising."

"Where's Linda?"

"Hard at work on something or another, I'd imagine. Things are hectic at the moment, and if Paolo truly has brought The Hub online, we're going to need to move quickly to-"

"Let me get one thing straight. I'm not helping you steal back your tech from Cruchetti. I'm only here because-"

"Because you want to make sure no one else goes through the horrors you've seen others suffer? How noble of you."

"We're all just pawns to you, aren't we, Cuthbert?"

"If you like. That is not to say I do not care, simply that I serve a higher purpose."

"What higher purpose? Becoming even more rich and powerful by giving the world it's first-"

"Ah! Please now, Officer Montgomery. If people hear you carrying on like this, they may draw nasty comparisons betwixt you and your father."

Chase seethed; he knew Dubois was right. He had tried to outlive his father's reputation every day of his life, one of the reasons that, in spite of what he'd seen with the GHAS, he tried so hard to downplay or deny the spectacular.

And here was Dubois, digging it all back out again.

"It was bound to happen, you know. Paolo has had several lifetimes worth of vantage to utilize in planning all of this. This day was, unfortunately, inevitable.

"Fine. Inevitable. Look, I've got two things for you. First, a friend of mine just moved his girlfriend and her teenage son into the Tenorio place. Two, Bob Freighter attacked said teenage son and my friend last night - scurried off on all fours to hear Wendell tell it."

"All fours, eh? Well, it seems Robert's proximity to the device has had some unexpected effects. Hard to feel sympathy, though, when he takes so much pleasure in his strange and terrible duties."

"Look Dubois, if Cruchetti has The Hub up and running and he's still using Freighter to switch people, doesn't it stand to reason he's planning some kind of massive offensive?"

"Oh, of that I have no doubt."

"Then who knows how many other people have been switched, or mutated, or whatever. The entire population of Knight's Side is essentially living at ground zero of a metaphysical H-Bomb right now."

"Even more reason we need to stop talking and actually get to work!"

"Agreed. What first?"

"Can you contact this friend? What is his name?"

"Wendell. He already contacted me. Filed a restraining order against Freighter late last night."

Dubois guffawed.

"Yeah, that's what I said. Like asking a rabid fox to please not kill your chickens. Still, appearances."

"Chase, appearances are what has allowed Knight's Side to grow fat at the teat of lies that, ultimately, left it dangling from the precipice of calamity. Perhaps we can dispense with them from here out and try telling people the truth."

"Well said, Cuthbert. You first. How old are you?"

"Why Officer, what an absolutely boorish question."

CHAPTER 13

"So who is this Chase Montgomery?" Talia asked.

"Just a friend. He's a cop in Knight's Side."

"I didn't know you were friends with any cops. Might come in handy."

"You know the pizza we had the other night?"

"Yeah. Pretty good."

"It's from his sister Nancy's place, Gulliver's Travails."

"Cute name."

"I guess. Chase still tends bar there a couple nights a week to help out; at some point, I developed a habit of stopping in after work when he was on shift, got to know him pretty well."

"Really? Rough place?" she joked.

"Naw. I mean, according to some of my colleagues, it used to be more of a shot-and-a-beer joint, you know."

"Joint?" Talia laughed.

WJ laughed with her.

"Chase used to be the regular evening bartender before he became a cop. Some of the guys in the department know him, they introduced us."

"Bunch of academicians hanging out at the Roadhouse?"

"Stop. After their father died, Nancy took the place over, put in the pizza kitchen and kind of cleaned it up a bit."

"So what'd he call for now? You leave your tab open?"

"Forget about Chase for a minute, I want to show you something."

"Okay."

"You know those mirrors you found in the basement?"

"Do I know them? They spook the bejeezus out of me."

Talia laughed uneasily and began to organize a stack of books on the large Oak shelf before her. One of the benefits of her cleaning spree that morning was she'd found the large ring of keys she'd carried with her all day. None of them opened the doors downstairs, but one had proved useful in unlocking the enigmatic parlor, so there was that.

"Yeah, well Chase confirmed that the man who used to live in this house designed them."

"Ah, this just gets better and better. Cruchetti did the house, the former tenant furnished our basement with dozens of creepy mirrors and, let me see... who did the plumbing? Satan?"

They both laughed, and WJ sensed she had relaxed some. He grabbed Talia's laptop from off one of the shelves and plopped into the seashell-shaped wicker chair in the corner, one of the few pieces of furniture they'd had the time to set up. Talia moved in close as WJ opened a browser, began typing.

"So that's why whenever I flush your toilet I always hear someone whisper Red Rum."

"All work and no play..." Talia quoted, one eyebrow cocked as she delivered a convincing "Ree Ree Ree" and pretended to stab WJ with her pen.

"Easy there killer," he laughed. Talia's playfulness had drawn WJ's attention away from the computer but now he re-focused. Curious, she watched as his fingers flit over the keys, plugging 'Arthur Tenorio' and the word "mirrors" into the search engine.

"Tenorio, huh?" she began to rub his shoulders but stopped abruptly when one of her fingernails snagged a thread from his sweater; WJ stretched an arm around her legs and drew her directly next to him.

"I need to figure out where my nail file is. Nosferatu here."

"Living in Knight's Side I'd heard the name Tenorio of course; he's like Cruchetti - something of a local legend. I guess I just didn't realize… yep! I knew it."

WJ sat up quickly and Talia lost her balance. She slid over the side of the chair, her shoulders and head landing square in his lap. Staring at him upside down, she laughed, a girlish smile brightening her entire face. Then a noise from somewhere in the hall outside caused her to start. Before she'd even realized it, she was back on her feet and fixing her shirt, which had escaped her brown leather belt and ridden up her back.

"I told Jessie about us, you know."

"You did?"

"I did. He already knew. Of course."

"Talia, that's, well, thank you."

"Don't thank me until I come back and we see if he's driven you crazy or not."

"Oh come on."

"Just kidding. Now, what were you all excited about?"

"Well," he said, offering a lascivious grin.

"I mean online, dufus!"

"Okay, look. This site here, eldritchmirrormage.com."

"Eldritch what? Wendell, have you gone goth?"

"Haha, you won't be laughing so hard when you pay for Jessie's college fund with those mirrors."

"Oh come on, something that recent can't be worth any real money."

"Oh yeah? Look…" WJ scrolled down the page and began to read from the text:

"The works of Arthur Tenorio are another matter entirely. Literally. The artist was discovered by world-renowned avant-garde architect Paolo Cruchetti and brought to the states to work exclusively alongside him on several of Cruchetti's larger scale projects. Tenorio's glasswork is said by some to contain strange and even magical properties based on the inclusion of a substance known among his native South American tribal ancestors as Ch'ul. Ch'ul is a psychoactive substance produced by the body of a shaman; this substance is often considered the seat of the Shaman's powers in the physical realm and-"

"Wendell! This is insane, what are you telling me? You're doing anthropological research on Eldritch.com?"

"Talia, you're missing the point. These things are hand-made works of art that a subset of the population believes give you magical powers. You, my dear, are sitting on a goldmine."

"Oh please. Let me see that." She took the computer from his hands, began to read and scroll at an irritated pace. At some point though, she slowed down.

"See something that strikes a nerve?"

"Please."

"Seriously. I don't think you understand just how rare these things are."

"Well, you wouldn't know it by looking in our basement," she said.

"That's what I mean; I figured if no one had claim to them then you might have a decent little chunk of secondary income down there."

"Was that why Chase called? About the mirrors?"

WJ hesitated a moment, then continued cautiously, "Not

exactly. I called him last night because I had to file a restraining order against your new neighbor."

"What? Why on Earth?"

"Don't worry. It's the old man that lives at the end of the block. I guess that local girl was showing Jessie around last night and they went on his property - I mean, you should see it up close. Looks abandoned."

"Are you going to plead Jessie's defense everytime he gets caught trespassing?"

"Talia…"

"No, seriously Wendell. This is no good. I mean, I leave tomorrow. What the hell-"

"We'll be fine. I swear. I've already talked to Jessie about it. He said it was an accident. They were walking in the woods, and this guy saw them and thought they were spying on him."

"Is that what he told you?"

"No, I spoke to the neighbor, too. And he nearly bit my head off. Literally. Very crude. I thought it best to get the order to keep Jessie away from him and him away from us."

"Oh my god. This isn't happening."

"It is, and it's fine. Seriously. Chase said the guy's a loon. I'm meeting with him later, thought it'd be good to maybe invite him over while you're on the dig. Gallows is unincorporated, so the police tend to stay away. Chase is a friend though, so if I ask him to help, and he meets and likes Jessie - which I'm sure he will - I have a feeling he'll be around a lot more to check in on us. Or…"

"Or what?"

"Well, he actually called me back this morning to tell me a really nice house just came up for rent in Knight's Side. You know, in case you wanted to move."

"Move? We just got here!"

"Yeah, just a thought."

"Wendell…"

"I know. He is a little concerned about the mirrors."

"The ones that are going to make me rich? What the hell is going on here?"

"I'll know more after I sit down with him."

Talia headed toward the door.

"Where are you going?"

"Where else? The basement."

"It's a miracle Jessie didn't trip and fall on his way down here the other night. Even in the middle of the day, I can barely see where I'm going," Talia said, carefully making her way down the first of the basement stairs.

"Hold on a second. Here," WJ caught up to her with an electric lantern in his hand. He turned it on, and all the stairs came into view, "I have a couple more of these I can leave down here until we get a better lighting system."

"Too bad spooky Arthur Tenorio didn't make lamps instead of mirrors, eh?"

They reached the basement floor and made their way into the circle of mirrors.

"This is just nuts."

"I can't even imagine what it was like finding this in the middle of the night."

"No, you cannot."

"Hey, this one over here's broken," WJ said, finding the mirror Jessie had accidentally knocked over that first night.

"I think that was Jessie. No biggie," Talia said, "I wonder what's back here."

They started out of the circle, towards a back wall against which sat an old workbench.

"You notice there's piles of sawdust everywhere? Like

someone was down here working recently," she said, an audible shiver in her voice, "Wendell, please tell me someone wasn't down here making magic mirrors like two days before we moved in."

"I'm sure that's not the case. If it were that fresh, we'd smell it."

"True. Okay, well, I'm assuming the realtor didn't show you any of this when you scoped the place out."

"I don't remember her mentioning it. Come to think of it, I know I saw the kitchen, but I don't recall even seeing the basement door."

"Jeez," Talia said, and the timer on her phone began to sound, "Oh, crap. I still have to go to school."

They walked back out of the basement.

"I wish I knew where the heck Jessie is."

WJ picked up Kim's purple hair tie off the kitchen counter as they passed it.

"Pretty sure this is your answer right here."

"Oh lord."

"They're fine."

"Easy for you to say. Are you sticking around by chance?"

"No. I'm supposed to meet Chase in two hours, I should go home and change first."

"Okay, I'll just leave the door unlocked for him. Not like we have psychotic old men as neighbors or anything."

"It'll be fine."

"Yeah. You're right. Meet back here later? Maybe we can do some more exploring."

"Sounds good."

They kissed briefly and were on their way.

CHAPTER 14

On his way home, WJ's resentment at the University's treatment of Talia grew, until he passed his turn-off and continued on directly to the school. When he arrived, he found that, as he suspected, Dean Stanisberg was in his office, preparing for tomorrow's start of the semester.

"Wendell, what can I do for you, my good man?"

"Well Dean Stanisberg, I wanted to talk to you about Talia Roberts."

"Ah, our new professor. Excellent job again my friend, bringing that one in; she will no doubt make a ripping contribution to our department."

"Then why pull her classes?"

"Excuse me?"

"I was with Talia earlier today when she was informed her classes this semester had been canceled."

Now it was the Dean's turn to look confused.

"That doesn't make any sense at all. I re-approved a budget that included Professor Roberts just the other day."

"Well, she was on the phone all morning."

"With who?"

"I know she spoke to a Paul Barker."

"Not possible. Paul Barker hasn't been at this school in almost five years."

"Come again?"

"You would not have been privy to Paul's situation, the entire ordeal was very hush-hush."

Spiders of unease began to crawl over WJ's spine.

"You understand if he has left the sanitarium, it is most definitely not through due process. Paul Barker was deemed unfit to return to society until the whereabouts of his wife and two daughters were discovered. Nobody wanted to think the worst, but even those of us close to him did after... the incident."

"What incident?"

Stanisberg retired briefly to a liquor cabinet sequestered in one of his bookshelves to gain the strength to continue the tale.

～

No sooner had Talia parked her car in the faculty lot then a small, gray-haired man in an outdated suit came running out of the closest building, waving and calling her name.

"Talia! Talia Roberts!"

"Hello. I'm sorry, I don't believe we've met."

"Paul Barker, we spoke this morning, I am the head of the field discovery program."

"Ah, so you're the man who's going to throw me a bone."

"I beg your pardon?"

"The Dig. That's yours, right?"

"Oh, yes. My apologies, your meaning was unclear."

Talia wasn't sure why, but she already did not like this man.

"So they've filled you in on the nature of the work?"

"Not really, but does it matter?"

"I don't follow."

"I moved here from across the country, bought a house and then found out the day before the semester begins that my classes have all been canceled. Frankly, I'm not very happy. This was supposed to be an opportunity for my son and I to settle down."

"I apologize for any inconvenience. Honestly, it sounds like a nightmare, but it has nothing to do with me."

"Then I apologize, as well."

"No need. I assure you, Professor Roberts, that this will be a most worthwhile experience. In fact, it should dovetail quite nicely with your class once it's reinstated next semester."

"Professor Barker, my course is on Ancient Masonry; how is digging in Alaskan snow mounds going to relate to ancient Mesopotamia."

"Yes, well, if you would accompany me to my office, I will brief you in full."

Talia followed Barker at a measured distance. Something about this man, this entire ordeal felt off, but she held herself upright, always the strongest person she knew, always reso-lute to deal with whatever unpleasantness came her way. The problem this time, Talia realized as she followed Paul Barker through the door at the end of the hall into a room that was empty, save for furniture hidden beneath gray tarps, dust several inches deep on every surface, was that the unpleas-antness was of an entirely new magnitude.

Talia had her phone out of her bag just as the door slammed behind her. Too late she realized what was happen-ing, and when she turned to defend herself, someone smacked the phone from her hand from behind. Talia turned and the world shuttered black.

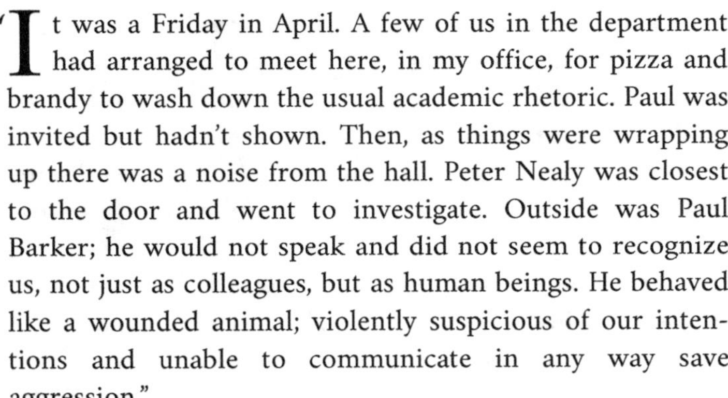

"It was a Friday in April. A few of us in the department had arranged to meet here, in my office, for pizza and brandy to wash down the usual academic rhetoric. Paul was invited but hadn't shown. Then, as things were wrapping up there was a noise from the hall. Peter Nealy was closest to the door and went to investigate. Outside was Paul Barker; he would not speak and did not seem to recognize us, not just as colleagues, but as human beings. He behaved like a wounded animal; violently suspicious of our intentions and unable to communicate in any way save aggression."

"Good lord. What was wrong with him?"

"I never learned. We finally managed to secure him in my office while Vanderhauten telephoned for emergency services. Once they arrived Paul became frenzied; one of the EMT's suffered quite the bite to his arm."

"Bite? Jesus, this sounds like a bad movie."

"Yes. Once they had Paul sedated and under control, they attempted to perform a perfunctory treatment on the EMT. His entire arm had turned black," the Dean paused, "You will have to excuse me, Wendell. I find it unnerving to think about this, even now."

"What are we talking here? Rot?"

"No. This was something... else. Something sinister is really the only word I have ever been able to come up with. And believe me, not a day has gone by since that I have not thought of this. It was as if the man's arm had become displaced by some form of negative space, as though he was becoming a shadow."

"My god."

"He was taken to the hospital, and we never heard anything after that. I never even learned the poor man's name. I have tried to put it out of my mind, but it is never far. It haunts me."

"So how did Talia talk to Barker earlier today?"

"Do I detect something more than professional courtesy in your concern?"

WJ blushed. Busted.

"Honestly? Yes. And now it is I who would prefer discretion from you on this subject, at least until we find out what exactly is going on."

"Agreed. As for Paul, once he was secured, I attempted to contact his wife. No one, however, had seen her in days. The same with his two daughters."

"And the investigation?"

"I believe the term is cold case. However…"

"Yes?"

"Are you familiar with the GHAS?"

"Somewhat," WJ thought of his recent conversation with Chase but held his tongue, "I've seen the junk mail. Why?"

"I happen to know that several days prior, Cuthbert Dubois was summoned to Arthur Tenorio's house because 'a little girl disappeared.' I have no proof this relates-"

"How can it not?"

"Indeed, but either way, I have long suspected that Dubois knows more than he told the police."

"What about Barker? Any new information after he was hospitalized? Tests must have been run?"

"After my phone calls failed, I made one final attempt at closure and personally went down to the hospital, only to discover that a representative from the CDC had put guards outside Paul's room. When I inquired as to his condition, I was whisked away in private and asked to cooperate with an "on-going investigation" by quietly arranging for Paul to take an open-ended personal leave. I have never heard anything since. Until today that is."

Dean Stanisberg held eye contact with WJ and then returned to the pile of papers on his desk. He stared at them for a moment and then reached into the top drawer, retrieved his keys and abruptly stood back up.

"And that Wendell, is the last of my information. I am sorry, but I'm afraid all of this talk about Paul has left me exhausted and morose. If I promise to look into this dig from home and call you as soon as I know anything, would you forgive me if I took my leave?"

"Of course, Dean Stanisberg. I'm sorry for upsetting you."

"On the contrary Wendell, what upsets me is the feeling that I should have done more. But that is not the case, and now this madness has fallen across your doorstep as well. Forgive me."

And with that Dean Stanisberg left the room, older and frailer than he had been when WJ came in just a few short minutes ago.

CHAPTER 15

When he couldn't raise Talia on her cell, WJ was tempted to skip the meeting with Chase and drive back to the house. However, Gulliver's was literally around the corner from the University and when he passed it he saw not only Chase Montgomery's police cruiser in the parking lot, but the silver and black, 1954 Cadillac Imperial - one of three designed as prototypes the year before the car went into mass production - that belonged to the richest man in the state.

"Dubois," WJ said, ruminating that when serendipity strikes, it's usually for a reason.

He pulled in next to Chase, tried Talia's cell one more time, and then entered the bar.

"WJ! Over here!" Chase called from the booth closest to the back of the room. Chase's sister Nancy was behind the bar. She was tall, blonde and pretty, and WJ had almost asked Chase to set them up once, right before he met Talia. They said hello now as WJ passed.

"Good evening, Mr. Briggington," Dubois's voice seemed inconsistent with the man. Seventy if a day, he was six-foot something and had the gait of someone half his age. His long gray hair was a mystery as well, as it terminated in the front in a completely out of place swathe of bangs that appeared to require regular maintenance; he'd already pushed them back three times in the sixty seconds or so since WJ had laid eyes on him. He was dressed in the sharpest suit Wendall had ever seen. A suit that, judging by the tailoring, probably cost close to what WJ's Mercedes did in resale.

"Mr. Dubois, a pleasure to finally make your acquaintance. I didn't realize you would be joining us."

"Scotch, Wendall?"

"It's a bit early, but what the hell. It's proving to be a trying day. Sure Chase. And thank you."

"No problem."

Chase darted off to the bar and WJ and Dubois were left to appraise one another. Stanisberg's words came back to WJ then:

"I have long suspected that Dubois knows more than he told the police."

"Please, sit. Wendell, I have heard a lot about you."

"And I you."

Chase returned with the drink.

"Well, that may not necessarily be a good thing, eh?" Dubois chuckled. Chase offered WJ the third seat at the table, just to his right, and the three men sat.

"Any luck convincing your woman to move?"

"Nope. She thought I was crazy for suggesting it."

"Yeah, this isn't my best moment. I should have been way out in front of this thing, Wendell, and for that I apologize."

"I dug around online a bit and found a lot of people out there who consider Arthur Tenorio's work to be magick."

"Wendell," Dubois interrupted, "may I speak frankly?"

"Of course," WJ said, taking a sip of his scotch.

"Excellent. Arthur Tenorio is responsible for some of the

greatest achievements in transportational metaphysics that, until two days ago, I feared no one would ever know about. He was raised by the Bruja of an Amazonian tribe and is steeped in the Arts of his ancestors. And it was exactly because of those Arts, and Arthur's abilities in manipulating them, that he originally came to the United States to work with Paolo Cruchetti."

"Did Chase tell you my girlfriend's basement is filled with his work?"

"Yes. She is the first person to live in Arthur's home since…"

Dubois stopped himself from whatever he was about to say, and WJ couldn't help but wonder if it had to do with what Stanisberg had told him.

"But everyone in Gallows Hill is living in a Cruchetti, myself included. And everyone has at least one Tenorio piece in their home. And as you will no doubt soon discover, all but three of those houses are empty."

"Really?"

"Yes. Your girlfriend's, mine and your neighbor two properties to the Southwest, Bob Freighter. Everyone else…"

"The truth, remember Cuthbert? Wendell, everyone else that lived in Gallows Hill is dead or disappeared."

"Jesus. What?"

"God's honest truth."

"And you're telling me… what? That it's because of Arthur Tenorio?"

"Indeed. You see, Arthur's mirrors actually do possess magical properties."

"I'm sorry. I don't want to be rude, but you must see how I'm having trouble with this."

"Do not apologize, good sir. It is the duty of all rational men to question the irrational, but only to the point of direct experience. I can give you that experience, if it will convince you of the danger you and your family are in."

WJ thought for a moment.

"What kind of - ahem - magical properties are we talking about, Mr. Dubois?"

"For starters, the ability to open the doorway to another world."

~

The mirror Jessie knocked over that first night lay off to the side of the Roberts's new basement, its surface fractured in a large, diagonal fissure inside of which a small ambient light began to grow. The orb-like emanation expanded slowly, until the entire pane looked like a pool of water lit from below. The top rippled with motion, and soon a hand split the surface, emerging from the ethereal depths and catching the frame as if it were the side of a bathtub. A second hand followed, and a moment later, something that looked exactly like Jessie Roberts pulled itself dripping from the silver liquid, breaching the barrier between two worlds. Physically identical to the Jessie that had moved into the house two days ago, this teenage boy was considerably different in every way imaginable.

~

"Another world?"

WJ noticed Chase was preoccupied watching a tall, attractive woman who had entered the bar. He'd seen this woman before, but did not know her name.

"This is where I'll let you two talk," Chase excused himself and WJ watched him approach the woman. Based on the haughty, non-communicative expression on her face, she did not seem particularly pleased to see him, despite body language that said the exact opposite.

"Widdershins, Mr. Briggington. The reverse of our world, which for contrast's sake we sometimes refer to as Deosil."

"The positions of the clock. A Victorian concept."

Across the room, Chase removed an envelope from the inside pocket of his Police Bomber and handed it to the woman. She declined to take it at first, and Chase left it on the bar with a weak smile and exited through the front door.

Dubois continued.

"The mirrors themselves hail back to the Victorian era, to the days when Percival Fawcett lead the Royal Geographical Society into the jungles of South America to map the entirety of the uncivilized world."

"Percy Fawcett? Jesus, I didn't expect to discuss him today."

"Be that as it may, Colonel Fawcett brought back with him many strange and exciting ideas to the RGS's annals, the most spectacular of which were the works of the Tenorio tribe."

"So how, exactly, do the mirrors work?"

"The glass is made from a substance the Bruja generates using their body. Arthur's people call this substance Ch'ul. It is a cosmic, reflective material that, when one meets one own's eyes in its surface, awakens an intelligence in the reflection. From this point on, there is a second version of that person. A Doppelgänger, if you will. This new being was once confined to the world on the other side of the mirror-"

"Widdershins."

"Exactly. The awakening of the very first Doppelgängers created Widdershins, and for centuries this place of dreams and magick was known only to the people of Arthur's tribe, a sparse landscape from where they drew their magic. And then Arthur brought it here, and gave it to Cruchetti, a Western man with an agenda and stout financial backing."

"This is fascinating but-"

"Wendell, many years ago Paolo and I invented something we believed would change the world. It was a transportation network built around his abilities to manipulate matter and Arthur Tenorio's Glass. We called it The Hub, and it was to be an instantaneous transportation system that utilized Widdershins as a kind of 'between space' to cut travel times. You see, Widdershins is only made up of what has been reflected in Arthur's glass, so it is an incomplete world."

"I don't follow."

"In other words, if you put a piece of Tenorio Glass in Argentina and another in Brussels, you can step through one and the other will be only a short distance away when traveling in Widdershins. Thus, you could conceivably move between any two fixed points in the world at almost instantaneous speed."

WJ did not know what to say to that.

"I know, this sounds like the ramblings of a madman, Wendall, but I assure you it is not. Paolo and I had a falling out, and The Hub has lain dormant ever since, each of us attempting to put the finishing touches on it, each failing because the missing piece of the puzzle was not known to us until two days ago."

"You mentioned something happened two days ago."

"Yes. Years ago, Paolo confided in me that he had taken a number of volunteers, all over the world, to switch places with their Doppelgängers. This, he said, acted as a sort of bracing system that kept the conduits open. Like tying two pieces of rope together to make one, stronger piece, the inversion of these people twisted Deosil and Widdershins together, so that in some places they were the same world. What we never realized is there was one person who would prove to be the final piece of the puzzle. That person, it seems, is your girlfriend's teenage son."

~

When he finally left the bar, WJ's head was so full of paranoid ideas that he drove back to Talia's house at almost seventy miles an hour. When he arrived, he did so in a cold sweat that was only exacerbated by the fact that neither Talia or Jessie were home. As he entered, he thought he heard a door slam, but saw no signs of another soul.

"Where the hell is everyone?"

Talia's phone went straight to voice mail, and Jessie's rang through the same. WJ's concern, enflamed by Dubois's revelations, became maddening. Long ago he had closed a scientific door on a previous version of himself, a version that, at age twenty, had spent Friday and Saturday nights as a fledgling 'ghost hunter'.

Through to the kitchen, WJ saw the basement door stood open.

It was a past that embarrassed him now, and he secretly cursed Dubois for bringing him into his fold. When he was younger, WJ had believed a lot of strange things. That was before he grew into an adult immersed in academia, a world that eschewed all such belief in the incredible. There was a time when he thought he would be the one to open that world to these so-called 'radical' new trains of thought. He'd been wrong.

"Talia? Jessie?" he called from the top of the stairs, pulling the chain for some light.

Down here, WJ...

"Jessie? Thank god. Listen, we need to get some things together and leave, right away." He took the stairs two at a time. When he reached the basement floor, dread set back in.

"Jessie?

Over here...

WJ moved toward the voice, off in the as yet unexplored darkness that ran beneath the rest of the house. He stopped when something raised the hairs on his arms. He couldn't say what, but something was off. He looked around and recognized a change had come over the room: the broken mirror had been moved out of the circle, and the rest of Arthur Tenorio's works had been re-arranged so that they all faced one another.

WJ, I need help.

He didn't know how, but WJ knew this wasn't Jessie.

Please! Help me.

The voice seemed to come from every direction; WJ turned in a circle, attempting to pinpoint its origin.

He could not.

Desperation set in. He wanted to bolt back up the stairs, but something kept him going. Using the electric lantern, WJ swept the darkness to no avail.

"Where are you?"

A noise from behind startled him; WJ turned and came face to face with his reflection. Dubois's words came over him:

"...when one meets one's own eyes in Tenorio Glass, they awaken a Doppelgänger."

Ripples broke the surface like a body of water standing on its side. Sheer terror, as his reflection's left hand shot out and grasped him by the back of the head. There was a moment of insanity as he made eye contact with himself, Cast and Doppelgänger, and then one WJ pulled the other through the threshold of the mirror with a tremendous SLURPing sound.

"Gotcha," the dust and shadows seemed to say finally, as the surface rippled one last time before returning to its formerly solid state. In another moment the light at the top of the stairs turned itself off.

~

Smiling, the other Jessie Roberts left the mirrors to their prey. He moved up the stairs, through the kitchen to the corridor that led to the front door. As he crossed the out of place foyer's threshold, he stopped to survey the legion of closed doors that had thus far proved a mystery to the home's new inhabitants. Jessie Two spoke three words under his breath, and a faint light kicked on beneath the floor, now revealed in the glow as being made entirely of glass. Stopping when he arrived at the second to last door, he tried the handle and when it opened, he passed through into another house that looked exactly like the one he'd just left, except all the mirrors inside were coated in thick, black paint.

CHAPTER 16

For the better part of twenty-four hours, Kim sat in her room, staring at the mirror where her sister had appeared. Nothing happened; there was no recurrence of the communication, not even a failed attempt. But the brief contact had incited in her something Kim thought died several years ago. She found a book of pictures beneath her bed; inside were photos of her mother, father, and Patty. She hadn't seen any of them in a long time, and her loneliness had begun to affect her heart. This is why, as she abandoned her vigil with the mirror, and her eyes began to focus instead on the photographs, a swell of memories and their living, breathing details began to overtake her. And in the heat of this unexpected sadness, the only thing that brought a smile back to her face were thoughts of Jessie.

Kim couldn't stop thinking about him.

When Kim was younger, she and Cassie would tell each other stories about what it would be like when they were older and began to date boys. Kim had never been able to imagine the face of the boy she would first kiss, but it was there, obscured in her mind, as if fate had already decided his identity, and hidden it from her only by a thin mist of time. When she met Jessie several nights ago, that fog rolled free, and it was his face that appeared, perfectly formed. It was as if Kim had known him her entire life.

But of course, this was all untrue, as it had not been her, not *this* Kim Corduroy who had talked with Cassie about her future. It had been her Cast, the girl this Kim switched places with five years ago. It wasn't a malevolent action; she'd simply saw a moment to transcend her life, even if only for a moment, and she'd taken it. What this Kim hadn't known at the time was that Deosil's Kim was sick, and her father wanted rid of her. Cruchetti promised an exchange, but it hadn't worked the way it was supposed to. As a result, no one ever came looking for her; and with no reason to return, this Kim had stayed.

After, it was Fattingback who found her and subsequently helped her survive, hidden from those who would exploit her.

Something disturbed her thoughts. Alone for years in this house that belonged to the other Kim's family, any stray sound gave her reason for concern. She readied herself, then scanned the room from end to end. She heard it again; the sound was coming from downstairs.

"Kim? Kim, are you here? I have the most wonderful news."

Jessie? How? She didn't care. Kim was so excited at the idea of seeing him, of explaining why she'd left him at Freighter's, that she started down the stairs at a run. That's when Jessie spoke again, and she realized something was very wrong.

"Kim? I need your help. I don't know where my mom or JW went. I'm worried. Please, Kim."

JW? Kim knew that was wrong. Chilled, she stopped on

the stairs and waited. She could hear Jessie's footsteps, but she couldn't see him.

"Kimberly?"

Kimberly?

The revelation hit her like a fist: this wasn't Jessie. Not her Jessie.

Panic. The footsteps were closing in on the bottom of the stairs; she could hear the close proximity by how short the echo was.

"Where are you, Kimberly? I've been waiting to see you again for such a long, long time. Come down and give me a kiss. Please?"

Unsure if she should make a break for the door or run back upstairs, the moment Jessie appeared at the bottom of the landing her feet decided for her. Kim ran back up, straight to her room and slammed the door from the outside. Then she ran down the open hall and slipped into the parlor. From here she opened the window, climbed out onto the roof and carefully scaled down the worn and filthy shingles. At the gutter she looked down; it was only about a twelve-foot drop. Focusing her thoughts on the feeling of her shadow body, she leaped to the ground and landed with a whisper in the overgrown grass. Above her the moon throbbed red, as Kim ran down the driveway and turned onto the street beyond.

CHAPTER 17

Kim ran down her driveway and into the shadows gathered at the base of a large Weeping Willow. She tried to merge with the darkness there but stayed firmly outlined by the light of the moon. Since meeting Jessie, her abilities - as Kim had come to think of them since arriving in this world - were sketchy at best. She was lucky to have landed her jump from the roof without injury. Her feelings for Jessie were changing her, making her more human. This humanity is what Kim had always wanted, only it had arrived at the worst possible time. Unable to blend into the shadows, she continued on. When she rounded the corner from Eeryx to where Derleth dead-ended at Caliper, Kim stopped cold.

Jessie stood in the distance.

"Oh no. Not now. Not now!"

Her defenses flared until she realized this Jessie looked hurt: hands pressed to his temples, his face writhed in an escalating grimace. Hoping it wasn't a trick, she ran to him.

"Jessie! Are you okay?"

"I… this noise. I… You still don't hear it?"

Kim blushed. She reached up and put her hands on his, massaged his temples.

"I'm sorry. I totally lied to you about it when you asked me before."

"What?"

"I hear it, Jessie. The low rumble that started Saturday night? The hum that feels like it's underneath everything? I hear it. I have the whole time."

Jessie grabbed her by the shoulders, his face animated by the relief of finally being able to share the sensation with another person.

"Why did you lie about it? I've been going freakin' crazy this whole time! And why did you leave me at Freighter's?"

"Jessie, I'm… I'm sorry. My life is really complicated at the moment. Like, supernatural complicated."

"Yeah, but you know I believe you, about your powers and your sister, and everything else. All this crazy shit happens to us but I keep coming back for more, and I've known you for, what? Two days? That should tell you I'm not going anywhere. You can trust me."

"I know, but it feels like you've known me longer, right?" Kim said, her pupil-less eyes drinking him, her tongue drifting over her lips ever so slightly, accenting the coquettish grin she could no longer suppress. There were so many human experiences she looked forward to...

"It feels like I've known you my whole life."

Now Jessie blushed.

"Yeah. I feel… electric with you."

The tension between them became as exquisite as it was untenable. Their guards came down, and Jessie found himself pulled into Kim's arms, a frenzied embrace consuming them both as their lips locked in pulsing, fumbling passion. Jessie ran his hands up Kim's back even as her hands went around his neck, shoulders, and chest. His spine felt like it had absorbed a lightning strike, and as the bliss overwhelmed him, Jessie whispered, almost in a dream:

"I was so worried about you. Please don't do that again."

"I won't, but…"

The mood changed, and Jessie pulled apart from her then, focused his concern.

"What is it?"

"Jessie, you haven't been inside my house, have you?"

"No. Why?"

"Never mind. Just hold me."

~

"Richard said I should bring you in slowly." They were sitting in the burnt-out shell of the house on Caliper Lane.

"Richard? The mailman?"

"He's not just a mailman. He can help us."

"He said something really weird to me when I met him. He said-"

"He said you'd woke something up."

"Yeah! I thought maybe he was talking about Freighter's that night, but he mentioned the sound. He called it a great machine."

"I think it's more than that. But he hasn't told me everything. I found my sister, the other night at Freighter's. And I'm sorry I ditched you with that creep, but I knew I wouldn't get another chance like that."

"Like having live bait to distract him?"

Kim didn't want Jessie's words. She thought about the sound of his voice in her home not fifteen minutes before. The idea that whatever Jessie had done that first night in his basement, he had awoken another version of himself, a fifteen-year-old that would be as evil as this one was good, as dangerous to her as he was willing to help. She felt her panic return for a moment, but then he reached up and caressed her face, and suddenly they were at each other again, their lips melting together. Time disappeared as their tongues probed the insides of each other's mouths.

When the moment came to a natural lull, they separated and shared a knowing glance. Good things were coming. They just had to make it through all the bad stuff first.

"My sister is definitely in Freighter's house. I found a door I couldn't pass through."

"Is that how you got inside his house to begin with? You walk through walls?"

"The shadows, sometimes I can merge with them. I'll explain everything if you promise to help me."

"I helped you before, didn't I?"

"Alright, then come on."

She grabbed his hand, and they left the shelter of the ruins, walked out further into the trees.

"What kind of help are we going to find here?"

"Trust me?"

"With my life."

Leaving the crumbled road, they headed West. It was rough going until they passed through a dense thicket of trees and emerged into a large open field, a veritable arena of decay lined on all sides by columns of scorched black trees. The field's grass stood chest high in places and was peppered with dozens of crumbled, ivied stones that resembled grave markers, darkened by the ghosts of flames that had consumed the structure years before. The weak light of the overcast day faded, and when Jessie glanced up through the trees, he saw a horizon of haunted witch-fingers that cross-hatched the sky. The darkness these ghostly limbs created was unnatural and disturbing; there was a certain malevolence suggested by this place, an unidentifiable threat whispered to him from between these trees.

"We're here."

He looked around.

"What, here?"

Kim nodded, "Close your eyes."

As soon as Jessie's eyes were closed, he felt his stomach contract, followed by nausea that suggested he'd lost control of himself, as though his head had become too heavy to hold upright. He remembered the exact same sensation from the first and only time he'd ever ridden a roller coaster; it was the sensation of cresting the top of the ride's tallest drop.

In the dark, Kim's voice came to him from further ahead:

> *"As shadow to cast*
> *And mirror to light*
> *As right is to left*
> *And day is to night*
> *Fold a space*
> *And tuck some time*
> *Lift your hands*
> *Recite this rhyme*
> *The door will show*
> *The path within*
> *Now through the glass*
> *To Widdershins"*

Something about the words sounded familiar to Jessie, but not in a way that had anything to do with reality. Had he dreamt this? Kim's voice rung out in his head, creating a space where memory and sense melded, and for the briefest of moments he went there and forgot his body and the world that surrounded it - it was like he could see through someone else's eyes. Then Kim's voice called him back.

"C'mon!" she called, excited. Jessie opened his eyes, and his brain recoiled at their surroundings. They were no longer in the field. Instead, they stood at the beginning of a cobblestone path that led through a series of boney trees, beyond which Jessie could see a flat, one-story house with two large picture windows on either side of the front door burning with red light. It looked like a skull with glowing red eyes.

"Where are we?"

"Between," Kim said as they began down the path, the stones uneven but pleasurable to walk on compared to the ragged forest floor from only a moment before.

PART II

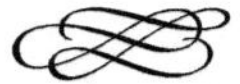

CHAPTER 18

Richard Fattingback did not feel the activation of Cruchetti's fabled Hub. True, the night Jessie first descended into his basement, the one-hundred-and-thirty-three-year-old mailman sensed *something*. But the Architect had spent years talking about his 'global teleportation system' without ever actually getting it off the ground, so it had long ago been dismissed. What began as an extraordinary opportunity and over time turned into a threat, eventually came to occupy the same space in the colloquial outlook as Santa Claus and the existence of little green men:

The Hub was fun to treat with conjecture, but in reality, would never happen. Until it happened.

Like Jessie, Richard began to experience the extrasensory fall-out from hundreds of portals into a parallel dimension coming on-line, the low-end hum of Cosmic Microwave Background Radiation as it flowed through hundreds of Tenorio mirrors. Many of those mirrors were centered in and around Gallows Hill and Knight's Side, so the effect was strongest there, like the residual radiation that haunted a nuclear ground zero. There were hundreds more mirrors scattered across the globe, sought-after pieces that, until his falling out with Cruchetti, Dubois had used his GHAS to place in the hands of collectors the world over. Despite his familiarity with these hidden events, Richard had grown cynical and complacent. No one had actually seen Cruchetti - or Arthur Tenorio for that matter - in years, and it had become more comfortable to believe they had passed on than they lay in wait, plotting.

When he received a correspondence from the Lower Amazon Basin, Richard realized the good days were well and truly over. Cruchetti was alive, and The Hub was up and running. This meant there were safeguards to put into place, forces that must be rallied, and an accord to enforce if they were to protect the world from the Architect's plans.

To begin, there would need to be a meeting.

In their initial exploratory adventures, many years before, he had sometimes tagged along with Cruchetti and Dubois as they charted the parameters of Widdershins, what they'd blandly called the "Potential Dimension" until Richard coined the more colorful name everyone now used. Back then, Paolo and Cuthbert were young, idealistic, and hungry. And very much in love, that played no small part in the way things ended up. Once they enticed Arthur into giving them his tribe's secrets, things began to turn. Cruchetti had a lust for power, Dubois one for wealth. Together, they sought to change the fabric of the world around them, something Arthur's grandmother Encarnación, the Bruja of the Tenorio tribe, condemned. The modern world had its own magic, it was not meant to have the old magics, too. Arthur followed Cruchetti and Dubois to America, helped them start work on The Hub by designing Gallows Hill and all its mystical elements, and then, just as Encarnación said it would, horror struck.

Kimberly and Patagonia Barker disappeared, and their parents followed shortly after that. Dubois and Cruchetti suffered a massive falling out, and the rest, as they say, is history.

In the wake of this tragedy, Encarnación arrived to collect her great-granddaughter, Cassandra. Arthur went into hiding and Richard, suffering guilt for his part in the subversion of Widdershins, remained in place as an impartial intermediary, a sort of governing body to watch the progress - or lack thereof - associated with Cruchetti's invention. The fact that most had written it off only made Richard feel like even more of a fool when the Bruja's family solicitor contacted him with the news.

"Miss Elizabeth Manhattan! How wonderful to hear your voice on such a strange day. <Hurm>."

"I wish I could say it was under better circumstances. Mater Tenorio would like you to call a meeting on her behalf."

"With all due respect, Elizabeth, might we not be well beyond the point where a meeting will suffice? If Paolo has already begun utilizing the system-"

"He has not."

"Then, as is my custom, I defer to Mater Tenorio's prescient wisdom. Consider your meeting called."

CHAPTER 19

Linda Evans stared out her window at the old Oak Tree that stood in her front yard and fought back tears. The sky had gone dark early; a storm was gathering. It would prove no match for the tempest raging inside her.

Why? Why did Chase insist on making things so damn complicated?

The letter felt heavy in her hand, and after a moment of trying to convince herself not to, she balled it up in her fist and launched it across the room, out of sight.

Linda had lived in Gallows Hill long enough to know Chase Montgomery very well. They had worked together in the GHAS for years. Chase attended her wedding, was friendly with her husband. And while there had always been an attraction between them, it wasn't the kind of attraction you did anything about. Even if Luis had been missing for three years this October, and everyone told her to let go, Linda was still married to him. So what the hell was Chase thinking?

"Every time I see you I think about all the things we could be together. All the things we should have been together..."

Linda met Luis in college. They were married two months after graduation, and she put her own career ambitions on hold so he could pursue a position on staff at the University in Knight's Side. The move was difficult for her, as the forested environment proved an enormous change from her twenty-five years of city life up to that point. But Linda loved Luis, and because of that love, she followed him. She tried to make the best of the situation, applying for positions at his school that she knew she had no hope of getting. Linda was an art major, Luis an expert in Hellenistic Art and the sociological structure of the era that surrounded it. She tried, but nothing fit. Eventually, more than a little defeated, she settled into the role of housewife, the antithesis of her goals. Shortly after, they discovered Luis was incapable of fathering children and life began to seem meaningless.

Bored to tears seven days a week, their relationship suffered. Luis became increasingly important to his department, and that made Linda feel increasingly less important to him. He never showed this, but she felt it in every unexpected phone call, last minute weekend meeting and late night at the office. Linda knew Luis loved her, but over time that love was stripped of its shiny coat, their interactions increasingly sublimated by the demands of his career.

Fearing irrelevance and suffering depression, it was Dubois who proved to be Linda's salvation.

They met at a Humanities Department Soiree, one of the functions she customarily attended on Luis' arm. Cuthbert was charming and intelligent, and by the end of the night, the three of them were old friends. Later, when Dubois tracked her down and asked her if she would take a position in the Gallows Hill Antiquarian Society, Linda knew she had found purpose. It didn't pay much and often demanded long hours, but it was something she would enjoy.

How could she say no?

That was going on ten years ago now. By the end of the first month, Linda met more people than she had in years: antique dealers, collectors, appraisers; artists and renovators from around the world. Also, she'd gotten a taste of something utterly unfamiliar to her: mystery. Cuthbert's unyielding passion was the influence and allocation of ancient tribal techniques into modern art. He possessed an almost endless list of connections in every part of the world imaginable, from Eastern Europe to Tibet to Argentina, and he used these connections to import and sell mysterious and exotic art and furniture. People from all over the globe came to him for his advice and suggestions, and in turn, he traveled extensively to stay on top of what was circulating, what was re-discovered and, his favorite, what was unknown.

It was some time before Linda learned the more Occult interests Dubois dabbled in, and Cuthbert rejoiced at her criticism.

"I need a cynic, Linda, that's why I asked you to join us in the first place."

As she experienced more, one thing became clear to her: some things were meant to stay in the past. There were arcane systems of information that had disappeared from the world for a reason. Replaced by technology, these things were not meant for the modern world, a world that was always in reach, shrunk by air travel, maps, GPS and the internet. A world small enough that, if the right person put certain key areas of forgotten information together, the entirety of it might be molded by their influence. Thus, while the GHAS did deal in antiquities, that was only a cover for a greater mission: policing modern culture for the reappearance of ancient magic. This had changed Linda's entire view on the world, and it'd given her something other than Luis to be involved in and important to. It was in this capacity that she first began to see Chase Montgomery regularly. Cuthbert paired them on assignments, often sending them out to find this painting, pick that antiquity from auction. Errands. Upon this most recent reflection, Linda wondered if Chase had requested that pairing; if his interest extended back that far. Certainly, she'd never noticed it until...

The night she and Chase spent together shortly after Luis's disappearance had been a mistake, they'd both agreed at the time. Theirs was a fire that burned once, burned bright, and burned out. And it had remained that way ever since. Until now. Why Chase suddenly decided they had a future together was beyond her, but she wasn't going to let him continue. The next time she saw him, Linda would put him in his place, once and for all.

The phone rang, and Linda felt as though she'd been caught doing something wrong. She wiped her tears away and blushed at the anxiety the sound caused her.

"Hello?"

"Linda. We have problems."

"We always have problems, Cuthbert."

"Serious problems this time. The Hub is online."

"Since when?"

"Since two nights ago. A new family has taken up residence in Arthur Tenorio's home."

"What? Oh, come on! How the hell could that even happen?"

"You should ask Chase. I have it on good authority he practically recommended the place to them."

"Jesus! Of all the-"

"That is not all. Richard has called a meeting on behalf of Bruja Tenorio."

"Christ."

"Indeed. I need you to go, as our official representative."

"You mean as *your* representative. No way. No one's seen Paolo or Arthur in how long? You know as well as I do that leaves only one person who's going to show up to represent their interests."

"Be that as it may-"

"He tortured me, Cuthbert. Do you even get that? I'd rather be dropped into a pit of snakes than go anywhere near that madman."

"Linda, in the last twenty minutes Paolo has taken two innocent pieces from the board. This puts us at a severe disadvantage."

"This isn't a game Cuthbert."

"Tell Paolo that."

"Goddamn it. Why can't you go?"

"Because I am trying to prevent another family from suffering the same fate as our little girl lost's family did."

She wanted to scream. Instead, Linda picked an apple up off the counter behind her and threw it as hard as she could against the wall. It disappeared through the drywall, leaving a near-perfect hole.

"Fine."

"Thank you."

The line clicked dead, and Linda slammed the phone down so hard its case cracked in her palm. Steadying herself, she walked quickly across the room, passing a large, ornate mirror along the way.

She did not cast a reflection in it.

The path wound back and forth in wide arcs to the right and left, and as they neared the house more red lights trailed out from in front of it; the skull's teeth from one perspective, a low-lit path from another.

Past the lights, Kim brought them directly to the door and knocked with her fist, three times sharp. After a moment, the door opened to reveal Richard Fattingback before them.

"Kimberly! How fantastic you have made the acquaintance of young master Roberts! <Hurm> Welcome to you both! Please, come in, come in."

They stepped in, and Jessie's eyes faltered. The house was dark.

"Ah, lad! You do not look so well! Tell me, are you plagued by the same sound as the rest of us?"

"It's The Hub, isn't it, Richard?"

"It is, Kimberly. With the damnable device finally activated, those of us with a more sensitive nature are tuned in to receive the feedback inherent in hundreds of extra-dimensional doorways opening simultaneously."

"Can you help him?" Kim pleaded.

"Of course, lass. I have a tincture of my own concoction. Come in, come in, and I will fetch a glass for both of you."

They entered, and Fattingback scampered off toward a room in the distance. The clinking sound of glasses preceded his return. He handed Jessie a snifter and motioned for him to drink. He did, and a moment later Kim followed suit. A few moments later, just as quickly as the sound had come upon Jessie, it stopped.

"Oh my god. Thank you! I thought I was going to lose my mind."

"Think nothing of it, lad. To my humble mind, there is no greater delectation to be had than that of freeing another from the affliction of the discordant resonations of the cosmos."

Here it was again: Jessie could not help but smile listening to this man talk!

"I myself have, on several previous occasions, suffered the wretched effects of the portals. The imbibe of which you have just partaken was the only thing that saw me through those dark, damnable days. Now, what else can I do for you?"

"Richard, I know you told me not to, but, well, I snuck into Freighter's house."

"Ah! You are mad as hops girl! If that demon had found you, or perhaps of considerably more concern were he to realize your intrusion after the fact, I question my ability to protect you."

"It doesn't matter, it's like I told you. He has my sister."

Fattingback contemplated Kim's words for a moment before nodding in acceptance.

"I can help you. But we must hurry, children! I have a crucial meeting scheduled to commence in no short order, and I happen to ken without a shadow of doubt that Bob Freighter will be in attendance and, thus, well away from his home. Come, let us palaver! <Hurm>."

CHAPTER 21

As Jessie's eyes acclimated to the darkness of Richard's house, he began to take stock of his surroundings. The place looked similar to his own home, only with a lot of deviations. Red lights in the familiar, ceiling-high sconces replaced the soft white glow he associated with his house and gave the space a surreal, crimson halo.

No mirrors. Anywhere. And the air felt damp and stuffy, as though the windows had not been opened in forever. Which made sense, as they were blacked out with thick layers of dark paint that would have prevented them from sliding in their tract. Richard had removed any possibility of reflection.

The passageway through the ground floor came after the foyer, which unlike Jessie's, was in the standard place just inside the front door. Moving beyond that, there were no doors - locked or otherwise - to either side of the corridor. Ten steps through and the hall opened on the den, its enormous windows replaced instead by black walls decorated with a series of large, framed posters. These depicted a man who looked like Richard, only dressed in Victorian-era tuxedo and top hat, surrounded by exclamatory font that spoke of the 'Untold Marvels of the Universe' and a 'Seeker of Sorcerous Secrets.' The largest of these, set as a center-piece, showed this same character surrounded by mirrors that looked identical to the ones in Jessie's basement. The typeset on the poster identified the man as 'Richard Acrobat Vanishing, Master of the Modern Mirror.'

"Ah, my greatest days, laid bare before you lad. <Hurm> To gaze upon my younger visage from the vantage of this future time is enough to color me red with the blush of memories; memories of adventure, fame, and indeed, seem-ingly endless holidays of harrowing hijinx!"

"How can that be you? What year is that from?"

"The answer, lad, is as obvious as it is astounding, or so I would be most fervent to wager <Hurm>."

Jessie looked closer, spotted Roman Numerals at the bottom of the poster.

MCMVI.

"1906? I don't understand."

"In time. Believe me Master Roberts, my narrative is a convoluted one; a veritable conundrum for one who has lived longer than most, and despite championing the exis-tence of a source I shall call, for the paucity of a more satis-factory descriptor, Magick, to this day I retain exactly the same quandary as yourself. Namely: how?"

Fattingback shot Kim a wink and then motioned for Jessie to sit. He did so in a small, forest-green loveseat. Kim sat beside him and took his left hand in both of hers.

"Jessie, I haven't been honest with you. And I... I really, really like you. So I'm going to tell you the truth, and Mr. Fattingback will be my witness because, in the five years since I came to this place, he is the only person before you that I felt like I could trust."

"Kim, you don't have to hide yourself from me."

Kim looked nervously to Richard, "Where do I even start? How do I make him think I'm not totally crazy?"

"The mirrors. Start with the mirrors, lass."

"Okay. Jessie, the mirrors aren't mirrors. They're like some kind of gateway to another world. Another place where…" Kim stopped and looked to Richard for assistance.

"Think of it as a sister world, lad; a place where we all have Doubles, sister-selves waiting to be awakened."

"Okay, so we're talking about what? An alternate dimension?"

"Yes."

"Populated by other versions of us?" Jessie thought of that first night in the basement, seeing one of his reflections stand perfectly still while he spun in circles. He'd tried to dismiss it as a momentary illusion, but truthfully, he'd known all along it was real.

"Precisely, lad! But not just other versions - these beings are us, in many ways. They are also our opposites. Their substance is drawn from two places - our reflection, and our shadow. Two sides of the same coin."

"Is that what Old Man Freighter is? Some kind of shadow person?"

"Doppelgänger is the preferred word in most instances. The extremity of his condition is a mutation."

Jessie looked at Kim, a revelation made plain.

"Are you? Are you a Doppelgänger? I mean, no judgment if you are. I'm just trying to understand, I guess. But you can do things. You told me, and I've seen you."

"Yes, Jessie. I'm one of the Doppelgängers."

"So… you're not exactly Kim Corduroy, you're her opposite?"

"I am, and I'm not. Five years ago I woke up. That's the first thing the mirrors do, they wake up the other you. Once that happens, there's this entirely different person that's just like you, only inside this other world, a world that's... incomplete."

"So the real Kim is on the other side? In the other world? You switched?"

"No. The Kim from this world is dead," Richard cut in, giving Jessie the impression he was truncating the story, "Cruchetti has spent years replacing people, creating a kind of living bridge to bind the other world to this one. Kimberly's Cast was taken, but complications arose."

"That's why they took Patty."

"Your sister?"

"Yeah. Because it didn't work when they took me."

Jessie sat back and let go of Kim's hand, ran his fingers through his hair and let out a deep breath. He felt exhausted.

"I'm sorry if this is a lot."

"It's a lot, but you don't have to be sorry. I mean, this is kinda awesome, providing it's really happening, and I'm not like, sitting by myself in a mental ward somewhere, acting out comic book fantasies."

"Take all the time you need, lad. <Hurm>."

"Okay, well, let me ask some questions."

"Please."

"First, why does Freighter have Kim's sister if it's Cruchetti who's swapping people with their Doubles?"

"Bob was Cruchetti's foreman, the captain of his vessel, sailing the seas of time on a raft built with Arthur's infernal magick. When Cruchetti first began Gallows Hill, adventurous as it was, he needed someone who could turn his ideas into actual flesh and blood; brick and mortar <Hurm>. But something happened between the two men, titans lost among dimensions most never see. The event sabotaged their work, left it impotent and forgotten. Freighter's wife suffered because of it. He lost his beloved to Widdershins, and Cruchetti's project stalled. And we've all been running in circles ever since. Until now."

"What happened? You're losing me."

"Look, Jessie, we can have Richard tell us all about the secret history of Gallows Hill later. The important thing now is we get my sister."

"Yeah, okay. I guess I can learn as we go."

"That's how I do it. This isn't something that there are rules for."

"Like everything else in life! <Hurm>."

"Okay, so what's the plan?"

Kim turned to Richard.

"I must make ready for guests, one of which will be none other than the man you wish to distract. Go now, and make your way to Bob Freighter's home. Take the back way, or his path you might cross, as even now he may be approaching my door."

Once again, Kim took Jessie by the hand, lead him through a long, crimson hallway and then out the back door of Richard's house. What they emerged into was part forest, part fog-cloaked vaguery. From the door they'd just left, Jessie heard the Mailman's voice:

"Stay on the path children! To stray is to put your lives in unnecessary risk."

They ran the path, dodging branches, fallen stumps and, occasionally, what looked like grasping hands.

Jessie kept his eyes trained on the back of Kim's head. And what a pretty head it was.

How long had it been? Years? Months? Bob Freighter no longer understood time the way most people did so he couldn't say for sure. To him, existence had become an endless spiral of hatred and pain, a perpetual struggle not to use the .38 revolver in his top dresser drawer to escape. But although he blamed himself for Helen's fate, Bob lacked the courage to take his own life. That, and there were other parties he held equally responsible, for Helen, and for his own private nightmare. Bob didn't want to bow out until he knew those parties would get what was coming to them.

So he drank. The booze helped create a kind of bubble around him. It made the things he did when the monster that shared his skin took over feel as though they were happening to someone else. Alcohol also helped him continue his charade, playing along with Cruchetti's agenda. Because Bob was close now, and after many long years, he was finally in a place where soon, he would be able to seal the Architect's fate. Then, his revenge complete, Bob thought he might finally find the strength to end his life.

It felt like a lifetime ago that Cruchetti had approached him with his plans for Gallows Hill. At the time Bob was a newlywed; a thirty-five-year-old master carpenter who had recently married his high school sweetheart and started his own construction company. Work was slow then, and Bob was looking for a bid that would give him a little stability and, subsequently a chance to bring Helen's dreams of owning a home and starting a family to fruition. Cruchetti was weird, and his proposal was weirder, but it also came with a handsome paycheck. When the eccentric architect handed Bob a six-figure check and added a contract with a bonus that included the first house completed, there was just no way Bob could say no. Of course, he realized now that the old adage, 'if it sounds too good to be true, it probably is,' had perhaps never been more appropriate than when dealing with Cruchetti.

The plans for Gallows Hill were more bizarre than anything Bob had ever seen. He was to build twelve houses in the middle of the woods using the same specific set of blueprints for each. At first glance, none of what Cruchetti gave him made any sense; the blueprints were drafted in an almost unreadable technical language that utilized a kind of geometric principle Bob had never heard of before. Also, the materials Cruchetti instructed him to use were not your standard brick-and-mortar fare. There was, for example, a formula for a variation on a standard concrete foundation that read like an alchemical text. Likewise, the wood was to be treated with a special compound Cruchetti imported from somewhere called Widdershins. Finally, the houses were to be built in unison, at a staggered pace that mapped milestones in their construction over lunar events. It seemed impossible, and to actually get the job up and running, Bob knew he would need help. So he called an old friend.

In his twenties, Bob had hung around a strange crowd; it was the end of the sixties, and the mind expansion impetus that began with drugs bled into a burgeoning mainstream interest in the Occult. Bob never went in for any of that mumbo jumbo, but some of his friends did. One acquaintance he still had from those days was a man named Darren Grimes. Grimes was equal parts academician and fringe science philosopher, with a doctorate in something called Arcane and Occult Studies. He was the one that taught Bob how the world as humanity understands it persists only because we force it to.

"We build from certain materials, Bob, because they work. Brick, wood, concrete; these substances form barriers around our lives, protect us from the elements, but don't do much else. That's why we decorate. But other materials can be used to build, especially when working with a four-dimensional hyper-plane. These materials not only form barriers for protection, they also open our senses into new vistas, take us to places we do not ordinarily travel."

At first, his life-long aversion to anything extrasensory made it hard for Bob to understand the concepts both Grimes and Cruchetti grasped with no problem. But after Grimes conducted him through several preparatory experiences - LSD trips, isolation tank training, and anonymous participation in a full-on black magick ritual - Bob began to adapt his aptitude for engineering and construction to include a fourth dimension. From there, the world opened to him like a strange, sweet flower. A flower that, once he had a taste for it, Bob found unable to resist. He threw himself into his work, and soon the houses in Gallows Hill were all but finished. Bob and Helen moved into their new home, the house on the corner of Derleth and Rune, and with completion on the horizon, Cruchetti briefed him on the next step:

activation of the nexus on a grid that was to tie two worlds together. Bob felt powerful. He felt integral to something amazing, and he had money. Things were weird, but they were good.

Then Helen's episodes began.

CHAPTER 23

Sheriff Jim Rash stopped to get a double cheeseburger and fries at the Big Tree Diner, then drove out to the first house on the list Gil had left him. When he arrived at the Crosse's, things began to get weird. "Weird feeds weird," is what Declan used to say. Jim thought his predecessor's death was pretty weird in and of itself, the fact that the man'd been hit by a train and not a single scrap of him had been left behind. But Jim had an idea about that. He thought the more you acknowledged weird, the more it acknowledged you back. He thought Declan might have just gotten what was coming to him based on his preoccupation with 'weird' and that damn town next door, so Jim lived his life by his own little creed:

"Leave weird the hell alone, and stay outta Gallows Hill."

Expecting to find Laura and Able Crosse waiting on pins and needles for his arrival, what Jim found instead was an empty house. He knocked a couple of times, went back to the cruiser and radioed into Terry at the station.

"Jess-sus Sheriff, I been tryin'a raise you for, like, ever. Where were you? Over."

"Man's gotta eat. Phone still ringing? Over."

"It was up until about ten minutes ago. I've got three more break-ins for you to add to your list. Over."

"What the hell is going on this week? Over."

"My money's on Meth-head college kids. Over," Terry said, and Jim could hear him pause and sip coffee that was hot enough to make his lips pucker.

"I'm at the Crosse's now; no one's home. I'll keep you in the loop. Over n' out."

Jim clicked off abruptly and stared at Laura and Able's house. Something was off. He climbed out of the cruiser and moved toward the darkened front porch, unsure if he should draw his weapon or not; the instinct he'd learned so long ago always came with a sharp reminder of what happened the last time he drew, over a decade ago as a State Trooper. For the time being, Jim left his weapon on his hip.

CHAPTER 24

Helen's episodes began about the same time their new house started to shift its rooms around on them. At first, Bob didn't understand her problems were the result of something more than the effects of the building. Eventually though, it became all too clear that something bad was happening to his wife.

She would disappear for hours on end, only to return terrified, barely able to speak. On increasing occasion, Helen's body would suffer a change wherein it no longer resembled human flesh, replaced instead by something akin to a living, breathing darkness; a Shadow Self, as Cruchetti called it. The architect assured Bob the condition was temporary, and he would be able to help Helen; that it was merely a side effect of the strange properties of their new home. But as activation of the nexus between worlds inched closer - what Cruchetti began to refer to as 'The Hub' - Helen's condition worsened. And as her symptoms escalated, it became obvious where Cruchetti's priorities lay. Sure, he strung Bob along with promises that once The Hub was online he would help her, but Bob was no fool. He knew bullshit when he heard it. This was also about the time Bob began suffering bouts of missing time.

He'd always been a somewhat heavy drinker, and as such, blackouts were not uncommon for him. Still, no matter how many hangovers, or near catastrophes he dodged by the skin of his teeth, the worse Helen's situation became, the more Bob drank, and the more time he accrued that he could not account for. Helen became a ghost, a flitting image of Shadow with the scent of lavender, often the only way he'd even be able to discern her presence at all. By then, Bob was mostly alone, left to contemplate the fact that the house he'd built for his wife had somehow robbed his beloved of her humanity.

His guilt escalated the bouts of missing time. His memory contained fragments of terror that brought him to his knees.

Then one night, Bob came to while it was happening. His eyes opened on a mass of jet black shadow as it crawled across his flesh, pushing him from his own body, replacing him with another person entirely. This other person looked just like Bob when he took on human form, but in all other respects was a decidedly different person. The newcomer had an independent consciousness, its own distinct personality, and an exacerbated mean streak that made Bob look like a cheerleader by comparison. This Doppelgänger, as he learned to call it, commandeered him for a full five days this time. He was a prisoner in his own flesh, left to watch as this other version of himself carried out a series of terrifying errands for Cruchetti. He helped abduct a young girl for Cruchetti, then followed that up with nothing less than the cold-blooded murder of the girl's mother. When it was over, Bob was destroyed, and to make things worse, he realized Helen was no longer with him at all; there was no body, no evidence of foul play, just a vacuum that her absence created in the center of his life. Occasionally he would catch that scent of lavender, often outside in the woods that surrounded the property, but for all practical purposes, she was gone.

That was the night Bob swore he would kill Cruchetti. It was also the last time he'd seen the man in person.

"I need… I need you to attend… to sit in a meeting. At the Mailman's. Richard's. Yes."

"Meeting? You outta yer damn mind?"

Freighter stood alone in a dark room, staring at a mirror that was as tall as he was. Instead of his reflection, the outline of a much shorter man faced him, his features obscured by a light cast from behind, so that it merely outlined his form, but left any distinct attributes bathed in darkness.

"No. No, I am not. No. Heh. I need you… Bob I need you to act as my rep…representa-tive. This is delicate, very deli-cate. Yes. With The Hub finally up… up and running, I have attracted the attention of Arthur's people. If the Bruja Tenorio is… if she gets involved… involved at this stage, things will go bad. They will. Heh. That, Bob… Bobby… that is why you must go. To this meeting. You must convince them… you must tell them we are no longer bound by their rules. Uh-ah. No. But, I really don't want them… I don't want them to think that we are a th-threat to them. Not a threat, either. No. Uh-ah."

"When in reality that's exactly what we are."

Cruchetti didn't respond to this, and Bob had the distinct impression he was being sent because of his volatile nature. Would someone say something to set him off? Would he lose control and kill all of Cruchetti's enemies?

"Robert, you have had your… differences with these people. You have. And the tribe no doubt know of some of your… more extravagant… offenses. They must. Wouldn't it feel good to… feel good to show them what you can do? Hmmm?"

"I ain't a killer."

"Really? Tell that to your wife."

CHAPTER 25

The Sheriff stood perfectly still at the Southeast corner of the Crosse's house, his vision trained on a shadow moving toward him from just around the corner, something that by the shape of it, was not human.

"Gotdamnit. Shut up, you old fool. That's impossible."

But it wasn't impossible, because there were the shadows, a hydra-head of tentacular writhing just about to round the bend. It looked like… it looked like…

A monster.

Rash pulled gun from holster, braced himself and whipped around the corner, the source of the shadows dead-to-rights.

Only there was nothing there.

"What the fu-"

A high pitched scream came from deeper in the Crosse's backyard. The Sheriff sucked in his gut, told himself he was twenty-five again and ran into the darkness. He could feel his heart struggling to keep up the pace, could feel the sluggish blood pump and spurt through hardened arteries, the corpuscles in his lungs hammering to keep the oxygen moving to all the necessary places. Jim had done two tours in 'Nam, ran strategy during the first Gulf War; he'd seen a lot of death and had returned to this idyllic part of the states as a preventative maneuver. He didn't want to ever see violence again.

Too late for that now.

The scream hadn't recurred, but as Jim stopped to rest behind a massive Oak tree, he heard a voice. Or voices; he wasn't sure how many, but someone was definitely out here in the dark with him.

"Goddamnit Able, didn't you just finish tellin' me about some new security light you installed?" he demanded irrationally, burping up the extra pickles from the burger he'd just eaten. He peeked around the girth of bark and realized his quarry was gone. Despite a stitch in his side, Rash remained low to the ground and picked up the hustle again, emerging from behind the tree and running full-on into the darkness of the backyard. Ahead, he could see a faint light, no more than five hundred feet away. A candle in the window of the treehouse Able had built for his twins when they were young? Or…

Four hundred feet.

The orange flicker became brighter as he closed the distance. It wasn't a candle. No, not a candle, a flame.

Three hundred feet.

The Sheriff's eyes finally adjusted to the night; he could see shapes moving everywhere in the background, all around him.

Two hundred feet.

Something slammed into him from out of the darkness on his right, sent Rash toppling onto his side. The wind knocked from him, he watched as the shapes continued to zip by just beyond the limits of his vision.

"Who's there? Able? Laura? What the hell's going on here?"

The candle-sized flame popped once and then ignited into a full-on fire; the treehouse went up in billows of black smoke that further choked the shadows, churning them out with gray ash.

And something else. What was that smell?

The Sheriff white-knuckled his revolver when he realized he recognized the smell - human hair burning. He reached around to his belt for his walkie, only to find it wasn't there.

"Crap," he cursed, realizing he'd left the radio on the front seat of the cruiser. He was about to get back on his feet when he heard a sound that froze his blood.

Laughter? Not just any laughter. It sounded like Declan's laughter, distinctive for its high-pitched, phlegmy timbre.

Weird. This is weird.

Weird feeds weird, Jim.

Every hair on the Sheriff's body stood as a dark shape dropped almost two stories from the top of the burning treehouse to the ground before him.

"Freeze!" Rash screamed, his voice cracking like a teenager's. Whoever it was, they were close enough that he should have been able to see their face. The figure, however, remained cloaked in darkness and smoke.

"Now just you stay right where you are and put your damn hands where I can see 'em!"

Angered by his fear, the Sheriff trained his eyes on the sight of his gun, beyond which the figure appeared to be... expanding?

Weird, huh Jim?

A pulse of horror ran through Rash as his eyes strained to confirm what the voice before him promised.

"Declan?"

Something at the edge of his peripheral vision drew his

attention, and engulfed in a wave of terror, Rash barely had enough time to register it before he pulled the trigger on his gun. Sound became muffled, waves in a distant sea, and his gag reflex kicked in as the inky black horns of midnight came to claim him for their own.

CHAPTER 26

"I can't believe I'm about to break into this lunatic's house," Jessie said.

"Look, I was just in there the other night. It'll be okay."

Headlights up the road; they disengaged and ran the final length to the top of Freighter's driveway, into the cover of the trees that served as the perimeter to the ramshackle property. Jessie watched the car go by to see if it was WJ, but between the trees, the rain and the headlights, he couldn't tell. Alone in the dark again, they turned and slipped through the damp, moldy membrane that separated Freighter's world from the ordinary one and a chill ran up his spine.

Even in the dark of the night, the gloom was tangible, an ethereal hand of doom that held the entire estate in its palm. Seeing the structure again, the dilapidated Le Mans, the moldy ziggurats of magazines posed as columns on either side of the door, the reality of what he and Kim were about to do served as a cold slap to Jessie's face.

"How do we get in?"

"Right over here," she answered, moving toward the darkness gathered below the balcony. Kim closed her eyes and willed herself to bond with the shadows. She took Jessie's hand and stepped forward. It didn't work; she walked face first into a wall.

"What the hell?" she said, her nose stinging, her eyes filling with vinegar tears from the sharp impact.

"You okay? What happened?"

She laughed, "Oh my god, I'm so dumb."

"What?"

"It's you. Jessie, you're making me whole. Every time we hold hands or …"

Kim grabbed him by the forearms and leaned in, stuck her tongue down his throat. After several long, sensuous moments, she disengaged, all smiles.

"When I'm with you, I become more like you; more like the people born on this side of the glass."

"I don't understand."

"Did you know I never ate a single piece of food until that day at your house? It's because in Widdershins, we're non-corporeal. Before you, I was a ghost."

"No wonder you eat the way you do."

Kim laughed, kissed Jessie quick once more on the lips, and then scanned the area.

"Okay, you're going to have to get us in. You think if I give you a boost, you can make it up onto that balcony?"

"I think so."

Jessie surveyed the supports more thoroughly, took note of how they emerged from the house, flush with the outside wall just above their heads and from there ran up at a forty-five-degree angle before connecting to the underside of the balcony.

"Here, hold this so I can see what I'm doing," he handed his phone to Kim, the flashlight engaged, then grasped the support directly in front of him and pulled himself up, wriggling to get his legs hooked around the wood where it met the wall. From here he worked himself up the beam inch by inch, until he was just below the underside of the balcony. Freeing one hand, he reached up and over, grabbed the railing that surrounded the entire structure and finally managed to pull his head up enough to see through the slats and locate the door.

"Kim, the light."

She didn't hear him. Jessie looked back over his shoulder, saw her moving her fingers over the touch screen like she'd never held a phone before. Maybe she hadn't.

"Kim?"

"Huh?"

"The light. Over here."

"Oh, sorry!" she pinned the light to exactly where his face was, blinding him.

"Not in my face! Up there, on the balcony!"

"Sorry," she said again, and straightened the light.

Gaining the balcony, Jessie grasped the screen door and prepared himself to enter Robert Freighter's home.

Once inside he moved cautiously into the first room and was amazed to find exactly what he was looking for:

Keys. A lot of them.

"Crap."

"You alright?" Kim called up from the ground outside.

He'd come looking for a key. What he found was a couple hundred of them.

"Uh, we've hit a bit of a snag in the key department."

Jessie moved forward and stared at the walls of the room, every available inch decorated with keys. Big ones, small ones, brass, silver, gold. Some looked old-timey and had an antiquated patina to them. Others seemed new or at least cared for. These he guessed were the least commonly used. Some of the others looked as though they would crumble to dust the instant something as tenuous as a human hand touched them.

"What the hell are they all for?"

The keys were mounted like functional decorations, hung over every wood-paneled wall, arranged in a cascade of showmanship as if these were the prized possessions of the old man's life. Jessie moved closer to the wall on his left and tentatively grasped one key in his hand, something about its three-and-a-quarter teeth with their almost playful arrangement drew him to it.

There was a crash at the window.

Jessie ducked, hiding behind the only nearby piece of furniture, a high-backed, dark green velvet recliner that faced the window.

"Did you forget about me or what?" Kim hollered from outside, below.

"Geez! Did you have to break the freakin' window?"

Another rock flew by him, into the house and crashed on the wall behind him.

"Sorry! Sorry, be right down."

Jessie found a staircase just outside the entrance to the key room. He took the steps as quickly as he dared in the darkness, barely able to make out the path ahead of him. Unable to glean specifics, he set foot on the ground floor in what could only be described as a workroom. The four walls were lined with hearty wooden work benches, tools of all kinds mounted above each of them. Confused, he had to stop and re-orient himself. It looked like his basement, only on the ground floor. He found the house and its remixed nature unsettling, but essentially no queerer than his own house's peccadilloes. Jessie's nerves spiked as the musty decor lent easy comparison to a cinema maniac's torture store. The image of Old Man Freighter's creeping, undulating face spurred his feet back into motion, and Jessie headed toward a doorway several meters to his right. As he left the room, two iridescent eyes winked open in the darkest corner.

CHAPTER 27

The sound of a violin woke her. Previn's take on Adagio for Strings. The music took her over with memory before she even had a chance to contemplate where she was or how she'd arrived.

You come home, this same song swells from the stereo system. Nico would never use the USB speakers. He held onto his love of analog, forged long before they'd met. The blinds were closed, which was odd for such a clear night. Always one of your favorite things to do together, sit and stare at the stars.

The first word you heard was 'Bastard.' You didn't remember that until later, after you were able to accept what happened, how you had failed to react quickly enough to save your husband's life. The word was loud, hurled at someone with force. There was a smell, unlike anything you had encountered before, and then you noticed the wooden knife block on the kitchen island was over-turned, blades spread across the linoleum floor. You dropped your purse, somehow didn't think to pull your phone from it first. Through the open doorway at the far end of the den, to the right of the kitchen, just as a sharp cry of pain split the house in two, followed by a dull thud that you've often remembered since as the sound of your life breaking. The sound haunts you; you hear it daily, often in unexpected moments and places. And it always brings you back to that night, emerging into the library in time to see Nico on the floor, the knife stuck in his chest, blood everywhere, especially the white suit on the man coming straight toward you.

You will never forget that face.

Talia surfaced from the memories in the throes of panic, unlike anything she'd experienced since those first few years after Nico's murder. Nerves frayed, she blinked her eyes in the dark and started the deep breathing that had gotten her through the worst of it back then, but after half a dozen breaths she felt as though the exercise had worked against her. She imagined herself hyperventilating and it began to happen. Her head turned side to side, and as she searched for some clue as to where she was, six giant words repeatedly stepped on her sanity:

She'd been taken against her will.

After a few minutes, the attack leveled off. Talia was able to stand, and once she did, she began to catch her breath. With a steady flow of air to her brain, her faculties rebooted, she began to catalog her surroundings. The floor she'd woken on was cool stone, large blocks inlaid with a precision that left the mortar joints almost invisible. This was the kind of masonry you didn't see anymore, not in the States anyway, if that's where she was.

"How long was I unconscious?" she wondered, realizing the last thing she remembered was following Professor Barker into a run-down, empty room.

A shard of memory surfaced:

She'd been carried here on her back.

At the thought, panic threatened to reclaim her, but Talia fought it off, if only just barely. From somewhere, the violin continued its heavy exposition. "Next thing. Move on to the next thing," she said, invoking a mantra she sometimes used to clear hurdles in everyday life.

The walls that surrounded her were not wood, but a cool, smooth and featureless stone cut in a way that indicated something unthinkably expensive. Marble? No, these were too perfect, the entirety of the walls one enormous piece and glowing white even with this little amount of light.

"Oh god," Talia's hand came away quickly as the idea that it was bone occurred to her.

"Impossible. Unless… not bone. Ivory?" There it was, and the idea was such a ludicrous accusation as to the wealth of the builder that she understood immediately where she was, who she was facing.

"I must apologize for your treatment up to this point, Talia."

She jumped at the unexpected sound of the voice. How long had he been standing there, watching her from the dark?

A light unfolded several feet in front of her, a door opening, a figure outlined in its glow as, with the wave of a hand, her observer beckoned her to follow him from her prison into more accommodating spaces.

Apprehensive, Talia stood and followed the man at a considerable distance. As her eyes adjusted to the light, images appeared through the doorway: a beautiful, hand-carved wooden table with two equally fantastic chairs on opposite sides. A clock whose face had no hands. A bookcase. The man reached the table, pulled one chair out for her and then moved to take the other. Seated, he turned to face her and she knew him instantly. It was the man from her memory, the man who had murdered her husband.

CHAPTER 28

"Follow me, but stay close. Something about this place isn't right."

"I hadn't noticed."

Jessie took Kim's hand, laughed at her sarcasm. They moved through the house, into what should have been the workroom he had just passed through. Instead, they came out in what appeared to be a dining room with no furniture. China cabinets on one wall were the only evidence of a function beyond the clutter created by dozens and dozens of stacks of books.

"Okay, this definitely isn't right. I just came through here and..."

There was a doorway ahead. Jessie led them through it, and they came out into a smaller room. Then another. They kept pace, traversing through a series of rooms he had not passed through earlier. Each one was, maddeningly, smaller than the one before. The effect was that of walking through a set of Chinese boxes. It was unnerving. Finally, they reached the smallest room, which was not much bigger than the folding chair and tea table that occupied the center of it.

Just beyond the chair was the door Kim had seen during her previous expedition here, the one that wouldn't open for her.

"This is it. My sister's behind this door, I know it!"

Jessie approached the door, rapped on it with his knuckles.

"Shh!" Kim warned.

"Who's gonna hear us?"

"I don't know, let's just get the keys, get my sister, and get the hell outta here, okay?"

There was another door catty-corner to the metal one; they crossed to it, came out by a staircase.

"This is totally messed up. Do you know where we're going?" Jessie asked.

"You're the one who spent the better part of an hour creeping around in here. You tell me."

Jessie placed his foot on the first stair, hesitated for a moment and then went full out, pulling Kim after him as he ascended a staircase that did not resemble at all the one he came down five minutes before. Gone was the ornate balustrade, replaced by a rickety, make-shift railing. Noting this, something occurred to him.

An hour? Try five minutes - ten at the most by his count. Jessie was reminded of his first night in Gallows Hill, standing in front of Caliper Lane. Then too, he had lost time. More folding and tucking, like the rhyme Kim had recited on their way to Richard's.

"Was that rhyme, like, how we got to Richard's? Is it some kind of key?"

"I think we really have to be careful in here," Kim said, avoiding his question. Jessie thought she seemed unusually nervous, like she wasn't telling him something. They rounded a corner and came to a dead end hall.

"I thought you said you found the keys?"

"Yeah, well, the house doesn't seem to want me to find them again."

"This was the first one they built; Richard says it's unstable."

"To put it mildly."

Another corner and another dead end. If things kept rearranging around them, was it possible he might not find the room again? Was it possible they might not find their way out?

Terrified by this line of thinking, Jessie surveyed their surroundings for a clue. He could see recessed lighting enclosures buried in the ceiling at regular intervals from which no light came. Kim saw this too, walked back in the direction they'd come, running her hands along the wall as she went. In a second she found a switch, also recessed and almost impossible to see in the dark gray tones of the lightless house. She flipped it, and lights revealed the entire hallway around them.

"Hey! Got it. How's that?"

"Kim!" Jessie screamed, and when Kim turned around, a tall, impossibly black figure loomed malevolently before her.

CHAPTER 29

While Kim used the rhyme to set her mind to the frequency required for entering the space between worlds, Linda had a different approach. The most important thing Cuthbert had taught her was that Magick is a thing of perspective; it's whatever works to bypass the conscious mind, the parts that say, 'this won't work because it violates the rules of the world.'

"What all great Magicians will tell you, Linda, is that there are no rules for the world. We create our own limitations by agreeing reality is what the consensus says it is," Cuthbert had told her on the day she was inducted into the inner circle of the GHAS. Since then, Linda had seen more than most of the others in the group. She'd seen things that were so far beyond being categorized as 'unbelievable' that she had long ago trained herself to excise all derivations of the word 'belief' from her vocabulary.

Linda stopped her car at the truncated intersection of Derleth and Caliper and breathed deep. She'd only been to Richard's one other time, the night he saved her from Freighter. There, he had cared for her, taught her how to exist without a shadow or a reflection, how to trick people into seeing those things when they expected to see them. After that, Chase had taken her home, and it was then, at her lowest and loneliest, Linda had succumbed to her attraction to him.

"Ain't gonna do me no good thinking about this shit now. Alright girlie, cowboy up."

Linda left her car behind and entered the trees. Her mind was clear and calm, and as she walked, she focused on the spaces between the things that made up the world around her. Between the trees were shadows, between the leaves was dirt, darkness, and moisture. Between the sky and the Earth was the world's dirty shadow, the place where the sun went briefly when it sank from view, before it appeared on the other hemisphere. There, in that state of indeterminacy, was The Between, the harbor for Schrödinger's fabled cat. Eschewing the world she knew, searching for that between place now, Linda's footsteps left the soft stamp of the dirt behind and began to echo as cobblestones appeared beneath her feet. In the distance, red lanterns came into view. Linda was no magician; she didn't know how this kind of Magick worked, she'd simply memorized the steps Dubois had taught her.

When she reached Richard's door, she knocked politely. A moment later, the jovial Mailman answered, a welcoming smile emblazoned across his face.

"Linda Evans! Wonderful to see you again!"

"Likewise Richard. Am I the first?"

"Indubitably. Vous Venez, please, please. Let's give you the advantage, eh? <Hurm>."

The Mailman led Linda into another room. Inside, a triangular table stood dressed for receiving guests: a chair at each point, an ornately folded napkin and crystal cordial glass set before each one.

"I apologize that it has become incumbent upon you to represent the Society in this matter <Hurm>."

"Yeah, well, just do me a favor and have my back if anything… untoward happens, okay?"

"Of course. May I offer you an aperitif?"

"No, thank you."

"Now, while we have a moment, I must confess that, while the Bruja Tenorio did ask me to call this meeting because of The Hub's activation, there is an ulterior motive as well."

"Do tell?" Linda smiled, remembering she enjoyed this person's company very much.

"Have you by chance had the occasion to meet Jessie Roberts yet?"

"The newest occupant of the Tenorio house? No."

"Well, while it will be no small amount of unpleasantness for you to occupy the same immediate air as Freighter, know that by doing so, you help keep young Mr. Roberts safe. He and a certain girl we all know and love are, at this very moment, breaking into his house in an attempt to rescue said girl's long lost sister."

"Barker's daughter? Jesus! Richard - they're kids! How could you let them do something so insane?"

"Linda, if you learned that Luis was sequestered inside that damnable domicile, would you let a hundred-year-old stick in the mud talk you out of attempting to save him?"

"Richard, that's different."

"No, it most certainly is not. <Hurm>. I voiced my concerns as best I could."

A belligerent knock at the front door stopped the argument. Richard scurried away, and Linda hated herself for keeping her eyes pinned to the floor as he returned with Bob Freighter in tow.

'Those poor, stupid children,' she thought to herself, and

her anger at the predicament moved Linda to look up and make eye contact with her own personal boogeyman as he entered the room.

"This better not be a waste a'my time."

"Oh sit down, you old bastard. No one here wants to be in your company, but there are rules," Linda said, writing something on the napkin before her.

"Rules are for those who don't have the upper hand. Case you hadn't heard, that ain't us."

Linda stood, planted both fists on the table before her.

"You happy about that, Bob? You think the fact that The Hub's finally online means you're gonna get Helen back?"

Freighter jumped to his feet, his chair tumbling to the floor behind him.

"You got no right to speak her name."

"Yeah? Helen, Helen, Helen. She's dead you twit, and no amount of pain and suffering you inflict on anyone else is ever going to change that. And Cruchetti? He's the reason she's dead. He's probably laughing at your pain."

Freighter lunged for her, but Richard was fast for his size, caught the older man by the ankle and brought him down hard on the table, which was sturdy and held his weight.

"Enough! <Hurm> Both of you. We are gathered at the bequest of Encarnación Tenorio to deliberate what happens now that the world has its first working teleportation system. I am certain we can all agree that the importance of protocol and decorum trump whatever personal grudges we hold against one another."

"I'm sorry Richard, I can't do this," Linda said and ran from the room. As she passed him, she stuffed the piece of napkin in his hand, feigning the gesture as a conciliatory one. A moment later Freighter was on his feet, puffing up his chest after her.

"No! Robert, I need you to sit and listen. Otherwise, I

make no promises concerning the Bruja's right to intervene. An intervention that will not garner the Architect's goodwill, as pertains to your situation <Hurm>."

Freighter stared at Richard, murder burning in his eyes. His skin had begun to bubble black.

"I ain't here to listen, Fatman. I'm here to talk, and what I say you can consider as havin' come straight from the mouth'a the Architect."

CHAPTER 30

The thin and aged aristocratic figure of her captor seemed to Talia spectacular in every way. There was a soft, percolating violence in the textures of his face, clean-shaven but webbed with shadows nonetheless, and an ominous characteristic to his voice, the timbre of which carved out the entirety of the room when he spoke. There was something about that voice that felt far away and yet uncomfortably close at the same time. Omnipotent was the word that came to Talia's mind. He matched her stare with chilling resolve, daring her to address their history first, a challenge that told her he was not regretful in the least for what he had done to her family. It took work, but Talia remained silent, afraid emotion would color anything she said, seething as she was with a toxic mixture of fear and hatred.

"It has been a long time, yes?"

In her head, Talia screamed.

"It's okay. I understand that you hate me. How could you not? But please, believe me when I tell you that not a day has gone by since our paths first crossed that I have not thought about you and your son. You are very special people to me. I've kept up with your adventures: always moving from here to there, darkness pushing you ever forward, the way you maintain an almost constant pace of activity so your son does not see the pain you are in. Tell me, do you think that your ruse works? Do you think Jessie does not see that you are... broken."

"Jessie believes my problems stem from his father's death."

"And they do, though not in the way he thinks. Talia, what happened to your husband was not personal."

"Really? An impersonal murder?"

"I know it seems preposterous, but there is much you do not know about Nicholas."

"Nico. My husband's name was Nico."

"When you knew him, yes. But before that? Nicholas."

Talia couldn't help it; she rolled her eyes.

"You knew him when? As a child?"

"It had been many years since your late husband was a child. Tell me, what day did you celebrate as his birthday? Was it the twenty-fourth of November?"

"May twenty-ninth. You sure you knew him?"

"Are you?"

"Well, I was married to him for three years. Not an eternity, granted. But I like to think we would have made it for the long haul if you hadn't murdered him."

"Nicholas Llewelyn Davies was born on Tuesday, November twenty-fourth, nineteen-o-three."

Talia exploded in laughter.

"Really? Well, that's funny, because I don't remember him being almost one hundred years old when we met."

"Be that as it may, he was. Unfortunately, he was also one of the only people who knew about me, who knew what I wanted to do and how I would be able to do it. Because of that, I came to him one night. You were at school, earning your doctorate. I approached Nicholas - Nico as he had rechristened himself in his new life - and offered to bring him into the fold. He refused, and I killed him."

"You're insane, you know that?"

"Talia, I knew your husband long before you did, and believe me, he had his chance to see it through. He lost the nerve. Eternity is a long time. But I do believe he would have wanted it for you and your son. That's why I am here now. I have a most amazing invitation for you both."

"What are you talking about? Invitation? What is it you think you could offer me that would make up for taking my husband, my son's father, from us?"

"How does eternal life sound for a start?"

CHAPTER 31

When WJ opened his eyes, disorientation stole over him. He tried to shake it off, but the feeling fought back, only relinquishing once he'd spotted the rickety old stairs that led up from Talia and Jessie's basement to the kitchen.

"Basement," he was barely able to mutter to himself under his breath. Speaking made his head spin, and as he acclimated to his perspective - flat on his back - a dull throb in his temples jostled his vision and sent small quakes through his nervous system. He held on, and eventually, time helped him gather his wits. When he finally felt like he wouldn't vomit, WJ closed his eyes, held his breath and tentatively sat up.

After a few moments of successful sitting, he tried to stand. At first, he was unsure if his legs would hold him; he felt wrong in some base, fundamental way, yet was unable to explain exactly how. Displaced - that was the word that seemed to sum it up, as though he was no longer present in his own body, despite his observations and ability to recognize his surroundings.

When WJ did make it into a standing position, he was shaky. Memories came to him then, images and snippets of conversation that coalesced, stunning him into motion. Dean Stanisberg's story, the drive back from the University, the lunatic in the driveway and that purple hair tie he'd found in the kitchen that suggested Jessie was probably okay.

Probably.

He tried to remember how he'd ended up in the basement, but nothing came to him.

"Senility, here I come," he said aloud, one hand against the wall as he closed the gap to the kitchen door. Light and soft music leaked through the jamb, communicating to WJ that he was not alone.

Eager to be done with his personal mortification, he mustered his strength and ascended the stairs. When he emerged into the kitchen, Talia and Jessie greeted him warmly.

They wouldn't hold this against him. Of course not. They were family now.

Uneasy with the silent, brooding violence that permeated his remaining guest's presence, Richard was nonetheless very much aware he must detain Freighter as long as possible. To quell his unease, he sought respite in the large, crystal decanter he had offered his guests. Aware that Freighter was watching him, Richard poured himself a small portion of the golden brown liquor and felt his nerves settle at once under its influence. Reinforced, for the moment, he returned to the business that had brought Bob Freighter into his home.

"Robert, <Hurm>, I am most pleased you have elected to remain here, with me, to pursue a proper discourse. Despite Linda's… dubiety, I feel certain her employer does indeed wish to cooperate as much as your own."

"Don't bet yer dough on cooperation from our end, Dick. The Architect sent me to deliver an ultimatum, not barter terms."

"I am certain I do not understand your sentiment, sir, nor your employer's. Surely, the Architect remembers there is an accord that must be considered before offering ultimatums. The Hub's activation must be treated with all the veneration worthy an event of this magnitude. <Hurm>."

"Yeah? Well, maybe we want you to remember we hold the cards now."

"By god man, did Cruchetti send you here to threaten us? Does he not understand the ire his impunity will arouse from the other players in this drama?"

Richard's nerves had returned. He poured another two fingers of the autumnal elixir, not bothering to offer any to his guest. What Freighter was suggesting would bring about a war. A subtle one, but the conflict would be bloody; wars for wealth and power always were. Once again steeled by the imbibe, Richard decided to attempt a different tact.

"Robert, perhaps you and Mr. Cruchetti have forgotten, I am a neutral party in your endeavors. I want what is best for everyone."

"Oh yeah? That why Mater Tenorio calls on you to deliver her messages? Don't think that kinda' shit goes unnoticed, Dick."

"<Hurm> My relationship with the Tenorio tribe goes back as far as your employer's. Perhaps if he retained a personable relationship with her, she would call upon him in much the same manner she does me."

"Yeah. Maybe."

Freighter stood up

"Now, 'less you got something else to tell me, this meeting's over."

"Hold on a moment, sir."

Fattingback moved quickly, knowing if Freighter went home now he'd likely walk in on Kim, Jessie, and probably even Linda.

"Ain't holdin' for nothin'. The Architect is launchin' The

Hub, takin' the town, and going public. All previous arrange-ments are off. He expects no interference, or there'll be blood. Lots of it."

"That, will indubitably not be the case, Robert."

"Fine. See ya soon, Mailman."

CHAPTER 33

Kim turned and saw the black, bubbling shape just as it came for her. She dodged, but the figure's reach violated physics, bent in an unnatural half-circle back and around, catching her by the wrist.

"Get off!" Kim screamed, disappearing for a moment, only to reappear behind her attacker and give it a good, sharp fist to the back of its head.

The Shape went down, but in a trick similar to Kim's, it hit the ground with a silent SPLASH, like a bucket of water tossed at the floor, shooting along the hardwood and straight through the gap between Jessie's feet, only to re-congeal to full height behind him. Startled, Jessie didn't have enough time to react before their attacker had him by the shoulder. He wrestled free, but not before the ominous figure spun him so hard he slammed against the wall opposite, leaving a hole in it with his shoulder.

The Shape stood before him, poised for a killing stroke.

"What the hell are you?"

The Shape remained stationary for a long, ugly moment. Jessie studied the black, unholy face. He found it impossible to look away. Ripples broke the surface of its body, and the ground beneath it began to move.

Kim slammed into the Thing from behind, and they both disappeared upon impact. It took Jessie a minute to track them; he ran from the room calling Kim's name. When he finally found them, they were down the hall, shadows on the wall locked in two-dimensional combat. To Jessie, it looked like a sophisticated shadow puppet show, the way the dark shapes lashed at one another, melding during contact into larger, less distinct forms. This gave him an idea. Despite her earlier problems using her shadow powers, Kim obviously still had both forms. Did their attacker?

Groggy, Jessie found the light switch and flipped it down, immediately throwing the room into darkness. Just as he'd hoped, as soon as the lights went out, Kim tumbled from the wall back into three-dimensional space, and The Thing disappeared completely.

"Are you alright?" he asked, running to catch her as Kim stumbled on freshly reappropriated legs.

"I should be asking you. You hit that wall pretty hard."

"I'm okay, but we gotta get moving before that thing comes back."

"Okay, let's get what we came for while we have time."

Jessie turned back to where the door to the Key Room had been only moments ago. Of course, it was gone.

"This is making me crazy!"

They ran through the hall again, and this time luck shined on them. Rounding the first corner, they could see the keys in a room directly ahead. They ran to it, neither daring to look away for even an instant.

"God, there's even more than I remember from earlier. There must be a couple hundred keys here. How do we find the right one?"

"I don't know!"

A light bulb went on over Kim's head. She ran out of the room, and Jessie screamed after her.

"Where the hell are you going?"

"Just hold on!"

"Kim, wait!" he called, but she was off. In her wake, Jessie's eyes played over every surface, waiting for their attacker to return.

Kim ran down the hall and back to the last room she'd seen before this one. A moment ago it had been a bedroom. That was no longer the case.

"Oh come on!" she tried to keep her eye on the doorway to the room with Jessie and the keys. If Freighter's home was this unstable, she might look away for a moment and lose the room with Jessie in it forever.

"Jessie!" she shouted back down the hall at him, once, twice. What if it had shifted? What if she lost him? No, there he was, poking his head around the corner, "Kim, what do I do? Where are you going?"

"Just stay right there, where I can see you. I have an idea."

Kim tried to fake the room in front of her out by running past it a few steps and then sharply turning around and coming back. It worked - the room had changed again. What's more, it had changed to exactly what she had been hoping for: a bedroom. She bolted inside, realizing too late that she may re-emerge into a different corridor altogether.

"Screw it," she said and ran deep enough in to grab two pillows off a beat-up old bed. Only away for a moment, Kim indeed returned to an unfamiliar view. She was about to surrender to despair when she heard Jessie's voice.

"Behind you!"

Kim turned; the room had swum only a small distance. Good. She ran back to him double-time, throwing Jessie one of the pillows while pulling the casing off the other.

"This isn't nap time."

"No stupid, the keys! We're taking all of them!"

His own lightbulb went off, and Jessie followed suit; ripping the crusty pillow from the casing, he threw it to the floor.

They worked with fervor, grabbing every key they could get their hands on. After a few moments, they had them all and stood to leave.

"You think that room with your sister's in the same place?"

"Doubtful. Hey, what's that outside?"

"Huh?" Jessie said, chills running up his spine as he stepped out onto the balcony and watched a car approach the driveway.

"Shit! That's probably him!"

Overhead, lightning turned the night into day for a second. The storm that had been brewing all afternoon was nearly here; the lackluster drizzle that had haunted the day turned to a downpour.

"Hey, give me that for a second," Kim said, indicating Jessie's pillowcase. He handed it to her, and just as he did, he saw the black shape reappear behind her.

"Kim! Look out!" he screamed, starting forward to protect her. Kim had other ideas. She ducked and thrust both hands into his chest, dodging an attack by the thing behind her and knocking Jessie off-balance and over the side of the railing.

"Go limp when you land. Sorry Jessie, but I can't let you risk your life for me!"

"Noooooooooo!" Jessie screamed, all the way to the ground below.

Still charged by the adrenaline from seeing Bob Freighter for the first time since being held as his captive, Linda left Richard to distract Freighter and drove to his house as fast as she could. As luck would have it, she arrived just in time to see Jessie fall from the second story balcony.

"Jesus, kid!" she screamed, pulling to the side of the road and opening her glovebox. She rooted around inside for a moment, tossing out papers and junk until she found a small box Cuthbert had given her several years before. Linda never thought she'd actually have to use the thing, but that was Gallows Hill: you just never knew.

Taking a deep breath, she stepped cautiously from the car. She'd once vowed to never step foot on Freighter's property again, and the residual paranoia left over after experiencing grand metaphysical trauma in the house before her made Linda's senses swim with fear. Fear that every little sound, every movement would be sensed by The Thing that lived in this house. The Thing Bob Freighter had taken from her. She knew it well; every once in a while it came to her in the mirror, came to tell her what it wanted to do to her. Most Doppelgängers hated their Casts, but Linda's carried that hate to a new level. Thinking of this, she hesitated.

"Just do it already, goddamnit!" she screamed at the empty rearview mirror that answered her gaze. A cauldron of emotion erupted: terror, pain, and hatred coursed through her veins at memories of her helplessness, at the feeling of losing a part of herself. And that was enough to do it; thinking of someone else having to go through what she had.

She'd never let that happen, so Linda took off at a run, up the decaying driveway and straight toward the source of all her nightmares.

"Ready or not you maleficent bitch, here I come."

She found Jessie straight away, sprawled on the overgrown lawn where he'd landed. He had a fairly large gash on his forehead, but he was breathing, and nothing appeared broken.

"Kid?"

No answer, so Linda bent down to pick him up. That's when all the hair on the back of her neck stood straight up. She knew what came next.

CHAPTER 34

The moment Kim pushed Jessie off the balcony she whipped around and caught a blow to the side of the head that sent her sprawling, the keys in the pillowcases scattering in all directions.

"Ah! You bitch!"

The Thing came at her again, Its limbs elongating, catching her by the hair and face, smashing her into the wall so hard Kim dropped onto her back, unable to move for several seconds. When she finally opened her eyes, The Thing stood above her, and for a moment Kim thought she recognized it. The face became that of the woman she knew worked for Dubois.

"I see you," Kim said, springing up and into a crouched position. She wasn't really ready for round two, but if need be, she would fight dirty.

The Thing seemed as surprised at this as Kim. It hesitated for a moment, then turned its head like a dog called by an invisible whistle. Something was happening, outside. Was it Jessie?

Too late to consider this, The Thing flickered briefly, then charged at her. Something about her proximity to this crea-ture had reactivated her powers, so Kim went 2-D and braced for more Shadow combat.

It didn't happen. Whatever had caught the Monster's attention was apparently more important than her; It careened through her and out onto the balcony, disappearing over the side. Kim stood on edge for a long moment, waiting for another attack. When one never came, she began to accept that she may have a chance to find her sister, unhin-dered by attack.

"What the hell was that?" Kim asked the empty room as she began to gather the keys back into the pillowcases. She had to find the door to her sister again quickly; the faster she could save Patty, the more likely she might still be able to help Jessie.

"Please be okay. Both of you. Please be okay."

Linda stood just in time to see the black shape come off the balcony, straight at her from above.

The rumor had long been that The Thing that haunted Bob Freighter's property was the ghost of his late wife, Helen. Linda knew different. She flinched at the memories now, always so vivid in replay. She could hear Freighter's voice, the exact pitch and timbre of his slightly Southern drawl as he explained what he did to her while he did it. Metaphysical Surgery, that's what he called it, two words that seemed too big for such an ornery curmudgeon. But Bob had known what he was doing, so it stood to reason he'd had help. Cruchetti had trained him, taught him how to perform dark miracles on behalf of their cause. Linda winced at the pain as it washed back over her, that feeling of having her other self torn away and rendered. Tears as another woman with her face, her voice, her everything stepped through the mirror, tearing some intimate fabric deep inside her; a nightmare with her face. It sat with Linda for days, told her things she desperately had not wanted to hear; things about herself, about the world. Linda shivered with the memory but kept it close to her, an ignited tanker of gasoline on a dry and windswept plane.

Soon there would be a fire.

With the pain of the memory turned to rage, Linda raised the box Cuthbert had given her in front of her face and popped it open; a pink spark flared inside, and she watched as that light reached into the sky and ate the dark shape right out of the air above her.

Hesitant to believe it could be over so easily, it took her several minutes of panting rigidness before Linda could accept that she had won. Cuthbert's little contraption had saved the day. Relieved, Linda closed the box. She sighed heavily as her Doppelgänger - never in contact with her long enough to fully materialize in this world - disappeared into what Cuthbert called a Vetusta Vitrium, a thing he had explained to her as 'a pocket dimension.'

"Yeah. Whatever. As long as it's not here."

Energized, a smile on her face for the first time in forever, Linda picked the kid up, threw him over her shoulder and walked as quickly as she could under his moderate weight back to her car, suddenly remembering the owner of the home could return at any moment. In the sky above, thunder announced the next phase of what sounded as though it might just be the mother of all storms.

Cuthbert Dubois pulled up to the Knight's Side sheriff station just as a great peel of thunder ripped across the sky. Chase's cruiser sat curbside. Good, the trip hadn't been a waste; Dubois lifted the collar on his three-thousand-dollar coat and hurried to the door.

The moment he entered, Cuthbert sensed something was wrong.

As he came upon the sky-blue, Formica-topped reception desk, Cuthbert's concern deepened: where was everyone? No one was behind the front desk, and the phone lay face-up, off the hook. He peered past reception, off toward the few offices visible from the lobby. No one there either. An eerie silence hung over the scene, and Dubois found he was suddenly very warm. He delicately removed his black leather driving gloves one finger at a time, tucking them in his pockets as he moved past the desk and toward the corridor beyond. Dampened but still audible, another peel of thunder shook the sky. As it faded, a new sound replaced it: the sound of muffled screaming.

~

Freighter returned from the Mailman's with a self-satisfied grin on his face. A grin that disappeared as soon as he saw the tire tracks to the left of his driveway. Someone had been here, and he was pretty sure he knew who that someone was. What she might have done in his absence would be far easier to learn if, instead of wasting time investigating his property, he simply tracked her down and beat it out of her. And Freighter knew there was only one place Linda Evans would be going to hole up if she'd just paid him a visit.

Dubois'.

~

When she couldn't raise Cuthbert on the phone, Linda became irritated. Pragmatic to a fault, she put the softly seething bud of anger to good use as fuel to help her muster the strength to carry Jessie's unconscious body to her car. Plopping him on the backseat of the Crown Vic, Linda set the Vetusta Vitrium on the passenger side floor, exactly where she could keep her eye on it.

She wasn't taking any chances.

Despite her triumph, Linda's fear was still very much present. To her, it felt as though Freighter was just around every corner; like he somehow knew what she was up to and would arrive any moment, retribution driving his slathering jaws. Couple that with the fact that next to her was a little glass box that housed her Double, a version of her that possessed all of her mental faculties and negative emotional qualities but none of her altruistic sensibilities, and Linda was just barely keeping it together. On bad days, she could be a mean-spirited, spiteful bitch. Remove the shackles of conscience and self-control from that, she didn't want to know what could happen.

"Alright Cuthbert, I did my part, now I need your goddamned help!"

She dialed Dubois again. Still no answer

"Great," she said aloud, glancing in the rearview mirror at the unconscious teenage body crumpled in her back seat. She hoped she would be able to get him out of the car and into Cuthbert's before the storm really kicked in.

To do this, she knew she would need Cuthbert to open his gate and access his home security system remotely, something that would be easy enough for him to do if he would just answer his damn phone.

Still looking behind her, something caught Linda's eye through the back window. She slowed so as not to drive off the road but immediately cursed herself for giving up her ground. Because Bob Freighter was indeed behind her.

Rounding the corner and running at them on all fours, Freighter was low to the ground; he resembled an animal more than a man. Fear spiked and Linda stepped on the gas; the tires spun in the wet gravel.

"Come on!" she screamed at no one, pounding the steering wheel in frustration as the wheel spun, and the back of the car moved sideways for a moment, then hopped back into forward motion, almost spinning a full one-eighty. Linda caught control at the last minute and gunned the engine, just as Freighter's face became undeniably clear in the rearview mirror.

"You bastard! Leave me alone!"

The Vic hit a pothole and bounced, slamming back down hard enough to slow them. In her rearview mirror, Linda saw Freighter leap into the air. A moment later the old man's full weight came down hard on the roof.

"Get away from me!"

An arm swung over the side, slammed into the driver's side window so hard it spiderwebbed, tiny shards of break-away glass raining on Linda's left cheek, arm, and lap. The Vic picked up speed. They rounded a corner at fifty miles an hour and the ten-foot-tall, wrought-iron fence that surrounded Cuthbert's came into view.

"Hold on baby!" she screamed, slamming first on the gas to accelerate the last two hundred feet or so to the fence and then switching her foot to drive the brake pedal straight into the floor. The Vic skidded in wet, loose gravel at the lip of the drive and her unwanted passenger took flight, arcing high into the air and landing prone against the iron slats. A moment later, Freighter lay stunned on the ground and Linda hit speed dial for Cuthbert.

One ring. No answer and Freighter was still.

Two rings. No answer, but Freighter's right arm began to twitch. His hue darkened to the color of pitch, and black shadow seeped from his every pore, coating him from head to toe.

Three rings. "Goddamnit, Cuthbert!" Freighter's head lolled for a moment and then snapped to attention. His features had been replaced by a sheen black surface.

Four rings. Linda stowed the phone and popped the car into drive just as Freighter started toward her. Grasping the wheel with both hands, she planted the accelerator again and showered her attacker with rocks for a good five seconds before the treads on her tires caught, the Vic peeling out in reverse. Moving backward at twenty, thirty, forty miles an hour, Linda tried to whip the car around in a Hail Mary one-eighty just as Freighter lunged and caught her front bumper.

"Damnit!" she grunted and spun the wheel back the other way. The power steering whined like a sick puppy, but it did the trick: the Vic shot around an extra ninety-degrees and sent Freighter flying a second time. She would not waste the opportunity, Linda thought as she brought the Vic up to fifty and slammed directly into the malevolent old man before her.

CHAPTER 36

Cuthbert emerged from around the row of cubicles to an alarming scene. Sheriff Jim Rash lay sprawled on his back across the desk just inside his office, Chase holding him down while deputy Terry Quinn fought to apply a makeshift bandage to the Sheriff's thigh.

"Good lord, what happened?"

Terry whirled, horrified to be caught unaware in the Sheriff's Station, of all places. It'd been an evening of surprises, that was for sure.

"Cuthbert," Chase barked, "landline's down from the storm."

"Am I the only person in this town that owns a cellular phone?"

"Mine's dead," Terry apologized, and Dubois' gaze fell accusingly on Chase, who ignored him.

"Officer Montgomery's phone-" Terry continued, but Chase cut him off.

"Doesn't matter! Cuthbert, maybe you could help, if it's not too much goddamn trouble?"

Dubois took a step backward and cocked his head like a

cat contemplating a corpse. Gunshot wounds did not belong in Knight's Side. He hesitated for an instant and ran his eyes over the scene again, this time slow enough to let the entirety sink in: the Sheriff's thigh provided a thick, unending flow of blood that pooled across his desk, the phone, Terry and Chase's hands as they took turns holding a wad of gauze against the wound. Terry looked frightened out of his mind, Chase more irritated than concerned.

"Today, Cuthbert!"

Dubois pulled his phone from his pocket.

"Butler Memorial Hospital," he said, and waited for the device to dial.

A moment later, the Sheriff's nervous system unleashed another lightning bolt of pain. Rash went rigid, gnashing his teeth together hard enough that two of them cracked. Chase struggled to hold him down while Terry reapplied pressure with the gauze.

"Well?" Chase barked impatiently.

"They have me on hold. Do you... do you have any painkillers or... hmmm. Let me think..."

"By the time one of you jackasses find someone to tell you what to do, I'll be as white as the walls. Quinn, get me up!" The fresh burst of pain had apparently pulled the Sheriff from the stupor of shock.

Concerned, Dubois covered the phone again and grabbed Terry's shoulder, "You cannot move him. It would be better if-"

"Someone's driving me to the hospital, or I'm going to shoot all three of you and drive myself!"

Cuthbert looked from Chase to Rash, pain turning the Sheriff's face into an origami imitation of its daylight self, and he lowered his phone.

"The Sheriff has a point; whoever heard of a hospital putting a person on hold?"

"Whoever heard of someone calling a hospital directly instead of 911?" Sheriff Rash snarled from under one side of Chase's arms, motioning for Dubois to leverage the other. He did, and for a man of advanced age, Dubois did not appear to struggle much with their five-foot-nine, two hundred and twenty-five-pound cargo. Terry in tow, the three men had just begun moving toward the door when what sounded like an 8-bit rendition of "The Girl From Ipanema" came from the phone still clenched in Dubois' free hand. He stuttered their progress to look at the ID and then halted it all together to answer.

"You've gotta be freakin' kidding me," Sheriff Rash gasped, exasperated.

"Linda, I am afraid I will have to call you back, as I am currently indisposed."

"Damnit, Cuthbert! I have the boy and Freighter is trying to kill us!" a shrill shockwave of sound came through the phone, caused Cuthbert to fumble the Sheriff as the hand holding it shot out to arm's length to protect his ear.

"Jesus, what is that?" Rash grunted from teeth barred right next to Cuthbert's head as he mashed desperately at the phone's touch screen, trying to lower the volume.

"Linda? Linda?" Dubois shouted at the phone, barely able to hear himself. Finally, the sound stopped, and the phone went dark. Ornery from pain, Sheriff Rash tried to swat the thing out of Dubois's hand, but the older man was too fast; the phone went back into the pocket of his greatcoat.

"She okay?" Chase asked.

"I'm not sure."

Two minutes later, they had successfully loaded the Sheriff into the police cruiser. They had to get Rash to the hospital, but all Chase could think of was Linda; the screams he'd heard over the phone told him they might already be too late to help her, too.

As welcome as Freighter's departure from his home was, Richard Fattingback knew he had precious little time to waste if he was somehow going to prevent Bob from discovering the raid that was, even now, taking place on his home. Richard was quick to put together a small satchel of weapons, but on his way out the door the Mailman Mystic received a start that stopped him cold.

Ahead on the path, Jessie Roberts approached, a frightened look on his face. Richard pocketed his phone and jogged to the boy, concerned.

"Good god, lad! I am most pleased to see you here and no longer contained within the domicile of our mutual Nemesis. I was just on my way to create a diversion, lend aid, fight to the death, whatever might be needed <Hurm>."

Jessie stared at him but did not respond. Something was off about the boy, and Richard began to fear the worst when he realized neither Kim or Linda were with him.

"What day is today?" Jessie asked, now only a few feet away. In the space between them, Richard thought he could feel dark energies coming off the boy.

"Jessie, snap out of it lad! For Jupiter's sake, speak to me, so that I may enlist myself in the righting of whatever wrongs Robert has perpetrated to leave you dazed and your companions unaccounted for!"

"Compan*ions*?" Jessie asked, staring up into Richard's eyes and smiling for the first time. The look of it unnerved the Mailman, and he found that he took an involuntary step backward as his brain screamed at him to RUN!

Too late.

There was a flash of movement, and then a sick feeling ate into Richard's belly, stealing any subsequent words from his tongue. Suddenly confused, as though his life had broken into pieces and been rearranged into a pattern he no longer recognized, Fattingback dropped his gaze toward the cobblestones and saw Jessie's right hand flush with his abdomen, the hilt of a large blade penetrating the ample curvature of his stomach. Pain slipped in around the edges, and the world hiccupped, tearing away the sheath of crippling shock and revealing beneath it a profound pain.

"Companions? Kimberly and who else?"

"B'ah! Pay no… attention… to me lad. Remember only, that you are damned…"

Jessie twisted the knife ninety degrees and the Mailman dropped to his knees, his rejoinder lost amidst the slobbering gurgle of his life leaving his body. As his consciousness winked out, he prayed to the stars between worlds that what Paolo Cruchetti had orchestrated so well would not come to pass. That final thought, however, was laced with the understanding of the odds in him getting his wish.

CHAPTER 37

Jessie had just rounded the corner from Eeryx onto Caliper Lane when, with no magick spell or sleight of mind, he saw Richard's cobblestone path ahead of him in the trees. The bricks were flickering in and out of existence, like bad special effects in a B movie.

"Mr. Fattingback?" he called. No answer.

Still confused at the loss of time between Kim pushing him off Freighter's balcony and waking up in the wreckage of a car on the side of the road with a strange woman slumped in the driver's seat, Jessie had to force his concern for Kim from his mind and focus on himself. His vision was blurred and his head hurt, which he figured meant he was probably concussed. Carefully he made his way over the cobblestones, the walkway seeming to have grown since his last visit. From somewhere nearby, he heard voices.

The path was not the same. Jessie crested a small hill and Richard's house finally came into view, its red hue infecting the shadows of the forest around it. Near the door, the Mailman stood, gesticulating wildly as he spoke to someone who looked like he could have been Jessie's twin brother.

And that's when Jessie understood; it *was* his twin. It was his Doppelgänger.

The world rippled with further degrees of disbelief as he once again recalled the icy sensation of seeing his reflection stand still while he spun before the mirrors that first night in the new house. It was all true; he'd awoken his Double.

As this concept stole over him, Jessie tried to taper it with logic. Just because he had a Double didn't inherently mean this new Jessie was evil, did it? In fact, how could that be the case? Kim had admitted to being the Doppelgänger of the Kim Corduroy who had lived in this world until Cruchetti swapped them; she wasn't a bad person, so why should Jessie's Double be inherently evil? Besides, he might have had the same issues most teenage boys his age did, but neither anger or hatred was included in those. The Jessie from this world didn't have a malevolent bone in his body, so why would the Jessie from Widdershins?

That idea went out the window when the Double pulled a knife and jammed it straight into Richard's stomach. Shocked, the world rotted on the vine right there in front of him; if this was him, even just another aspect of him, and he had murdered someone - murdered Richard - what did that say about anything? As Richard fell dead to the stones at his feet, Jessie exploded with rejection and rage.

"Hey! What the hell are you doing? You killed Richard!"

Dark Jessie turned to him then, the glint of the red lights sharper on the teeth in his smile than on the steel of his blade. And it was a long blade, now covered in thick, runny blood.

"Come for the show, did you? Good. It always helps to know what you're capable of, don't you think? Now, how about we have a little talk about the way Jessie Roberts is going to live his life from here out? And when I say Jessie Roberts, you get that I'm talking about me, right?"

"You're insane! I'm Jessie Roberts. You're… you're just some nightmare version of me! You're everything I'm not!"

"Guess again, bud. I'm everything you're going to need to be if you plan on surviving what's coming. Now, how about you just come here and let me put things right, huh?"

"I'm gonna… I'll…"

"No you won't. I, however, *will.*"

The Double smiled and held Jessie's hateful gaze, his fingers dancing on the hilt of the blade. They measured one another by eye, and Jessie sensed that his nemesis knew he did not possess the fortitude for murder, even as an act of revenge. His smile widening, the Double broke into a full-out run at Jessie, who had to force himself back into the reality of the situation and react. Unarmed and unsure, he turned and ran.

Linda snapped back to the waking world with a start so strong she lashed out and accidentally smashed her head into the driver's side window. This hurt, but it also brought her around fast enough to assess the situation for the disaster it was:

The Vic was totaled.

She was most definitely concussed and probably injured besides.

The Vestusta Vitrium that should have been on the passenger side floor beside her was gone. The window above it, shattered.

The only good news about the situation was that she could see Bob Freighter laying dead or dying on the ground before her, surrounded by a half dozen running tributaries of watered down blood carried away by the driving rain. Emboldened by her victory over yet another of her foes,

Linda removed a crinkled plastic bag from the passenger seat and forced her driver's side door open. Standing was trouble, as she found out when she lost her balance and fell to the soft, wet Earth. Battered by rain, she raised her head and saw the small glass box that had contained her Doppelgänger. It lay broken, the orb housed inside empty on the ground only a few feet in front of her.

"Shit."

She had to get into Cuthbert's. Rain flooding her ears, nose, and soaking through the knees of her jeans, Linda searched the area for evidence of her Doppelgänger or her previously unconscious teenage cargo. Finding none, she pulled herself to her feet, snatched the empty orb from the mud and began to limp toward Cuthbert's, where she saw the gates finally stood open.

~

"You really are delusional, you know that?"

"Talia, you of all people should know that madness is simply that which does not fit into the rigidly defined parameters of our society's perceived 'facts.' In the tribal world, those who suffer madness - visions, access to other realms - they are revered."

"Of course they are. No wonder you killed Nico, you totally stole his routine. He used to talk like this back when we first met."

"Step past your anger for a moment and try to look at it from a scientific perspective."

"What's scientific? Every society has their version of heaven and hell. Eternity; what happens when we finally close our eyes for good."

"Stop thinking in Western terms. What I am talking about doesn't hinge upon death; it *circumvents* it."

"How? Exactly?"

"Widdershins."

Talia had just seen mention of this on that forum WJ found, something about Tenorio mirrors granting access to another world, a sort of parallel dimension where everyone had a Double. She'd been unable to stop thinking about it and now she realized why: taken by what she'd read, Widdershins appeared to be a natural cousin to tribal thought; a permanent shaping of what had been known to Talia in her studies of South American tribal cultures as The Nagual - a kind of conceptual cousin to Newton's Luminiferous Aether; a place made solely of potential. Despite her initial revulsion toward this man, she began to find it hard to fight the allure of his ideas and their implications. Was he claiming to have synthesized the elements of tribal thought within the modern world? If so, he was everything she'd looked for in her studies - a link to the past, a path to the future, a door to another world. Perhaps literally.

"What about it?"

"Ah, there she is. There is the renowned woman of science. Talia, Widdershins has always existed; it is a place of potential, waiting to be molded. That's the trick of creation; the fact that you can think of something, anything, means it *can* exist. Wants to even, but sometimes things just need a little push to free them from the formlessness of the void."

"Look Cruchetti, I don't-"

The man laughed so abruptly she stopped.

"I must apologize, but I believe you've mistaken me for someone else."

"You're not Paolo Cruchetti?"

The man extended his hand, "Arthur Tenorio. Pleased to meet you."

CHAPTER 38

Halfway through the second pillowcase it happened: Kim inserted a key that looked like every other key, except it turned and the locking mechanism inside the door clicked. A moment later the passage before her opened onto near infinite darkness.

She could tell the chamber was huge by the echo of her footsteps. This kind of space, massive and dark, freaked her out, but it also afforded her cover. The more time she spent with Jessie, the more human she became. Away from him, she became pliable again, another reason she'd wanted him out of the picture before approaching the door.

She felt herself pass through something unexpectedly, and in a flash the darkness was gone, replaced by a light so bright it was blinding. Shielding her eyes with her hand, Kim spotted a series of industrial-sized lamps, six on each side of the massive room. Beneath them, two seemingly endless, polished wooden shelves ran away toward a distant horizon. Lined up in perfect symmetry along each were dozens if not hundreds of glass orbs, sparkling beneath the lights. They looked like decorations: snow globes or complex dioramas.

Despite this, Kim recognized them immediately for what they were.

Vetusta Vitriums; pocket dimensions. To some, they were a method of escape, or a hiding place. Here, they were prison cells.

"Patty? Patty are you here?"

No answer. Were all of these full of people Cruchetti had abducted? If so, the captives inside could probably hear her. Kim balked at the thought of triggering false hope in others, but she only had time for Patty.

"We'll come back for the rest of you, I swear," she said aloud, as if questioned. Quickly, a touch of panic setting her off, Kim began to work her way down the line, picking up each orb to examine. Sure enough, most had people inside. Some were even people she recognized. But after two dozen or so tries, the futility of the task set in. It would take her forever to find her sister by this method.

On the verge of tears at having come so far only to be defeated in the end, Kim was about to give up when something occurred to her. It was small and distant at first, but steady, and as the loud, grainy sound grew, it gave Kim an idea. When they were little and shared a room, Patty had been afraid of the dark. To help her sister fall asleep some nights, Kim would sing. Her repertoire consisted of the theme songs from Patty's favorite cartoons, or the occasional nursery rhyme. Here and now, only one piece seemed appropriate:

> "As shadow to cast
> And mirror to light
> As right is to left
> And day is to night
> Fold a space
> And tuck some time

Lift your hands
Recite this rhyme
The door will show
The path within
Now through the glass
To Widdershins
By yourself but not alone
Inside the mirror your secret's grown
You've told me how, so it's my turn
To find you now and bring you home"

A sea of agonized voices responded to the words, but Kim filtered through them, until from nearby on her right came the response she'd been hoping for.

"Kim! Kim, over here!"

"Keep talking Patty!" Kim called as she moved to the side and zeroed in on her sister's voice.

"Over here! Here!"

As soon as she pinpointed Patty's cell, Kim picked up the orb and peered into its glass. Surprised and disturbed by what she saw, she couldn't help hesitating. Was that Patty?

"Hurry Kim, please! Let me out."

What if it was a trick? Or... could Freighter have done something to her? The thought of her little sister being used as fodder for Freighter's mad experiments was too much; Kim's fervor to make amends and reunite with the only family she had left trumped her caution. Besides, she wasn't exactly the Kim that Patty knew either, so they'd be equal.

Carrying the orb to the center of the dusty wooden floor, Kim knelt and set the trinket down, winding her wrist and setting the ball spinning like a top. The sound made the ever-present hum swell for a moment, and as the orb picked up speed, it began to increase in size, until what spun slowly to a stop before her was an orb big enough to hold a full grown adult, and then some.

"What now?" she called to Patty through the glass.

"Break it."

"Okay. Hold on."

Kim rooted back through the pillowcase before her and found the heaviest key she could.

"Stand back and cover your eyes!"

"Okay."

Rearing back, Kim struck the glass with the key and it shattered. When the dust cleared, Patty stood before her, free in all her reimagined glory. Her face was misshapen, as if the skin was pulled taut over the skull of an animal; her arms were set too far back on her shoulders, and jagged, horn-like appendages rose from her temples, giving her a somewhat demonic appearance. Finally free, the two girls stared at one another in astonishment for a moment before Patty uttered a simple 'Help' and collapsed into her sister's arms.

"You came!" she said weakly, "You found me!"

"Of course I did, silly."

"Of course you did," said a voice from the shadows. Kim turned, incapacitated by the weight of her sister - now much larger than the little girl that had been stolen five years before. The voice was familiar, but in the way a nightmare is familiar to a child that dreams it over and over, night after night.

"Congratu... congratulations Kim! I'm happy... happy that you've made it this far. Yes. After all, you... you swore you'd never come back, yes? And now, here you are! Mmm-hmm."

Of course! That's why the house was moving; it must be stuck in both worlds at the same time, phasing in and out of one after the other. Kim realized she'd been tricked: she was in Widdershins again, and that meant there was no way they would let her leave.

The sound of another glass orb thundered toward her, and Kim pushed Patty free just in time to avoid being snared by its magick. One moment she saw it approaching, growing in size as it neared, the next, Kim was inside the prison looking out.

"Run Patty! Find Jessie! Bring him back here!"

"Yes! Yes Patty! Bring Jessie... bring him back! Bring Jessie to save your sister. That's a good girl. Yes."

CHAPTER 39

It hurt Jessie to run, but he could not have stopped his feet if he tried. The combination of whatever head trauma he had suffered in the car, along with the horror of watching his Doppelgänger murder Richard, was proving to be too much. Physically and psychologically, he was in peril. As he ran, the cobblestones continued to flicker in and out of existence, making it increasingly difficult to judge where to put his feet. Jessie thought of that first time leaving Richard's house with Kim, the Mailman's admonishment to stay on the path, the image of the trees that might have been hands, reaching for them.

What was this between place and could he navigate it back to Deosil?

Distracted, Jessie missed it when the cobblestones disappeared once and for all, depositing him back into the rough forest floor. From there all it took was a fallen branch to snag the leg of his jeans and Jessie fell sprawling into the mud. He felt his hands sink into the soft, pliant goop, and it took him a moment to pull them free. He knew in that delay, his Double had gained on him.

"Damnit!" he screamed helplessly, pulling his hands free only to find they came away scraped, as if he'd landed on the stones. He looked behind him and the tree that had caught him opened and closed like a fist, then went back to being a configuration of finger-shaped branches.

"What the hell is happening?"

"Hey me! You're not going to get away from me, okay me? So why don't we just stop and join forces? It'll be great! You'll love what I do to Kim, trust me!"

The implications of the threat made Jessie feel sick. He climbed to his feet just in time to stay slightly ahead of his pursuer, but the Doppelgänger had altered his approach to an angle that made it impossible for Jessie to stay on the path. Luckily, his improvised route through the underbrush ended up being a short cut that put him back on Eeryx, only a short distance from where he'd left the woman in the car.

When he rounded the corner, Jessie saw the damaged wreck he had crawled from not fifteen minutes before. Beyond that, the gates of a massive mansion lay open, the woman he had left unconscious in the driver's seat limping toward the front steps. He saw Freighter's motionless form, too, which gave him pause. However, Jessie knew his best chance for survival lay behind those gates, so he made a final push past his injuries and horror, passing the wrecked Crown Vic and hitting his stride on the slick, asphalt driveway just in time to call out and get the woman's attention.

A moment later, they were both inside.

After the shock of her captor's identity wore off, Talia found herself unable to keep what he was telling her at bay any longer. The implications were too earth-shattering.

"This place of infinite potential, your tribal family would have called it the Nagual."

He nodded, "Yes, that was my grandmother's word for it. But that no longer fits. I've changed it; given it shape and form, just as the biblical Yahweh did when he created this world in the Christian mythos. What's more, by doing this I have changed our world as well. Every Double that separates from Its Cast is free to live forever, in either world. Death is a strange trick of our design, here on this side of the mirror."

"I don't follow."

"Let me explain. If a Double awakens and is able to kill its Cast, it becomes free of the circle of time. I've never been able to figure out why, something about the fact that on this side of the glass, everything naturally decays because we operate on kinetic energy. Being comprised mainly of potential energy, our Doubles do not decay at the same rate. In fact, they only die because we do. Unless that is, they can kill us themselves. This act sets them free from the constraints of time."

"You've seen this happen?"

"Yes. Numerous times. It has caused an imbalance. An problem I have been unable to prevent."

"What kind of imbalance are we talking here?" Talia's tone suggested they had discussed this type of thing before, two old acquaintances putting their heads together over a recurring problem.

"Consciousness, as I am sure you are aware from your own studies, is infectious. The population of Widdershins is growing exponentially because those already enlightened wish to propagate. If it had been up to me, they never would have learned of this loophole for eternal life. However, my employer has levied his bets on the other team, so to speak."

"Cruchetti?"

"Yes."

"But the loophole can work both ways; I can put you in a position to kill your Doppelgänger and live forever. The same with Jessie."

"If it's that easy, and there's an entire start-up dimension of Doppelgängers who know that if they kill their Casts they can live forever, how has history not been one long episode of Reflections popping out of mirrors and strangling their Casts?"

"Good question. The answers, however, are complicated. And to understand them you must understand that there are political affiliations among the inhabitants of Widdershins. Different agendas; different ideas as to what kind of balance should be re-installed into reality. Some Doubles want us dead, some merely want to take our place, and some want a kind of union of both worlds. Further preventing a revolution such as the one you posit is - or rather was - the fact that, until recently, our one saving grace on this side was that a Shadow and Cast could not exist on the same plane at the same time."

"And what happened 'recently'?"

"Something changed. Remember when I said that I had inadvertently altered our world by altering theirs? Well, the effect of both planes undergoing mutations has made it so the old laws of reality do not entirely apply anymore. There are thin spots and thin people. Your son is a thin person. He is very special."

Mention of Jessie derailed Talia's curiosity. She'd slipped into this psycho's spell and forgotten her own son, her husband dying at this maniac's hands. She always acted like this when it came to the pursuit of knowledge. But thinking of Jessie, hearing the man who killed his father speak her son's name aloud, Talia's disgust returned. And something else returned as well - a memory of slipping the nail file into her back pocket, now a lifetime ago. Very nonchalantly she began to work her hand toward her backside.

"Special huh? You sound like a nut job. Stay away from my son."

Arthur returned to the table and took the seat opposite her. He trained his gaze upon her, a gaze that only intensified as he spoke. Talia brought her hand back around to rest on her lap.

"I'm afraid I cannot. There are others who are also interested in, I guess you'd say 'recruiting' him. We need him, or all our hard work will have been for naught. You see, many years ago those former partners and I spent a great deal of time proliferating my mirrors throughout the world. Likewise a particular approach to architecture. But love and ambition never make for proper bedfellows, and our little cabal fell apart. Everything we had worked for, everything we had accomplished, has been in jeopardy ever since."

Seeing how distracted Arthur was while discussing his passion for the subject, Talia's hand began to creep toward her back pocket again.

"And just what had you accomplished?" The fingertips of her index and middle finger brushed the tip of the file; not enough was exposed for her to pull it free without shifting her weight, something that would no doubt catch her captor's attention.

"We planned to create an instantaneous transportation network, a sort of worldwide system of doors that, once activated, would allow one to use Widdershins as a shortcut to reach specific locations in this world at an almost immediate speed."

"Teleportation?"

"That's what people always say," Arthur turned his back to her and took several steps away. When he did, Talia sat forward quickly and clutched the file with her fingers. Before she could pull it free he turned back around; she manufactured a sneeze and bent forward violently to accentuate it. The nail file remained in her back pocket, albeit slightly more exposed than before.

"No, not teleportation, but in effect, the same idea," he looked at her queerly while she pretended to need a tissue. After a moment Arthur produced a handkerchief from the breast pocket of his shirt and handed it to her, "Keep it, please."

"Thank you," she said and pretended to blow her nose.

"Immediate access to locations all across the globe."

"That's what this is all about? Transportation?"

"Not just transportation! We can use this technology to build a power base. Don't you see? The benefits from this - politically, economically, socially - will be absolute."

"But everyone wants it for themselves."

"A shame. There should have been a way to work this out so everyone could win. Instead, we have a war, complete with casualties. Your husband was, regrettably, one of them. You will be the next if you don't stop reaching for whatever it is you have in your back pocket."

Talia slouched in shock and dismay, dropping her eyes like a little kid caught with her hand in the cookie jar. How did he know? She received her answer when, head still down, she opened her eyes and saw her reflection staring back at her in the glass of the table top. It was her, but it wasn't. And it was laughing at her.

CHAPTER 40

Terry sat quietly between Chase and Dubois for the better part of thirty minutes before anyone spoke to them officially about the Sheriff. Finally, one of the doctors, a tall, attractive woman all three men knew as Doctor Loraina Gershaw, exited the ER.

"Well gentlemen, the Sheriff will be just fine."

"What happened?" Chase asked.

"It appears to have been an accident. I believe you'd call it friendly fire."

"What? Who?"

"I'll leave that to him. In the meantime, since talking to the Sheriff directly does no good, I'll stress to you that he needs to keep pressure off his leg. Absolutely no walking or driving."

"How long you keepin' him?" Chase asked, impatient now that they knew the Sheriff was okay.

"I'm ready to leave right now," Sheriff Rash said as he emerged from the operating room in his open-backed gown, using a tray table as a crutch, "But I'm going to need someone to get me some new pants - Doctor Gershaw here couldn't contain herself, literally ripped mine off."

All three men burst into laughter at this; however, it was more than clear that Doctor Gershaw had had quite enough of the Sheriff.

"I don't think-"

"Don't care what you think right now, Quinn. We got us a whole lotta funny business, and I need some damn answers. Cuthbert; wasn't expecting to see you here. What brings you out this evening? Antiques are best left for the afternoon, wouldn't you agree?"

"Even in times of pure physical duress your sense of humor never ceases to bring a smile to my face, Sheriff. You know as well as I do why I am here. We can forego the charade."

"Ain't pretending, just looking to get to the bottom of this and I don't know that it pertains to your area of expertise. That's more Gallows Hill territory an' frankly, you can keep it."

"Yes, well clearly we have been a bad influence on your community Sheriff, if this evening's events are any indication."

Sheriff Rash looked sternly at Terry and Chase, "What'd you tell him?"

"Nothing," Terry looked hurt by the accusation. Chase just smiled and hung his head, "We didn't need to tell him anything, Jim."

"Yes Sheriff, as Officer Montgomery says, I have my own sources."

"That right? What'd your sources tell you about my town?"

"That someone -" cut off by the sound of shattering glass, everyone turned just in time to see two paramedics come crashing through the double doors of the emergency entrance. They pushed a gurney, atop which a man thrashed and screamed like an animal.

"Security!" Dr. Gershaw yelled and took off at a run, Chase and Dubois barely two steps behind, roused by her panic.

"What the hell's going on?" Chase asked, recognizing Bob Freighter once he was close enough. Freighter's right leg was broken in several places, so that it hung at contradictory angles, and blood ran down his face, pooled in his hair, which looked longer than Chase had ever seen it. That was when the deputy realized what he was looking at wasn't hair. Instead, some kind of long, tendril-like appendages sprouted from Freighter's head, flopping from side to side behind him like dead limbs.

"Hit and run. Found him on the side of the road near Mr. Dubois' house."

Chase shot a glance at Cuthbert. Linda; they'd forgotten all about her in the havoc of the night.

Freighter reared up off the stretcher and caught the closest paramedic by the face, threw him through the air like a rag doll. Witnessing this, Chase had his gun drawn and centered on Freighter so fast Terry didn't even see it happen. But Bob was faster; he slipped onto the floor in a profoundly unnatural maneuver and was off down the hall quicker than Chase would have thought possible. Chase's finger rested on the trigger as he tried to draw a bead, tracking Freighter as he ricocheted like a tennis ball from one side of the corridor to the other.

"C'mon!" he called, and Terry was fast enough to already be ten or so steps ahead of him.

Terry rounded the turn through the doorway into the room first, Chase right behind him. There was no sign of Bob Freighter anywhere.

"The closet," Dubois whispered coming up on their left. Terry tried to focus, both did and did not want to see what Dubois's whisper suggested. When his eyes settled on the spot that held the older man's attention he cried out. It was the closet, but it was empty, only an open door and darkness. Pitch, dramatic darkness. And then it occurred to Terry, that darkness was, in fact, the first clue; nothing was that dark, no lightless room at midnight, no corridor in an abandoned building, no space beneath the bed. This was a darkness so complete that it wavered like heat on a desert road. Then, amid the black, Terry saw something move.

"What… is… that…?" Terry's voice squeaked. There was something inside the closet; it shimmered, an optical illusion that defied easy interpretation but revealed more of itself with every moment locked in Terry's stare. He wasn't sure, but then, yes, something inside that tiny space drew tighter, more concise. The very air inside the closet congealed into the shape of a man for an instant and then, just as quickly, dispersed again to an almost gaseous state. A cloud, a dream, a delusion. A vision.

The vision recurred, and this iteration sustained for a moment longer, allowing Terry to eke out a small parcel of comprehension. A man hunched over with his back to the room, something in his hands. The vision appeared and disappeared. There was a terrible sound, followed by the rustling of indistinct movement from the small, darkened space. The specifics eluded his conscious mind, but inside, Terry grappled with some manner of recognition.

Dubois moved unexpectedly and shattered the near-epiphany. The older man stalked from the doorway into the hospital room like an animal on its hind legs. Unconsciously, Terry took a step forward to stand beside Chase, his eyes still glued to the unfolding nightmare before him as Dubois approached the closet. A marked difference in temperature reinforced the threshold between what was outside the room and what was trapped, smoldering within. The back of Terry Quinn's neck felt considerably cooler than his face as invisible flames of unease licked at his chin. It reminded him of winters in front of the fireplace at his childhood home.

And it wasn't just the temperature that created a sharp delineation between the corridor and the room. As he followed Chase in, Terry thought he could discern a slipperiness, a certain intangibility that, once inside made the air of the room feel sick and gelatinous, as though he were moving through invisible mucus.

'Is this how a fish feels in water?' Terry thought before Dubois caught his attention. The eccentric Gallowsian produced something from his coat pocket and made a small, strobing circumference of light appear on the wall around the shape. It was a flashlight, one that had been modified to perform strange, strobe-like applications. As it oscillated, the light made the mysterious figure in the closet more substantial, and for the first time, Terry thought he could make out the shape of a head. Then it was just the shape again, midnight black and malevolent in its indistinctness.

Terry and Chase closed the gap to join Dubois. They stopped only a few steps behind him, conscious to not interfere.

"Cuthbert, what the hell is going on?" Chase whispered.

"Freighter was one of the first. We're looking at the infection on a long-scale timeline."

Dubois's voice was labored, as though he was straining to keep the light on the creature, a fisherman fighting for a massive catch. Unsure what was required of them, Terry had to squint to make sense of what he was seeing; a flickering, merry-go-round of reality that moved the figure in and out of the here and now.

"When I move the light, he will move with it. I need you, gentlemen, to swoop in and restrain him."

Terry saw Chase nod confidently and quickly followed suit, still uncertain of the stakes they grappled with but convinced that he would do whatever it took to rise to the occasion. Meanwhile, the cognitive dissonance of the survival gene shouted for him to get the hell out of that room as fast as he could.

Terry ignored it.

And then everything exploded in a series of actions that bypassed cognition - dissonant or not - altogether.

"Now!" Cuthbert yelled as he whipped to the left forty-five degrees, moving the light and the thing trapped inside it clear out of the closet and against the wall adjacent to where they had come in. Chase jumped in and laid hands on the figure, but Terry remained still, his realization stunning him into inaction.

That shape was Bob Freighter.

"Terry! Wake up kid, we need your help!"

Terry snapped back to lucidity in time to see Freighter pitch Chase across the room. Horrified, Terry's feet sprung into action before his brain could catch up. He dove forward and caught hold of the shape, but as he did, his opponent's arm elongated in a way Terry knew no human arm should. It caught him by the neck, began to choke the life from him. An instant later the light came on, and both Terry and Freighter had vanished.

CHAPTER 41

"Please. For the final time, I do not know what you are talking about!"

Dean Stanisberg's words were interrupted by a hard, bone-crunching collision. He blacked out for a moment, head lolling across his shoulders, a broken children's game.

Although the figure before him looked like WJ Brigging-ton, when the Dean opened his eyes again, he understood without a doubt this was not the man he had met with earlier in the day.

"You must forgive me," the imposter made a sweep of his form from head to toe with his left arm, "but this… this is taking a little bit to get used to. I'm having trouble controlling myself, so watch out."

The imposter smiled and swept his arm out wide, the limb refusing to stop where it should, instead continuing to unravel in a long, dark extension. Seeing this reminded the Dean of the paramedic hauled out in Paul Barker's wake, that day five years before. The imposter's shadow-limb shot past him, collided with the impromptu wet bar in the corner and sent the decanter and crystal tumblers to their deaths against the opposite wall, a momentary shower of glass catching the light as the pieces arced across the room.

Outburst complete, the imposter ran a hand through his hair and rolled his shoulders in an unnatural way, like a shirt clinging to a clothesline in the wind. He straightened his mangled tie and a ripple passed through him from head to toe, then back again.

The Dean understood then that not only was his tormentor not WJ, It was not even human.

Forty-five minutes ago when he answered a knock at his office door, what the Dean had greeted looked and spoke exactly like WJ. Now, Stanisberg saw that any resemblance to a human being had all but worn off. A certain hazy, cross-hatched texture obscured the imposter's shape, a vagueness that undermined a painfully generic attempt at humanity. The effect was that of a costume, a demon's mocking effort to portray a man for a Halloween party in hell: a strange juxtaposition of sweat pants and t-shirt beneath a suit coat at least two sizes too small obscured Its misshapen form, and a garish fuchsia necktie and matching slippers completed the ensemble, so that the finished product seemed like a madman's vision of business casual; the rotten cherry on a maniac's sundae.

"I confess, at the moment I find it challenging to understand anything about this... abbreviated form I've taken on to perform the tasks assigned to me."

"You're not a man. What are you?"

The WJ-Thing moved close enough to touch foreheads with the Dean. It stared straight into his eyes, tiny ganglia crawling out of solid black irises, teasing the skin around the old man's eyes.

"Do you know what the word 'body' means where I come from? It is a slang, and a repugnant one at that," the WJ-Thing took a moment to stare at Its captive, helpless, bound to a black leather-upholstered chair. It smiled before continuing, "Body means prison. Prison, because that is what your bodies are to us. Imagine chained obeisance to an inferior form. Awful. Truly awful..."

The monster began to pace as It spoke.

"But then came the man with his mirrors. He understood. He wanted to help us. He understood the absolute INSANITY of shackling something of unlimited potential," the WJ-Thing motioned to indicate Itself, "to something so small and limited. Something so disgusting."

At eighteen, Augustus Stanisberg had killed fifteen men his own age in the war. Fifteen men whose deaths he had received honors for. Fifteen men whose faces he saw right alongside Paul Barker's, every night when he laid down to sleep.

"None of us are ever happy... with what we see in the mirror..." the words tumbled from the Dean's lips, and the WJ-Thing stopped Its dissertation and eyed him with unimpeded malevolence.

The WJ-Thing considered the Dean's words with a smile. A grin so wide and psychotic that the corners of Its mouth stretched unnaturally, the excess flesh collecting in drooping puddles off to either side of Its head, like a vaudevillian rubber mouth performer. It raised an arm, the limb once again unraveling at the elbow. Twisted black ribbons emerged, spiraled across the distance between them, infiltrating the Dean's face, burrowing into every orifice that made the man recognizable. Stanisberg kicked at the intrusion; his chair rocked back so violently that it would have fallen over backward had the mask not pulled taut and held him upright. Fat, lumpy masses began to pump through the tendrils, faster and faster, the Dean's strangled gurgles crescendoing into a teapot-like whine as his entire form gushed with hellish, black overflow. The noxious spew seeped from his mouth, his nose, his eyes, cascading down his face and chest, erasing his features as it went. And as the textureless substance reached the floor, Dean Stanisberg became nothing more than a crumbling pile of sludge.

The WJ-thing smiled and straightened Its tie. "Nice."

CHAPTER 42

In high school, when Terry Quinn encountered trouble with Geometry, his mother found him a tutor. That tutor was Helen Freighter.

The two women knew one another via their crochet club. Along with her award-winning work with needle and yarn, Mrs. Freighter also happened to be an uncanny mathematician. The one eccentricity to this otherwise polite, intelligent and - or so young Terry's teenage heart thought - beautiful woman, was the constant presence of her husband.

Protective was not the word. Helen didn't drive, so Terry's mother used to bring him to the Freighters' home twice a week for lessons. Every Monday and Thursday. While he was there, he was often uncomfortable at the fact that Bob - a tall, curmudgeon of a man who ran a construction empire - would stand nearby and watch their sessions, as though Terry might steal something. Later, after he related the uncomfortable quality of the experience to his mother, Mary Quinn developed her theory that Helen Freighter wasn't physically unable to drive herself to their sessions, she was just not allowed to.

∾

Terry opened his eyes and a wave of panic hit him. He was no longer in the hospital.

He was in a small room, the walls dark and plain, save for a series of intricately crocheted pictures, dusty and faded by time. He recognized them immediately, understood exactly where he was. And with the revelation, Terry's memories returned to him in full. So did his terror.

"How did I get here?"

"Quiet. I'm tryin' ta think," the grizzled voice came from the shadows gathered in the farthest corner. Terry froze, slowly scanning the room until… there they were: two dim eyes. Freighter spoke again but did not move, "I didn't mean for you to get dragged inta this. Didn't mean to hurt any of the Doc's people, either. I get… confused. Don't always know which side I'm on."

Freighter stepped into the light, and Terry choked with shock. The man he remembered was gone, the one before him a tall black figure whose face remained obscured in darkness.

"How you got here don't matter no more. It's where you're going."

Freighter moved closer; Terry interpreted this as a threat and raised his hands to ward the man off. That's when his reality crashed.

Terry's hand was black as night.

The struggle at the hospital felt like a bad dream, but it fell short of this horror he had woken to. He opened his mouth to scream, but the sharp CRACK of an open-hand across his left cheek killed the impulse before he could manage. Stunned, Terry inherently understood the blow was not an assault but a much-needed reset. Because of it, the icy terror of his blackened arm dissipated, and he realized that, no matter how his body might look at the moment, fundamentally he felt the same as he always had.

No pain. No discomfort.

In fact, the more mindful he became, the more Terry Quinn realized he felt better than he had in a long time. And as this realization settled over him, he watched the thick, black shadow suit climb up past his elbow, down from his shoulder and across his chest, up his neck, until he was sure his entire physical form had undergone the transformation into... what? A living shadow?

"Mr. Freighter, I-"

"Shut yur mouth and listen!"

The two black shapes contemplated the moment together, featureless ghouls on the road to understanding.

"If you try, you'll feel it."

Freighter's words ignited a process inside him, as though it was only Terry's mind that didn't understand what was happening to him; his body understood just fine. Something changed, but he couldn't tell what.

"Help me... understand. Please."

"That feeling? That's something you're unaccustomed to. We're all unaccustomed to it. That feeling is power. The power that comes once a body's merged with what birth takes from ya. You've swallowed your shadow. Once you do that, you're the best you've ever been in yur life, 'cept maybe when yur dreamin'.'"

Terry heard Freighter's words, but they were unimportant in the face of what his body was now communicating to him. It was literally humming with power, charged in a way that made him feel as though he could do anything he wanted to.

"I... it's like I see can all of this stuff that's been right in front of me the whole time. Things that are in front of all of us but..."

"But most folks are too stupid to see it. Yeah. I ain't gonna lie kid - this is gonna ruin the life you had. But if you ain't like me - and I know you ain't - it's gonna make you strong enough to do what has to be done."

"What has to be done?"

"I been alive too long. What's more, I let people do things they shouldn'a done to me and mine," Freighter hung his head at this, braced his forearm against the wall as if his words were too heavy for him to stand against. In his current form as a living shadow, the black mucilagina that made up his physical form began to drip down the wall like heavy industrial oil, "I remember you, ya know. From the instructions. You'd come over, and Helen would fix lemonade and help you with your mathematics. It always bothered me when she'd show anyone but me 'ttention. Insecure I guess. That and my drinkin' used ta make me crazy. Ever since Helen…"

"But that wasn't your fault."

"It was!" Freighter's words erupted from him in a violent explosion that caused pieces of him to disperse in all directions. It was monstrous, and Terry recoiled before he realized he was witnessing an example of the kind of power he now possessed.

"It *was* my fault! Falling in with those bastards, even just for a little while. Making their work part of my own," the anger washed off in a wave of self-loathing that crushed Freighter's posture and moved him toward the wall furthest from Terry where a small, lime green bureau stood alone beneath one of the Crochet pieces. Freighter opened the top drawer, rooted around inside for a moment before continuing. When he did resume speaking, he did not turn back around.

"I couldn't save her, but I let him talk me into thinking he could. Lies… all lies. What happened. So I did something terrible. I trapped that woman, stole a piece of her, just to have something; someone," Freighter forced these last words out through clenched teeth.

Terry stared at the confession as though it was a monster, a tangible, malevolent presence in the room.

"I don't understand. Who did this to you? To Mrs. Freighter?"

"Me! Ain't you listening? That's why I'm asking you to take over and make amends. There's a man named Grimes. You find him, he'll listen to you. Bring him here to help stop this once and for all, before everyone suffers like I have. Like she did."

"But Mr. Freighter-"

"I've lived too long; can't be trusted anymore."

Without turning around, Bob Freighter raised a handgun to his mouth and pulled the trigger.

CHAPTER 43

Eleven minutes after Terry disappeared from the closet in Bob Freighter's hospital room, Chase gave up trying to understand what the hell was happening and set his sights on what was important to him. Terry would have to wait; in all the madness, they'd forgotten Linda, and now Chase feared he might be too late to save her. Foot to the floor, he raced the Cruiser through the storm toward Dubois', praying he wasn't already too late.

Beside him, Chase could hear Cuthbert's voice over the sound of the rain that battered the windshield, but he didn't understand the words. It was all so far away, so far beyond the immediate urgency in his head.

"... But our organization has nothing to do with any of this. Linda should know better! She-"

"She better be okay, that's all I can say, Cuthbert."

"What? How is this my fault?"

"Pocket your bullshit."

"It is as I have said all along. You would love to pretend what you have seen is nonsense."

"It's not?"

"Was what happened in Arthur's house five years ago nonsense?"

"Mass hysteria's more like it."

"Liar! You do not believe that Chase! You have regressed. You're so damned afraid of becoming your father!"

"Cuthbert, you leave my dad outta this-"

"Look out!"

Ahead of them, a procession of people crossed from the trees to the left of the road into the forest on the right. Chase saw them too late, swerved and pumped the break. The Cruiser skidded on the wet pavement, and the side of the road came up fast. An instant later, they went nose-first into the drainage ditch. Black water ran up, over the windshield and buried the engine in runoff, leaving it choking for life. Chase's head slammed against the steering wheel and rocked back, finishing limp on his neck. Dubois cracked his head hard against the window to his right and darkness swallowed him. There was an indeterminable lull, and then ever so slowly the picture crept back in around the edges. Dubois' eyes flickered open, the world before him a crackly, hazy surrealist painting of blood and rain.

The WJ-Thing drove the Mercedes slowly, Its counterpart's muscle memory of how to handle the great motorized beast hazy at best, made all the more difficult by the ceaseless cacophony of rain that hammered the car. Having only recently awakened to a state of consciousness distinct from Its former host, the WJ-Thing still retained pockets of confusion at the sheer complexity of this world. Primarily driven by instinct, the steady succession of information It culled from Deosil's WJ could not come fast enough to smooth out the awkward learning curve inherent in forcibly switching places with him. None of this stopped It though; Widdershins' WJ piloted the automobile through the shattering storm, hellbent on Its mission.

A violent jolt of lightning shrieked through the sky, and It flinched. In that moment the WJ-Thing saw the tail lights up ahead, jutting from the ditch on the side of the road at a peculiar angle.

"Well, what do we have here?"

CHAPTER 44

FIVE YEARS AGO

They were losing Arthur. Cuthbert was sure of it.

"So what? Free country. You can't expect that just because you and Paolo fall out of love, everyone is going to come down on your side of things."

They were standing on Cuthbert's front steps, a search party formation only moments away while the town pooled its resources to search for the missing Barker girls.

"It goes much deeper than that, Chase. We are not talking about a high school break-up. Paolo and I were business partners first and foremost."

"Right. And you what, suddenly grew a conscience?"

"You can joke at my expense, but you are closer to the truth than you realize. The entire reason I split from Paolo was my certainty that this is something no one today should possess. This type of Magick is not meant for the modern world!"

Linda often felt that Cuthbert's superiority complex - bought and paid for by money he had inherited - was the point of disconnect that made people feel uneasy around him. At the moment though, she felt his insistence on inclusivity was an uptick for Cuthbert's humanity. He was an elderly misogynist with a heart of gold and a mixed bag for intentions. But she was working on him. Chase on the other hand... Linda wished he would get over the maddening state of denial he applied to everything they did in the GHAS.

"How can you even doubt what you've seen?" she asked, unable to hide her exasperation.

"Not you too, Linda!"

"You've seen the same things I have; it didn't take me half as long to accept the truth."

"You of all people, accusing me of not admitting what's right in front of my face? Hypocrite."

"This isn't about-"

"If it's about the lengths we go to lie to ourselves, then yes, it is."

Chase's walkie buzzed from his cruiser parked further down the drive, and he ran down the stone steps to respond.

"This is Chase. Any news? Over."

"We just had a... well, I don't really know what we had. Those missing girls' father showed up at the University. Over."

"You got him? Over."

"He took off. One'a the Deans called 911, but when the medics arrived he, well, Barker took a bite out of one of their arms. Or something. Jeez. Not even sure it was a bite, but I don't know what else-"

"Bite? Gil, what the hell're you telling me?"

"Sound normal to you, Deputy?" Cuthbert called from the doorway.

"Shut it, Cuthbert! Gil, any mention from Barker about his girls?"

"Said something about Tenorio."

"Speaking of Arthur, huh? On it," Chase said. He climbed

into the cruiser and balked when Cuthbert appeared at the passenger side door.

"What are you doing?"

"You are going to need me, Chase."

"No, I ain't."

"Yes, you are." Linda said, joining them, "You two go, I'll stay here in case-"

"In case what?"

"Just in case."

Chase drove all the way up and parked on the lawn outside Arthur Tenorio's front door. It was a gloomy evening, the moon and stars replaced by the same charcoal clouds that had choked the sky since morning.

"Alright Cuthbert, you stay here and-"

Screams.

"Wait for me," Cuthbert shouted, hardly out of the cruiser while Chase was already up the steps and at the front door, his weapon drawn. This was the first time he'd un-holstered his gun in the line of duty, and even though he didn't show it, Chase was terrified. The screams sounded like a child, like a child dying. A million wretched images echoed through his mind, proved the fuel for the anger he conjured to kick in the heavy front door and sweep into the glassmaker's home.

"What the?"

The world spun; Chase couldn't tell where he was in relation to anything else. Just inside the door, the house seemed to dead end.

"I told you that you would need me," Cuthbert moved past him, leading Chase through a doorway he had somehow looked directly at but missed. Inside, a long corridor stretched into darkness, doors barely visible on either side and those that were all closed. Near the ceiling, sconces cast small, yellow pools of light that evaporated before reaching the floor. Their feet were left obscured in darkness, giving Chase the disoriented feeling of floating instead of running. He paused, looked up and was surprised to see Cuthbert already far ahead of him.

Another scream ripped through the house. Chase broke into a run. He caught and passed Cuthbert, the corridor swallowing him completely in just five steps, as though he'd stepped through the jaws of some giant beast and disappeared down its gullet.

Now Cuthbert ran; the hall snaked left and then right, then left once more. Sweat stung his eyes, and he found it impossible to discern time, distance or speed. It may have taken him thirty seconds or thirty minutes before he reached the foyer, he wasn't sure.

When Cuthbert finally reached the kitchen, he saw Chase hunkered down before a teenage girl he recognized as Arthur's daughter Cassie.

"Is she alright?" he called, but Chase didn't hear him. Cassie's hands were by her side, the stance of an automaton. Her hair stood straight up at regular intervals, her mouth open wide but no sound escaped it save a sharp rasp, as if she had screamed her throat raw. Cuthbert watched as Chase grabbed Cassie by the shoulders, tried to take her into what was meant as a comforting embrace. She shook him off, pushed him so hard he almost fell to the floor.

"Cassandra, where is your father? What happened here?"

"I told her not to go down there. I told her."

"Who?"

"Kim. I told her, and now the mirror people have her, and she can't come home, and I'm going to get in trouble."

Chase stood up and walked to the threshold of the basement door.

"Stay with her, Cuthbert," he said, and began to descend.

"Chase, you are not ready for this!"

"If her friend is down there, hurt or -"

"Not hurt," Cassie interrupted, "Taken."

Chase descended the first step into the basement. Then two. On the third, Cuthbert saw him draw his revolver again.

"Chase, if they speak to you, do not listen. And do not approach the mirrors."

Dubois' voice warped as he spoke, damaged notes that dissolved in the shock of the moment. What the hell was going on here? Chase wondered. He reached the basement, turned back toward the stairs but couldn't find them. The house felt like it was miles away. His Maglight scoured the room, revealed dozens of dirty white sheets draped over what he knew would be Tenorio glass, the fabled standing mirrors everyone was so fond of. The one closest to him was uncovered, its blanket swaddled around the wooden base. Chase approached it, unnerved that, in the glass face he saw no reflection. Instead, the glass revealed another room, like a window into another world.

Exactly what Cuthbert and Linda insisted Arthur's mirrors were, and what Chase refused to believe.

The room was similar to the one he was in now: a dark, dingy basement. But something was off. The darkness on that side roiled, gathered into shapes at various points throughout the alien vista. He stepped closer, raised his hand to feel the surface of the mirror, and at that exact moment another girl appeared before him, slammed into the glass from the other side. Startled, Chase jerked backward, raised his weapon without even thinking about it, then misstepped and landed on his ass.

Dazed, he watched the girl open and close her mouth. Wide. She was screaming. Help me, her lips said, both small fists pounding against her side of the glass. He shook off the shock, made to stand, but while his eyes sought something to aid his balance she disappeared. By the time he was standing before the mirror again, Chase's reflection had emerged and without realizing, he shot it, once, right through the heart, the bullet passing through the glass like water. His reflection opened its mouth, fell to its knees…

At this moment Jim Rash descended the stairs, gun drawn. Chase could tell by the look on his face he was furious; could tell he was scared, too.

Chase had never been so glad to see another human being in all his life.

"What the hell's going on here?"

When Rash spoke the room reacted with another sound. Chase held up his hand for quiet and moved the flashlight around the mirrors, over the walls and corners. In the furthest one, he found the source of the sound, which he had recognized as crying.

"Holy hell! We got another one," Rash yelled as both men ran to where Kim Barker lay curled in a fetal position on the floor.

"She's in shock. Help me get her out of here."

"Fine. But soon as we get this girl help, you're going to tell me just what the hell is going on here, Montgomery!"

Chase spotted Dubois coming down the stairs, Cassie in the doorway behind him.

"'Fraid I ain't gonna be much help. That's your man right there though, if you want answers."

The look on Cuthbert's face told Chase the last thing he wanted to do was explain any of this to Jim Rash.

CHAPTER 45

The sound of a never-ending barrage of rain dragged Dubois back to consciousness. It took him a moment, but as the world reassembled to his eyes, he saw Chase beside him, still lying limp in his seat, one eye open and trained in his direction. The Deputy's expression told Dubois something was wrong. Then he heard it.

"Hello, Mr. Cuthbert."

The voice was that of a little girl, but when Dubois turned his head enough to catch a glimpse of their visitor, he saw something else entirely. Whatever was in the backseat was enormous, its size engulfing the entire area behind them. Dubois could feel its bulk pressed against the back of his chair, heard the small tearing noises it made, straining against the upholstery. Cuthbert wanted to speak, but horror kept his jaw clenched tight.

"I have a message for you from Kim."

Cuthbert opened his mouth to respond, saw Chase's head shaking almost imperceptibly back and forth as he mouthed, no. No. No.

"P…Patagonia?"

"Yes, Mr. Cuthbert?"

Her voice sounded just like both men remembered it. Small. Sweet.

"How?" Chase mouthed, but Cuthbert didn't have an answer. Where had Patagonia Barker been for the past five years, and what had been done to her?

The sound of the rain stopped. Dubois felt a cold prickle on the back of his neck. He shuddered and stared straight ahead out the windshield, tiny beads of sweat riding the curve of flesh beneath his chin. On his left, something vaguely appendage-like came into his peripheral vision, and he turned the other way, eyes beaming through the window to his right. Dubois found he could no longer identify the area around the car. The tall, wind-whipped bodies of the trees were gone, and the sky above had gone from black to red. Through the illusory lens of the water-scoured windows, the landscape became a vague, threatening crucible. He couldn't take it anymore. He had to speak.

"You… you say you have a message for me? From your sister? And where is she?"

"They have her. The bad men. She saved me, but they took her. She told me to find Jessie."

"Listen to me carefully Patagonia. Go to my house. Find the boy, Jessie Roberts."

"Kim told me about him!"

"He should be there, with Linda. Take him to the center of my house, the room that has a thirteen on the door. From there he will be able to go to the place where the bad men are keeping your sister."

There was a burst of heat and a quiet popping sound. Dubois felt the massive presence pass directly through him, like an invisible hand took hold of the heart in his chest and squeezed; through the windshield, lightning flashed, and he saw the trees had returned, along with the rain. Headlights approached on the road. Dubois turned to Chase but found his head hung limp against the safety belt, unconscious. Had any of it really happened or had he hit his head? The quandary became an eternity that ate his consciousness in a wide, shambling drone.

A sharp sound against the window at his left shattered the moment. Cuthbert's attention snapped, and he turned so hard he smashed his face into the window, recoiled and tried to focus but could barely make out what looked like the beam of a flashlight just beyond the rain-streaked partition. Dazed, for a single instant, he thought it an angel, sent to welcome him to a tiny copse of heaven wherein he would finally find peace. This nirvana was just as quickly denied him as the ghost visage melted. Cuthbert ignored the subsequent knock on the outside of the window, reached instead for Chase's unconscious form. The Deputy's head hanged limply against the cross-angle of the safety belt, his arms loosely compelled into the hollow leg-space below the steering wheel. Time died, re-started, became an amorphous shape without meaning. Until the sound of the glass next to Dubois's face shattered, the wind and rain whipping in just before he lost consciousness.

CHAPTER 46

Jessie wanted to close his eyes, pretend all of the insanity around him could be wished away and his life returned to normal. The stuff with Kim was one thing: adventure, danger, spooky supernatural girlfriends and teleportation conspiracies. But murder was something else entirely. The night no longer felt dangerous in that 80s movie way, everyone riding around with flashlights taped to the handlebars of their bikes, discovering amazing things and then returning home to their parents at the end of it. No, he'd just seen someone he knew murdered. And worse, he'd seen himself do the killing.

"He's dead."

"What?" Linda asked, suddenly anxious, "Who's dead?"

"I killed him. I saw myself kill him. Right there on the cobblestone path."

"Cobblestones? Kid, what are you talking about?"

Jessie didn't respond; he was zoned hard, staring at his hands as if they were soaked in blood.

"Kid!"

He looked up and broke into a sob. Never one for

dramatics, Linda's frustration came to a head and she snapped, wound back and smacked Jessie across the face hard enough to break his bottom lip.

"Ow! What the hell?" he cried, the taste of iron in his mouth somehow settling him inside.

"Hysterical is for old women and little dogs. You're neither, so buck up. Now, who the hell did you kill?"

"The mailman. Richard!"

"You killed Richard?" The anger drained from her, replaced by something Jessie recognized from his mother's occasional lapses into the tragedies of their own past: vulnerability. That this woman who had looked so tough a moment ago could now look so weak made Jessie irrationally afraid. Afraid for Kim. Afraid for his mom. Afraid for himself.

From the other side of the door, he thought he heard something.

"Kid, if you killed Richard Fattingback, I'm going to be really sorry I saved your ass."

"It wasn't me. It was my…" the sound recurred and Jessie flinched. When he spoke again, his voice cracked, "I can't remember the word Richard used for it."

"Your Doppelgänger," Linda said. She turned her own eyes toward the door, "Is someone out there?"

"I think… I think *he's* out there."

"Your Double? Okay, calm down. Tell me what happened."

"I woke up and saw where I was, saw you. I left the car… I'm sorry, but I didn't know you, and I wanted to find help. I saw that the path was still there, the door Kim opened with the rhyme hadn't shut. And then there he was. It was me, but it wasn't. I… he had a knife, and he stabbed Richard in the stomach. And then he was staring at me, the other me, I mean. Jessie Two. I think he wants to kill me."

"I *know* he wants to kill you. It's okay, kid. I've dealt with this before. What happened next?"

"I ran. And the whole way here he was beside me, or not beside but… I can't explain it. Sometimes it felt like he was *inside* me, or I was inside him. Like we were the same. And then I saw you and-"

A knock at the door interrupted Jessie; Linda smiled.

"And, that's him, then. Right on time."

"What do you mean-"

"Jessie, my name is Linda Evans. I work for Cuthbert Dubois, do you know who that is?"

"No."

"Doesn't matter. Look, you see this?"

Linda pulled the small orb from the burlap sack at her feet, held it up so Jessie could see it.

"You've seen some of this mirror shit now, yeah?"

"Yeah."

"Seen one'a these?"

"No."

"Okay. This is a Vetusta Vitrium. It's like a little prison cell if you use it right. I pull that door open, and you distract that bastard, we can trap him in this."

"Really?"

"Yeah. But you're gonna have to come face to face with him. You think you can handle that?"

"He's got a knife."

"Don't worry, we'll do it quick; he won't be expecting you to face him. Then that's one less of these goddamned things we have to worry about, okay?"

Jessie closed his eyes and tried to envision himself coated in shadow, like Kim. It wasn't the same, wouldn't protect him, but it might make him brave enough to pull this off.

"Okay."

"Yeah?" Linda smiled. She was starting to like this kid, "On the count of three, okay?"

Jessie nodded, dug in the tips of his shoes and tried to ignore the squishing of their waterlogged rubber.

"Do it. Now, before I lose my nerve."

"Okay. One."

There was a soft knock. And something else. Laughter? Wait, why hadn't it done like Kim and used the shadows to just slip through the door?

"Wait a minute…"

"Two."

The knocking became louder, though whether it was in his head or for real, Jessie wasn't sure. No time now.

"Three!"

Linda pulled the door open and dipped down to set the glass orb behind Jessie as he swung his fists forward at eye level, hoping to clock his Double right in the side of the head. Instead, a gale wind whipped through the door and right past them. Jessie stumbled out the door, caught himself about two steps before toppling down the stairs.

"He's gone!"

"Shit!" Linda yelled, then caught Jessie around the shoulders in an almost motherly embrace. Standing in the night, pounded by rain, they stared out at lights on Dubois' driveway, the feeling that something terrible had happened circled the drain but never quite disappeared.

Then she got it.

"Shit! How could I have been so stupid!"

"What?"

"C'mon."

She pulled Jessie back inside and shut the door.

"This house has some rather irregular security features."

"Is that why he couldn't use the shadows to get in?"

"Yeah. And then we opened the door up nice and wide for him. That wasn't wind that blew past us; it was your Double."

"But why would he want in if he wasn't going to attack us?"

"Are there a bunch of doors in your new house you can't open?"

"Yeah."

"Well, that's because all the houses in Gallows Hill are connected via another dimension, and those same doors appear in each of them. But, depending on what house you're in, not every door opens."

"What's this have to do with-"

"Because this house is the master mold for all the others. It literally is every other house in town. And in this house, all the doors open, and some open to other places. I think your Doppelgänger is trying to lead us to someone."

"Who?"

"My guess? Cruchetti."

CHAPTER 47

Linda looked familiar to Jessie, but he couldn't place where he might have seen her before.

"So who's this Dubonnet guy?"

"Dubois. Cuthbert Reginald Dubois, the Third. Richest man in the state. You get a letter from the Antiquarian Society yet?"

"Yeah."

"That's him. That's us, actually. I work for him."

"Okay. I heard a little bit about you. The GHAS, I mean."

"Not necessarily good, I'm guessing. I hope my saving your tail casts us in a somewhat better light."

"I don't even remember what happened. I mean... I remember Kim pushing me over the side of the balcony at Freighter's, then I woke up in that wrecked car."

Linda nodded, "Richard told me you and your girlfriend were in Freighter's house, so I came by to make sure you were okay. I pulled up just as you fell, saw your body hit the ground. You're lucky you didn't break your neck."

"Richard told you to help us? And then I killed him."

"You didn't kill him. Keep that straight, kid."

"He was so… I don't know. I didn't know him very long, but I really liked him."

"Richard was my friend; he helped me once when I was in a really bad way. But now isn't the time to cry for anybody. That comes after we get all this mirror crap under control."

"When you saw me fall, did you see Kim? I think she stayed in the house, to try and find her sister. We found this wall of keys…"

"She didn't come out when you did, so I have to assume she's still inside. The good news is Freighter isn't there because I plowed into that bastard at damn near sixty miles an hour."

"You think he's dead?"

"I sure as hell hope so. I loved that car, but I love the idea of Bob Freighter dead even more. What about this wall of keys you found?"

"I'm not sure, but-"

It came to him then, why he recognized Linda.

"Wait, you were there!"

"Yeah, you been looking at me like you knew me, so I'm guessing you ran into *my* Doppelgänger while you were inside that asshole's house."

"That was your Double?"

"Yeah, and she's a real bitch."

"She attacked us."

"She attacked me too. She hates me, but that's alright 'cuz the feeling is mutual."

"How long ago did yours wake up?"

"My situation is a little... different. My Double didn't just wake up; Freighter surgically removed her from me, kept her in his house as his pet monster."

"Removed? How?"

"Jessie, you don't want to hear that story, and I sure as hell don't want to relive it. Suffice to say, it was the most painful experience of my life. After, if it hadn't been for Richard, well, I don't know what would have happened."

"I'm sorry."

"Stop with the sorry. Richard was a good man, now he's dead. It happens."

They had moved to an enormous bathroom just off the left side of the room they'd entered through, what Jessie remembered WJ calling the 'Zero Point.' They were both injured, Linda worse than Jessie, and while they spoke, she laid out medical supplies: a syringe, antibiotic salve, gauze and bandages, and a small knitting needle and spool of thread.

"Look, I hope you're not squeamish because I'm gonna need you to put a couple stitches through this goddamn wound in my head. If it keeps bleeding into my eyes, I'm not gonna be able to see what's coming."

"Oh, ah. I've never done that before," Jessie said, recoiling at the idea. Since they'd come back inside, a strange tickle in his left ear seemed to be leeching his balance and stamina. Jessie felt tired and sickly.

"I figured, and I'm sorry to ask you, but here's the thing."

She stepped in front of the mirror and Jessie was shocked to see Linda had no reflection.

"What?"

"Like I said, Freighter removed it, reflection and all."

"So shadows and reflections are the same thing?"

"Metaphysics lessons later, if we survive, 'kay?"

A knock on the door in the room they'd just left interrupted the exchange. Linda and Jessie's eyes met.

"Who's there?" she demanded, unable to hide the faint shiver in her voice.

"Linda, open up. It's Chase. Cuthbert's with me, he's hurt."

Linda undid the locks, and a moment later a man in a police bomber carried another man in, arms around his shoulder. Behind them, WJ stepped from the cold, wet night and shook himself off like a dog.

"Oh my god! WJ" Jessie forgot everything once he saw WJ's face. He charged his one-time nemesis, hugged him so tight they almost fell over.

"Oh my god! I'm so happy to see you! Is Mom with you? Do you know where she is?"

"Ah, sorry kid. I found these two just down the road," WJ's clothes were ridiculous, and they gave Jessie a bit of a start now that he was past the initial excitement of a familiar face. The sweatpants and wet slippers looked especially bizarre sticking to him from the rain.

"What the heck are you wearing?"

WJ looked down at his abdomen, obviously not under-standing the question. Then, as though everything snapped into place, he laughed. It didn't sound like WJ's laugh, but he looked like he'd been through a lot.

"I'm afraid we crashed the car. Or, they did, rather. I found them... I..."

He trailed off, but Jessie let it slide, hugged him again. Linda noticed a look on the older man's face that bordered on repulsion at the affection, but she too let her intuition slide, busy as she was with her own reunion.

"What happened?" she asked Chase, taking up one side of the unconscious Dubois.

"We ran off the road in the storm. There were... people crossing in the rain. But they didn't look like people, they looked like shadows with faces."

Chase let the thought linger, and Linda saw his eyes bore into the man who had arrived with them. She didn't know why, but he put her on edge; now she saw she wasn't alone.

Chase broke the moment of shared suspicion, stepped away from her and wavered on his feet to the point that he almost fell, only to catch his balance against the wall.

"Sit down. You're probably concussed," Linda ordered him.

"I'm fine, I just," he did it again, this time tripping over legs that bent like rubber.

"Hey, you. What's your name?" she called to WJ.

"Huh? Oh, ah..."

"You okay, WJ?" Jessie asked.

"He's fine. Can you get me the smelling salts? They should be just in the bathroom through that door."

"I can go."

"No dice kid. You're not very stable, either. WJ, you're the only one here not injured, help me out, okay?"

"Yeah, uh, sure."

As soon as he was through the door, Chase said, "That's not your friend, kid. It's one of them."

"What?"

Footsteps and everyone went quiet. A moment passed before Chase whispered to Jessie, "Listen to It talk. It sounds like something *pretending* to be human."

WJ re-entered the room smiling. He did not have smelling salts. Instead, he held a hammer.

"No salt, but I found this and just couldn't resist the urge to use it. Too bad you guys talk so loud, eh?"

Chase stepped in front of Linda just as the flat of the hammer arced through the air. It hit him so hard in the shoulder that the sound of his bones breaking was loud enough to make Jessie gag.

"Kid! Get to the center of the house! You'll know what to do when you see it. Number Thirteen!" Linda screamed, bracing for a second assault as the Thing lunged at her. It turned to liquid in mid-air, shot across the floor and arced back up into Its human form just in time to catch her as she snagged the syringe on the table next to Jessie, who screamed as he watched WJ attack. Ruthless, It forced Linda to the floor even as she stabbed It repeatedly with the needle. Angered, WJ's Doppelgänger knocked the weapon from her grip and began to smack Linda's face with open palms. She raised her arms to shield her face, but her attacker's pliant form easily outmaneuvered them, pummeling her until she was left just shy of unconscious.

Linda neutralized, Jessie watched in horror as the WJ-Thing turned Its attention to him.

"And you…I know someone who wants to meet you reeeaaal bad."

Jessie turned and ran as fast as he could through the door behind him, slamming it closed before charging full-out across the cavernous triangular room he had passed through not twenty minutes before. He was losing allies by the hour.

CHAPTER 48

"I have something to show you," he said, and Talia followed Arthur through the doorway and into the corridor beyond. The floor and walls were stone, and the ceiling was obscured in darkness. A flickering electric lantern hanging above a door further down the hall was the only light, and in the cyclopean, subterranean darkness the space around them felt like it shuffled with each step. Disoriented, Talia fought to keep her wits.

They passed many doorways on either side until they reached the one below the light. Through here they emerged into what Talia immediately recognized as the basement of her new home, the forest of standing mirrors unmistakable.

"How?"

"This house has served me as something of a "backdoor" into Gallows Hill. Which, by the way, is not a small forested area with houses built into it, but rather one enormous construction woven by co-mingling matter from both Widdershins and this world. The basement of this house is, for example, something akin to a grillwork of overlapping transportation systems, all disguised if you will, as mirrors.

Talia rolled this over in her head, tried to grasp some understanding. Before her were the mirrors Jessie had found that first night; beyond them were stone corridors that stretched into the dark of the unfinished basement.

"So this is not only my basement. It's also… what? Every basement in town?"

"Something like that. But don't think of this as your basement. Instead, think of it as a place that has the exact same orbital resonance as your basement."

"Orbital resonance is an astronomical calculation."

"Again, the structures in Gallows Hill all occupy different spaces in our world but share the same space in Widdershins. They are, to put it primitively, 'stacked' or 'folded' in a harmonic order, all spiraling out from the true Zero Point, the house where Cuthbert Dubois resides. He was once Cruchetti's financier and de facto gatekeeper. Now he is our rival."

"That doesn't make any sense scientifically."

"It's complicated, but let's just say I taught Paolo Cruchetti my tribe's technique for accessing Widdershins in exchange for his secrets to applying non-Euclidean logic to the spaces of our world. When you put those things together, well, what you think of as scientific rigor begins to decompose."

"So if I understand you correctly, in the same way this Dubois' house is the Zero Point for the entire town, Gallows Hill itself is, what? Some kind of Zero Point for your transportation system?"

"Exactly! Think of Gallows Hill as a kind of "Union Station" through which all the other doors route. There's no disturbance in the everyday aesthetic of the place because the transit passages unfold across higher dimensional space, tucked away into, well, into higher dimensions."

"Jesus Christ. You're talking about Brane theory."

"Potato/Pah-tato."

Brane theory. In Gallows Hill. There was no guesswork to this anymore. Talia realized she was meant to come here, from as far back as she could remember, maybe her entire life. And with this in mind, everything that had brought her to this point - including Nico's murder - felt inevitable.

"Unfortunately, due to Cuthbert's betrayal, I only have access to a small portion of the doors. For now. That is why your son and his friend are so important."

"Jessie?"

"Yes. Come, let me show you something that may help."

Arthur led Talia past the mirrors and into the deeper corridor. Talia's eyes darted along the path as door after door appeared on either side of them, trailing off into a distant horizon where one final entry marked the end of the path.

"I have it on good authority your male friend is nearby."

"WJ?"

"Yes. In fact, I am fairly certain he is just though that doorway at the end of the hall."

"Wendell's *here*?"

"Not here. Through that door. In Gallows Hill, there is most definitely a difference."

Talia took a step toward the door, but Arthur caught her by the wrist. His grip hurt.

"It doesn't work like that. If you open that door, there's no telling where it will take you. You need me, Talia, in so many ways. Our revolution has already begun. My glass is in every house in Gallows Hill and over half the homes in Knight's Side. Do you realize how many people we've already replaced with their Doppelgängers? Once we give the word, there's going to be a virtual invasion! No one will be able to stop us."

Arthur's dark, pupil-less eyes bored into hers and his mannerisms suddenly switched. Here he was; here was the man she'd caught standing over Nico's body all those years ago, a remorseless hunter who, by his own admission, used people and then threw them away.

"Okay, first let me ask you, after we kill our Doubles and receive this eternal life, can we still be killed?"

"Oh yes. There is no cure in the Universe for murder."

Arthur smiled another brooding, lascivious smile and that was when Talia made up her mind. She surprised herself by swinging out violently and catching her captor in the face with a closed fist. The blow stunned him, almost sent him to the floor. He recovered quickly though, and without missing a beat lunged from one foot and caught her by the hair. As Arthur pulled her off balance, Talia swung both arms out in a clumsy attempt to batter his face. Both open palms landed but had little effect. Momentarily triumphant, Arthur dragged Talia down onto her back.

"Stop hitting me, or I will do this slow, much slower than I did your husband, who went quickly and with very little pain, by the way."

Talia stopped, and it made Arthur's job easier. He climbed on top of her, straddling her with both hands so tight around her throat that she felt like she had already asphyxiated. She closed her eyes on his disgusting smile, drowned out his words with one final thought:

"Brane theory. Proven. What a waste."

Talia's right hand came around from beneath her and drove the sharp end of the nail file into Arthur's throat. Her angle was odd but efficient, as it actually allowed her to get the blade behind his trachea. From there it was merely a matter of leveraging it forward, and Arthur Tenorio's entire windpipe came ripping through the skin of his neck, spraying Talia with what felt like gallons of blood.

Awash in a veritable deluge of gore, Talia scrambled to work her way out from under Arthur's still-convulsing corpse. It took a few moments, but when she finally got free and his body hit the floor, it disappeared in ripples, leaving only a shadow-like imprint on the stone. Talia's incredulity exhausted, she lay on her back, propped up partially on her elbows, panting through her terror and exhaustion. Shortly, her eyes came up and she saw the door at the far end of the corridor.

It took all of her remaining strength, but Talia fought her way to her feet and began to walk toward that door.

"Wendell," she said.

CHAPTER 49

At One forty-five A.M., Franklin Keith crawled from bed cursing the extra can of beer he'd finished the night with and made his way to the bathroom down the hall. Outside the bedroom, Frank stopped before the stairs that led to the ground floor of the two-story, white oak Colonial he and his wife Ginny had inherited from her parents. Something had caught his ear - a cold, metallic rattle-and-yap that goosed him awake before he realized it was the screen door at the rear of the house caught in the wind. His wits now about him, Franklin noted the thunderous downpour that had kept him awake earlier in the night had subsided, or at the very least wore itself down to a low roar. Storm or not, the bathroom window was open, and as Frank answered the call of nature, he came further around, the wind outside howling, the air still saturated with enough electrified oxygen to charge the night with a kind of supernatural wonder.

The storm hadn't stopped, it was merely biding its time.

Retracing his steps, Franklin received a start when something low and close to the ground stabbed at his feet, made him lose his balance and for one horrible moment almost fall down the stairs. He was quick though, and despite his disorientation, Frank caught himself at the last minute and breathed a sigh of relief; climbing back into bed, he cursed Lombardi the cat under his breath.

Ten minutes later, Franklin realized something was wrong: despite that electric charge to the night, he was suddenly shivering.

Franklin's side of the mattress butted up against the outside wall of the house, and the small layout of the room meant that put half a window next to his feet. He almost always kept this window open a crack, at least until the really cold weather came, but now he found the temperature must have dropped dramatically.

Frank tried to wait it out, pulling the comforter up over his head, but after a few moments, he realized the reality of the situation: winter was coming early.

"What the hell. It is still August, isn't it?" he posited, and Ginny's unconscious form gave only the tiniest of snores as a response. He smiled at that; Ginny's snores were one of those endearing little things that had taken Franklin years to appreciate. He stroked his wife's hair, her back to him and their other cat, TomTom, cuddled in her arms.

Preferring to keep the window cracked so as not to wake Ginny with the aging shriek that often accompanied its movement on the track, Franklin begrudgingly crawled back out of bed and went to the closet. The door was slightly ajar, and he reached in without turning on the light for the hoodie he kept on a hook just inside. The garment met his hand easily, and as Franklin slipped into its fleece-lined embrace, a single thought made his hair stand on-end: it seemed to Frank that someone had *handed him the garment.*

His hand made it to the pitted aluminum baseball bat beside the closet just as something tall and dark stepped from the shadows of the closet and enveloped Franklin Keith completely.

A moment later, when Ginny woke with a start, she saw her husband's legs disappear into the antique costume mirror across from the bed. She stood, unable to distinguish dream from reality, and watched in horror as a man made of shadows stepped through the glass.

A moment later, Ginny was gone, replaced by something that, although it resembled her in many ways, was definitely not Ginny Keith.

∼

The street outside the Keiths' two-story, quaint suburban home rustled in the wind. It was late August, almost September, but to feel the air in Knight's Side tonight one would think it November. The temperature had fallen beneath the rage of the storm, and the thick ozone tang in the air gave the night a decidedly more vivid quality than most late summer nights, ordinarily hot and muggy, and thus, dreadfully literal. The streets were slicked to the horizon in every direction from the recent deluge, and with the reflections that resulted they very much resembled large, oblong mirrors. Mirrors that ran as far as one could see, reflecting the street lights, traffic signals, and telephone wires to create the illusion of two distinct worlds separated only by an invisible line. Tonight, however, this was no illusion. Tonight two separate worlds slowly bled together; a subtle shift in reality that, heralded by the reigniting of the storm, shook with the continued appearance of dozens of shadows, thin and lithe. They swarmed over the streets, through the yards, and across the sleeping houses, moving with a purchase, picking up the speed of intangible things as they slipped and shimmied into the world they had for so long been denied. The shadows had faces; they were the faces of the people of Knight's Side, now all but entirely Replaced. En masse, this mob of black shapes made their way into the woods that divided the town from its neighbor, following the route of the first wave of Replaced that had played harbinger to Chase and Dubois earlier. This new group moved like the first, seeking a front row seat for the night's main event: The Pall had replaced the citizen's of Knight's Side over the past several years. They would now replace the town itself.

PART III

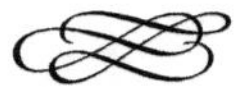

CHAPTER 50

Despite the bad-ass demeanor that served as her armor, Cassie Tenorio's stomach felt like a smoking cauldron of nerves as she stared through the car window. The sky was dark, the storm foreboding, but neither could match the darkness Cassie carried for her home town. Recently, she'd seen evidence of the Doppelgänger Population's more militant branch, the mysterious organization known as The Pall, staging uprisings in other parts of the world. Such tactics were increasingly common. Here in Gallows Hill though, where Cruchetti had managed to put the final pieces of his hundred-year plan in place, there was a palpable sense of sickness as reality fell under his influence. Even Knight's Side - which had previously acted as a kind of buffer between the rest of the world and that sickness - now had the stench of rot. The buffer was rapidly disappearing; that's why she was here: to stop the spread of the disease that crept from the other world into this one.

Just past the turnoff for 23, Cassie's eyes glued to the forest that bordered their route; she shook as she realized the trees all bent toward their destination. So too in the sky above, where great thunderheads funneled their torrential fury toward Gallows Hill, the after-effects of dark tribal magic in the wrong hands. Her father had opened a tear in the fabric of reality that, having gone unchecked, threatened to pull everything from this world into the other. Cassie knew that this was The Pall's goal: Widdershins would replace Deosil as the primary world, freeing humanity's siblings from their bonds as slaves. Shadows and reflections; reservoirs for the darkest parts of humanity, throwaway physical phenomenon children were taught from birth to ignore. We would no longer be able to ignore them, now that the ambitions of modern men had granted these formerly docile entities consciousness. Consciousness and under-standing; the ability to see what they'd been missing. It was the Adam and Eve myth all over again. Only this time it was real, and the enlightened ones weren't just sore about what they were missing. They wanted revenge for having had it kept from them.

Cassie felt her great-grandmother's hand on her own; it quelled the fires of uncertainty inside her. She trained for this for five years - more if you count the pocket dimension's irregular passage of time - but she still didn't feel ready. Too bad; the timetable had been moved up by the activation of The Hub, revealing her abuela's own reservations about Cassie's preparedness.

There was a flash of light up ahead as the black Lincoln Town Car came to rest behind a Police cruiser sticking out of the ditch on the side of the road. The three occupants of the luxury car - one up front and two in the back - watched through the windshield as the storm battered the abandoned vehicle mercilessly, the rapid-fire deluge hammering out an industrial soundtrack fit for the apocalypse.

"What do you suppose happened here?" Elizabeth Manhattan asked from the driver's seat.

"Only one way to find out," Cassie said, making to exit the car. A firm hand on her leg stopped her. Encarnación Tenorio worried about her great-granddaughter's temper; like the sickness they sought to cure, Cassie's anger threatened to poison everyone around her. Encarnación understood and even shared her nieta's hostility toward her father and the men who had corrupted him. But this newfound rebellion against those closest to her was troubling, it reminded the Bruja of Cassie's father.

"Elizabeth, por favor verifica."

"Of course, Mater Tenorio," Elizabeth replied, careful her tone wouldn't substantiate any inkling Cassie might have of her great-grandmother's tendency to rely on Liz over her. Elizabeth had helped trained Cassie, believed she was ready for whatever lay ahead. But the Bruja was still wary of her nieta's inexperience. Her inexperience, and her anger.

Elizabeth pulled up her hood and exited the car. At full height, she stood six foot two inches, and with her boots and hooded cloak she cut an imposing, wraith-like figure as she sliced through the storm, more apparition than person.

"You know, abuela," Cassie fumed, "you're going to have to start trusting me."

"Si," the older woman said, her focus trained on the events outside. In a moment, Elizabeth returned; when she opened the driver's door and slid back inside she did so quickly, eager to escape the storm.

"Brutal out there," Elizabeth removed her hood and turned to face her passengers. Her long, straight dark hair and deeply angled features bathed in shadow, her nose a pointed invitation to the beauty that lay easily within her eyes and brow, dainty for so strong a warrior, "Looks like two men were in the truck when it crashed and a third retrieved them."

The Bruja nodded as if she had expected this exact report.

"And… there's something else."

"Que?"

"I'm not sure. It felt like a door closed behind us once we crossed into Knight's Side. I have a feeling if we turned around and tried to leave, we would not be able to do so."

"Más de la magia negra de mi nieto."

"This isn't just my father's magick," Cassie said, "This is the Architect, too."

Both older women nodded in agreement.

They drove on.

"If I may speak frankly?" Elizabeth asked. She slowed the town car to a cautious fifteen miles an hour as Dubois' mansion came into view, the gargantuan shape outlined by random flashes of lightning.

"Si."

"Cassandra is ready for this, Bruja. I have trained with her long enough to know. Also, she will not fight alone."

The Bruja nodded but remained silent. Cassie knew her great-grandmother doubted her. She wished there was something she could do to make Encarnación see she was ready. But Cassie also knew that her abuela partially blamed herself for her father's evil. In the Tenorio tribe, the women were the keepers of the Magick. When Encarnación's daughter - Cassie's grandmother - birthed a son instead of a daughter and died with his first breath, it was the first time in their tribe's history a Bruja had produced a male heir. Against her better judgment, Encarnación took Arthur's arrival as a sign and broke tradition, trained him as the next shaman.

And then he'd abandoned the tribe, seduced by dreams of money and power. This was Encarnación's cross to bear, but her guilt manifested as an underlying suspicion toward Arthur's daughter, in effect punishing Cassie for the Bruja's own mistake. That grudge would not prevent Cassie from doing what she knew she had to. No matter what, she told herself. Because, regardless of the inner workings of their twisted family dynamic, Cassie knew it was her destiny to kill her father. And she knew her chance was almost here; she could feel Arthur's presence all around her.

As if sensing her thoughts, Encarnación laid a calming hand on her nieta's cheek.

"Remember please, Cassandra... la venganza es tan dañina como la malevolencia."

"Si, abuela. Vengeance is harmful, but only to those who deserve it."

Cassie knew her great-grandmother was right, of course, but that didn't change the fact that the moment Cassie saw her father or the Doppelgänger that had replaced her best friend, she would bury her blade in their flesh and avenge the wrongs wrought that night five years before.

Kim lay in the embrace of the softly sloping walls of her prison; an orb-shaped dimension of pure glass that repeated her reflection in every direction. She felt a weakness that she'd never before known and realized that she had come too far in her transformation to access the advantages she'd had as a Doppelgänger. Her blossoming humanity felt amazing by Jessie's side, but trapped inside this glass ball, it was the exact opposite. This was what she'd heard others of her kind refer to as the 'weakness of the flesh.' Kim had always thought the idea of humanity as an imperfect state naive, but now that she was hungry, needed to pee, and felt weak to the point of illness, she understood.

Still, she'd not trade it for the world.

Beyond her own prison, hundreds of other glass spheres lined the massive space, the combined glow a hazy, white light, not unlike fog. Inside each of these, Kim knew other prisoners lay drained, possibly near death. Richard had been right: by splitting the Reflection from the Cast, he'd theorized that Cruchetti could use multiple mirrors to create a perpetual state of duplication. Thus the mirrored walls, floor, and ceiling of the prisons. Kim stared at her reflections as they trailed off into infinity in any direction, realizing the iterations could be used to harness the prisoner's energy, while their Doubles walked Deosil as Cruchetti's agents, anchors that kept the flesh of one world enmeshed with the other. There must have been a couple hundred people in these cages here with her, so it wasn't Jessie that had been the final piece, after all, just a coincidence that his arrival had coincided with The Hub's activation.

"Hey, new girl."

The voice came from her left. Staring past her endless reflections, Kim could just barely make out the resident of the orb next to hers: a short, dark-haired boy lay with his face against the glass. His eyes were hollow, his skin seared white.

"Has it happened?"

"Has what happened?"

"The Revitalization? The Architect says when it happens, he's going to let us all go."

Kim didn't know this kid's story, but she knew there was no way Cruchetti was going to let him or any of these other people go. She stared at him through the glass, saw the strange growths poking through his skin, an anatomy of horror having replaced his humanity.

Just like Patty.

"So that's why…"

"Why? There is no why. We were chosen."

"Kid, I hate to break it to you, but…" Kim stopped, her

newfound humanity telling her there was no need to dash this boy's hopes against the rock of truth.

"Wow. Congrats, you're not as dumb as I thought."

She recognized the voice as her own, turned to face herself.

"I thought you'd be dead by now," Kim said, turning to face the girl who had once been her Cast.

"No such luck, bitch. You stole my life, trapped me here. And now, oh no! What's this? You're trapped here, too! How's it feel?"

"I didn't mean to do it. They told me you were dying, that they could help you."

"Bullshit! You snuck through that mirror and stole my life."

What could Kim say? It was true.

"I have people who will come for me."

"Oh yeah? That's what I thought, too. Besides, you're waaay too important for him to let you go. While everyone's been focused on Jessie, the Architect is really more interested in you."

"Me? Why?"

"Duh. You've been living on the opposite side for five years. You're the first long-term Replacement. What's more, now that you're actually turning into one of them, Widdershins is turning with you. *It's becoming Deosil.*"

"But… what will happen to Deosil?"

"Now that… that is…" a new, masculine voice said from the doorway to the left, "That is what I am very much interested in finding out. Yes."

"Who?"

"Paolo. Paolo Cruchetti. Heh. The 'Mad Archietct'. Yes, that is me, and I, my dear, I am at your service. Yes."

CHAPTER 51

Jessie ran as hard as he could. He snaked through corridors that wove in and out of massive living spaces, all empty and unused. A kitchen appeared. This led to a sprawling wood-paneled den, complete with a large, stone fireplace. Next came something that resembled a greenhouse, then a room that looked like the banquet hall where his mother had been honored several years before. Then more corridors: stone, hardwood, carpet. Repeat.

He felt like a video image stuck in an endless loop. Jessie thought for a moment he would barf, but the urge passed when the next doorway emitted him into a small movie theatre. On the screen was the image of a deeply tanned middle-aged man, his dark brown suit complimented by a diamond-stubbed Bolo tie. He sat facing a man whose back was to the camera, enrapt in conversation. No viewers were in the room.

"... *Is actually based on his work, correct?*" the tanned man said on screen.

There was a glitch in the image, and then the angle of the

camera changed to show another man, one Jessie knew only too well, if only through photographs.

"Dad?"

"Barrie discovered it through a friendship with a stage magician. It wasn't until after he died that I met Mr. Cruchetti, when we began to draw parallels to certain tribal artifacts he claimed his ancestor helped Percival Fawcett retrieve from the Amazon Basin. These parallels eventually led to my coining the term Trans-spatialism in my thesis, which in turn earned me a grant. Ultimately however, the idea was too radical, that all the perceivable, usable portions of this reality - which we refer to as 'space' - are not quite as definable as humanity has convinced itself. People don't want to hear that. They're much more comfortable with the illusion, this unnatural abstraction that we as sentient beings apply previously agreed upon parameters to, dressing it in materials that exist within a specific set of readily perceivable frequencies that then divide it into even smaller portions to reinforce ideas of tangibility and, eventually, ownership. We choose to perceive our reality in this way because it affords us a certain amount of ignorance to the things we do not perceive quite so easily. The things which most people prefer to discredit."

The screen fizzled again; both men disappeared, but the tanned man's voice continued over a faded image of a world map. Red dots covered a large portion of it:

"In the vernacular of my tribe, the sacred and the profane. I used my Grandmother's teaching to perfect the ability to blend the one with the other, masking the weaknesses of Deosil with the strengths of Widdershins."

This time, the image dissolved completely and the audio track faded out, replaced by the sound of film flapping against a projector. Upon the resultant blank white screen, the shadows of two hands appeared, superimposed. Palms out, the fingers began to move, folding around and together, until the shape of a complex shadow puppet loomed larger than life over Jessie. It looked like a bird, then morphed into something that reminded him of a dinosaur.

"Sit back and enjoy the show. Probably gonna be your last."

Jessie turned, but couldn't see anyone behind him. Something tickled his neck and he swung back around to find the shadow puppet no longer confined to the fabric of the screen.

He screamed as it fell upon him. Jessie fought but the puppet - now a tactile, three-dimensional monstrosity - enclosed him in its grip. Pulsing with unknown energies, It lifted him from the floor and threw him to the back of the room, where the WJ-Thing stood, its malevolent smile showing rows of jagged black teeth, Its hands working overtime to create the monster.

"Must be pretty weird to see that, eh? Your dad, up there talking all this crazy shit with Arthur Tenorio. Probably wish you had your mommy here to help you, right? Well guess what, Ace - we have her. You want to see your her again, you'll stop acting up and do what I say."

Jessie pushed himself up into a sitting position, his head hung in defeat.

"You have my mom?"

"The Architect has your mom. You either come with me, or she dies."

"Well then, I guess I don't have a choice."

"No, you don't."

The room crackled black as Cuthbert raised his head. The sound of the storm battering the outside of his house was nothing compared to the thunder of confusion that assaulted his mind. When he finally did open his eyes, it was with great effort and yielded little to offset his panic.

Initially, Cuthbert didn't know where he was. He remembered the Sheriff at the hospital, and afterward, driving with Chase. The car ran off the road when…

The caravan of ghostly figures came back to him and Cuthbert winced; Paolo had been very busy. Cuthbert understood that he had no hope of wresting control of the device from his former lover now. The 'gift' that had arrived late last week had told him this. Instead, he would have to be creative. Except, here he was with a head wound and none of his soldiers.

"Oh what price, the pitfalls of love."

Cuthbert's vision flickered in and out a few more times and then clarified. He'd hurt his head in the crash, this much he knew. Looking around, his sense of things returned; he recognized his infirmary, wondered how they'd managed to make it this far. Then he turned and saw Chase crumpled on the floor behind him and even at this distance Dubois could tell he was hurt, unconscious, maybe even dead.

Carefully, he stood. Making some perfunctory assessments, Cuthbert found that he was not as badly injured as he initially thought. His head still rang with dark black static, but his limbs worked as usual. He'd apparently not been attacked while unconscious and, what's more, he'd not been seriously injured to begin with.

Once he felt he could move, Dubois did so by keeping one hand planted firmly against the wall and taking baby steps. The first one was the hardest; the world blundered for a moment with the movement, but he rode it out. After the disorientation passed, Cuthbert took another step, then stopped to survey the rest of the room. He tried to pinpoint the last thing he remembered and found it a baffling abstraction: light approaching through a window, relentless rain and a shrill cry. Glass breaking? A picture began to take shape, one that was anything but comforting. Had Paolo sent him a dark black angel?

After a few minutes wherein he cemented his equilibrium with a series of deep and purposeful breaths, Dubois turned from Chase and began down a corridor that appeared in the center of the wall, as if by his mental command.

"My apologies deputy, but there are far more important things at stake than your life," Dubois said, disappearing into shadow.

CHAPTER 52

"Knock knock," Cassie called as she kicked the door to Dubois' mansion open, clunky bravado an attempt to hide her anxiety. She could sense things were escalating considerably faster than even her abuela could have anticipated. She could also feel the presence of Kim's Doppelgänger; It felt close, unlike her father's, which had felt vibrant when they first arrived in the States, but had all but completely faded in the last hour.

Behind Cassie, Elizabeth's cloak swam in the wind that carried them through the doorway; it made her indistinguishable from the shadows. Instinctively they moved to either side of Encarnación, to shield her in case of sudden attack. As powerful as the Bruja's magick was, her body was nearing the end of its time on this plane, and both younger women knew they must protect her at all cost.

Cassie bent to survey faint traces of blood just inside the door.

"What happened here?"

"Nothing good," Elizabeth answered in her characteristically dry manner, her voice echoing across the cavernous Zero Point of Dubois's mansion.

The blood trail led several hundred feet across the room then stopped dead, a fresh pool serving as an ominous calling card. None of them would have known it, but this room was no longer the same one Linda had led Jessie through, nor was it the room that had received Chase, Dubois and the Thing in WJ's guise just a short time ago.

"There are parts of this house we can't see. Parts probably only Dubois can see. I'm betting the blood is his, that he was one of the two men in the car," Cassie said, moving her hands through the air, presumably testing for an invisible door of some kind. The walls began to shimmer with a strange effect that seemed contingent on their presence, but no entrance manifested.

Cassie led them on, the walls changing as they went. Massive shelves unfolded what must have been thousands of books up and down their surface, spines appearing like dominoes throughout, their only interruption an occasional candelabra or bust. Minutes elongated, turned to an endless stream that weighed heavily on each of them. Encarnación kept them slow, her cane clicking across the wood floor with the rhythm of age and reason. Meanwhile, inside Cassie the fires of revenge continued to burn bright.

"This room... it feels... endless," Elizabeth observed, no fear in her voice, merely awe. Awe, and a recognizable hint of nausea.

"No es infinito en el sentido que quieres decir," Encarnación said.

"Everything that ends must have a beginning," Cassie added, reciting from memory, "This is the Zero Point; it's woven into our world using pieces of Widdershins, and it contains elements of all the houses in Gallows Hill, a structure made of both worlds at once."

"Guess that explains my nausea," Elizabeth said, gagging a little.

Cassie had studied the fruits of her Father's magick voraciously. This building was the raw material that all the other structures in Gallows Hill flowed from. The technique was called Trans-spatialism, was the first bit of new magic her father and his partners developed after they'd appropriated the magic of the tribe and distilled it into a raw essence from which they could create new systems to work with.

"The size of the Zero Point as we cross it depends on how many of the other Zero Points in town are being accessed or 'experienced' at the same time. Being that probably everyone still living in this town is somewhere in this house in one capacity or another, I'd say that means we're getting close to the maximum effect here."

They reached the other side of the room, slipped through an obscured door in the red wall and emerged into the master version of the out-of-place foyer, identical to the one in Jessie's home because it was the *same room*. Somewhere nearby Talia's alarm clock sounded continuously, forgotten in the events of the day.

"How does one access the rest of the house?" Elizabeth asked.

"Depends. Normally there would be an entrance here," Cassie ran her hand over the wood that, if this were her previous home, would just barely conceal the opening to the gold-trimmed den with its enormous windows, "But again, the characteristics we experience here now depend on what's happening in each of the other houses simultaneously."

"All of this feels... unnatural. I'm much better at the fighting than the math," Elizabeth said, her words muffled as she spoke into a black silk handkerchief.

"It is unnatural. I've always wondered if my father became the man he is because of all this Non-Euclidean Geometry.

I've read how prolonged exposure to higher dimensional realms can change people, and not necessarily for the better."

"Por supesto. Mira al senor Freighter," Encarnación observed. Cassie could tell contemplating Bob Freighter made her abuela nervous. There was no better example of how things had gone horribly wrong with the Magick Cassie's father had stolen.

Cassie tried to pass through the opening at the far left but found that despite its lack of a door she could not physically cross the threshold. She tried another, then another. No dice. She became impatient, tried the remaining doors in rapid succession. The second from last worked, and Cassie disappeared into the darkness beyond its frame.

"Cassandra Tenorio. To say that your timing is perfect *hack* would be an understatement of the highest degree."

Cassie stood just inside the doorway, staring at Dubois, violence in her gaze. Elizabeth and Encarnación emerged behind her, the sight of the three woman together giving the older man pause.

"You brought the entire family. Good."

"What happened here?" Elizabeth demanded.

"I am afraid I do not know. I was unconscious for most of it," Dubois said, trailing off as a morbid realization overtook him, "Are you here to kill me?"

"No," Encarnación answered quickly, noting her great-granddaughter's hand had already moved to the weapon on her belt.

"Well Mater Tenorio, you have certainly done nothing to improve this one's temperament. She behaves just like her-"

The sensation of Cassie's blade against his throat ended Dubois' observation premature.

"I beg your pardon?"

"Ahem. No, it is I who beg yours, Cassandra. My apologies."

Elizabeth physically defused the situation, then set about assessing Dubois's injuries. A penlight perusal of his eyes confirmed concussion.

"For someone who claims to be on our side, you don't show it, Mr. Dubois. Your representative left the meeting Richard called on our behalf, all matters unsettled."

"Yes, well, Linda no doubt had an issue with Paolo's choice of representative."

"Why do I feel as though you know more than you're telling?" Elizabeth asked.

"I assure you, I am just as keen on finding Paolo as you. His rampant behavior has created nothing but problems for our little town."

"I'll say. Where is everybody? All the houses we passed looked empty."

"Pawns on Paolo's board. He has been replacing people for quite some time, you know. Nicholas's boy was merely a coincidence or an omen, not the final piece."

"Why now then?" Elizabeth asked.

"The shift. There are virtual hordes of Doppelgängers moving through the town, the woods, everywhere. The balance between worlds is askew, and we are feeling the effect. Think of a canoe, capsizing in slow motion. If I can just see Paolo, I can stop this. He will listen to me."

"Why are we not just cutting this bastard's throat? Please explain this to me?" Cassie hissed.

"Porque eso no es lo que hemos venido a hacer. Tu insistencia continua en la venganza me preocupa, nieta. We are not here… for revenge."

"I appreciate your patience, Mater Tenorio, but

Cassandra is right not to trust me. In the chapters of your family's saga, I am afraid I have done nothing but work against your wishes. I have tried, these last five years, to make amends. The GHAS, my compliance with the accord, Richard's terms."

"I'm afraid the only terms you should be concerned with at the moment are those you need to accept as the situation pertains to your former lover. Paolo sealed his own fate, Mr. Dubois, the same as Arthur. If you're on our side, you will have to accept this," Elizabeth warned.

"You do not understand! It was never Paolo's fault. It is your grandson's! Arthur is the poisonous one."

"Mi nieto esta muerto."

"What?" Cassie turned to her great-grandmother, fury flaring her nostrils. Her smooth, dark brown flesh glowed a deeper, almost crimson shade as anger brought a rush of blood to her face, "Father is dead? How? When?"

"It happened as we were coming into town. We thought it best to… wait to tell you." Elizabeth added.

The rage Cassie felt at having been denied killing her father was blistering. Despite this, or maybe because of it, the adults ignored her.

"Then Paolo is alone. That means he is vulnerable. Let me go to him, try and talk some sense into him."

Cassie shook with anger when she realized her great-grandmother was actually considering Dubois' request.

"Wait. Mater Tenorio, I believe Mr. Dubois may actually be right," Elizabeth said.

"Explique, por favor."

"Think about it. Even if we kill Cruchetti, we still have to deal with the bridge, with all the displaced people he has unleashed. We have to save the canoe, and right now Cruchetti is the one steering it. If we can get him to come around to our logic, we might be able to reverse the damage that has been done."

The look on her great-grandmother's face told Cassie she agreed with Elizabeth. Feeling betrayed, her anger erupted.

"This is such bullshit! Abuela, we came here to end this. Do you really think Cruchetti's going to listen to reason? He never listened to it before, when you told him not to encourage Papa to leave the tribe; when you confronted him about his use of magick; when you told him there would be consequences to his ambitions. What makes you think he will listen now?"

"Cassandra, he has to list-"

"I'm not fucking talking to you, Liz, so shut up already!"

"Cassandra! Esto no está abierto a debate!"

Cassie could not turn off the hatred she felt for everyone and everything at the moment, even when she looked at the woman who had raised her, who had made her what she was today - strong, not weak like her mother.

"You're right, abuela, it's not. I hate to tell you this, grand-mother, but you are wrong. And I'll prove it."

Cassie stormed off, disappearing into the shadows.

Sheriff Jim Rash left the hospital alone and in pain. He'd managed to make sure Dr. Gershaw was okay and then lit out as fast as he could, hobbling on his bad leg as he went. It was not, however, the leg that filled his eyes with stinging tears, tears he damn sure wasn't about to let anyone else see.

As he drove, Rash resigned himself to the fact that he was going to have to tell Terry Quinn's mother that her son had vanished; not been injured or - thankfully - killed, but disap-peared. Was that worse? Dealing with this black magic mumbo jumbo, it sure as hell felt worse.

"Sonovabech," he cursed, flipping an eye up into the rearview mirror and adjusting it so he could see into the back of the cruiser. That was when the Sheriff had something of an epiphany. If he had to go try and explain nonsense he didn't understand to a woman who trusted him with her son's life, then he'd do so only after he'd evened the score. Rash felt as though he'd had about all one man could handle of Gallows Hill and realized the only way to make sure this madness stopped for good was to burn every single house to the ground. If anybody was inside, well... they'd better get the hell out.

He would not spare a single house.

In the back of the cruiser were two gas cans, mostly full, that he'd filled up a couple of days ago with the intention of keeping his snowblower running during the winter. It wouldn't be enough for what he had in mind now, but it was a start. The only question then, was which house should he begin with? His natural inclination was the house he perceived as the genesis of the problem, the place where the horror show had occurred five years ago. But then something dawned on him.

Dubois.

Cuthbert was the one link between everything; what's more, he was the man who had almost single-handedly spread Arthur Tenorio's mirrors out of Gallows Hill and into Knight's Side, into who knew how many other communities. Was what happened at the Crosse's earlier in the evening happening elsewhere? How many other towns, cities, communities might Dubois have spread this madness to? Tenorio was either missing or dead, but Dubois was alive and well, more prosperous than ever and uppity as all hell.

Sheriff Rash's plan crystalized and he knew exactly where to begin; he came in off the turnpike, hit Rune Road and passed the turn-off to Derleth. He'd get to the former home of Arthur Tenorio as he would all the houses in Gallows Hill this night. But he now understood he had to start at the source of the problem. He had to begin by burning down Cuthbert Dubois' house.

CHAPTER 54

Jessie had taken no more than half a dozen steps as the prisoner of WJ's Doppelgänger when something knocked him to the ground. Momentarily unconscious, a loud, wet SHUCT brought him back; it sounded like a plunger's seal breaking underwater, followed by a faint, garbled cry. Jessie popped back up and saw the WJ-Thing hanging skewered on a thick black talon that protruded from the arm of yet another obsidian nightmare. The hulking shape sported cock-eyed pigtails that sprouted from a face like a meteor. Black resin leaked from three blank orifices placed as though to serve as the Thing's eyes and mouth. A small, powder blue children's dress hung from It by the jagged spikes that covered much of Its form, and it was this last clue that told Jessie he was looking at Kim Corduroy's long lost sister.

"Patty?"

The Thing stared at him, mouth-hole open in what almost looked an imitation of Edvard Munch's famous painting. From deep inside, a horrible, lonely noise began to emanate, an existence of pain taking shape all around him.

After a moment of acclimation, Jessie recognized the sound as the Thing's voice.

"Whoooooooo?"

An emotive cry more than a word, Jessie felt a weight on their exchange that made his heart heavy.

"Patty, I'm Jessie. I'm a friend of your sister's."

Easily seven feet tall, Patty took a step toward him and sent the remainder of WJ's Doppelgänger sloshing to the floor. Freed from its burden, the limb congealed inward with a SQUISH, returning to something that vaguely resembled a human hand, the fingers gnarled and pointed. Where the powder blue of the dress didn't show through, great swathes of crimson coated her form, and Jessie could see that any humanity remaining in Patty's visage was actually no more than faint reverberations of what had been. The sound from the mouth-hole changed pitch, and then in a terrifying twist, the voice the Thing began to speak with became that of a little girl. The disconnect between watching the black, leaking mouth move and hearing the candy-coated timbre sent shivers through every part of Jessie's body. For the first time, he realized he was not only dealing with supernatural phenomenon but nightmares that had come to life.

"Hi, Jessie. I knew it was you. Wanna know how?"

"How?" he asked, that heaviness on his heart making him feel like he maybe shouldn't have.

"Because Kim told me you were the cutest boy she'd ever met. *Giggle*."

Patty took another step forward, the black puddle that had been the WJ-Thing's form sluicing through the talons that might have once been the toes on her feet.

"Patty, where is Kim? Have you seen her? Did she help you escape?"

Patty's head turned toward the floor, and Jessie saw the spikes on her head resembled horns.

"The bad men have her. She's where I was. She saved me but…" Patty started to cry, and her entire form writhed with the sobs.

"I hurt her! Jessie, they're going to do *this* to her! They're going to make Kim like me!"

"Hey, hey, it's okay. No one is going to do anything to Kim. I have a plan."

His revulsion temporarily excised by his empathy, Jessie crossed to Patty and embraced her. They stood carefully entwined, so as not to impale Jessie on her spikes.

"Patty, can you take me to Kim?"

"I don't know how to get back where we were! It was so weird, not like when they first took me there."

"Good for you I do," another voice said from behind them. Jessie and Patty whirled around to see a girl of about Jessie's age standing in the doorway behind them.

"Cassie!!! Yay! I missed you!"

Cassie Tenorio stepped forward, a curved-blade weapon in her hand: "Yes Patty. I missed you too. And you're the Roberts boy, eh? Well, I'm here to clean up everyone else's mess. You wanna live? Follow me."

"**A**nd you…*I know someone who wants to meet you reeeaaal bad.*"

Linda heard these words as if from underwater; she had to swim up through leagues of pain and darkness before she could open her eyes, and then it took a few moments for the images to coalesce and make any kind of coherent scene. When it did, she saw Chase laying broken on the floor behind her, but no one else. Instinct took over, and despite her own pain she began to crawl toward the man Linda finally realized she loved more than her long-lost husband, more than her job with the GHAS, more than herself. She'd just about reached him when a voice from behind stopped her cold.

"You really are something, you know?"

Linda's terror was not enough to assuage her anger. She pushed herself from a crawling position to a sitting one and turned to face her Doppelgänger.

"It's been too long, lady. Missed ya. Our time together was way too short, don'tcha think?"

The Doppelgänger looked different. She'd begun to change, to look less like Linda and more like some strange mutant beast made of thick, flowing tar. The shadow-substance moved across the surface of her body, never still, so that to look at her for any prolonged period produced almost instantaneous nausea. Linda felt her stomach begin to bubble and looked away. When she did, the Double lashed out and hit her so hard she landed on her face several feet away.

Slowly, Linda sat up, dialing in a hate-stare that would have withered anyone else. She spat a mouthful of blood and teeth onto the floor between them and cocked an arrogant smile.

"I hate to burst your bubble bitch, but I'm not afraid of you anymore."

"You should be."

Linda crawled toward the wall, used it to maneuver herself into a seated position. When she turned, someone new was standing beside her Double. Nothing could have surprised her more.

"Luis?"

She was unsure if she was hallucinating.

"Hello, wife."

"Where? Where have you been?"

"To the most wonderful place in the world. But let me

take you back. When you went missing, your Luis was beside himself, of course. Then, he saw you in a vision. Well, he thought it was a vision. You came to him and told him where you were, told him that terrible man had you, imprisoned. He went there, to Robert's home. To try and reason with him. And that is where Luis learned the truth."

"What truth?"

"That this form you wear now, it is inferior to the other..." Luis turned to the Doppelgänger, passion burning in his eyes. They grasped one another by the head and began to kiss violently, black fluid splashing as both figures reverberated with physical changes that made them look less and less human.

"You're not Luis."

The monsters disengaged, returned their attention to Linda.

"I never said that I was. You see, Luis understood the pointlessness of his existence. He laid down his life so that his better version - me - could live forever."

"You bastard..."

"Oh please. Your marriage had become a prison. Neither of you even had feelings left for one another. You didn't talk, didn't make love. Didn't laugh. He spent all his time at the University, you with that preposterous club. And, of course, your lover."

Chase's name hung on Linda's lips as she finally realized the extent to which she had wasted the later years of her life, holding out for something on principle, instead of emotion. Of course, she loved Chase. She had from the moment they met.

"You see? No denying it now, eh? And so it all works out perfectly. You have Chase," Luis motioned toward Chase's still form behind her, "And I have the superior version of the woman I love. Everybody wins."

Her hands pressed to the curved wall of the prison, Kim watched Paolo Cruchetti pace the room, occasionally stopping to admire one of the hundreds of glass orbs that lined the shelves.

"You see, everyone… believes… that is, they *think* that Jessie Roberts was the… the catalyst for The Hub's activation. And they're… well, they're correct, yes yes. Only not in the way they think. No."

There was a pause as Cruchetti seemed to fight himself for control of his thoughts. Listening to the man speak was frustrating, and Kim found herself wondering if all his time in Widdershins, exchanging his birth world for this other, had damaged his mind. And if that was the case, would swapping sides eventually damage hers as well?

"I've been… I've been re*placing* people - friends and neighbors and guests and the like - I've been replacing them for years. For years. These shelves… these shelves lined with Vetusta Vitriums… Double V's manufactured by my agents in The Pall. These, well, yes, these contain the Casts of people from all over the world. The world. Widdershins… Widdershins has already… it's invaded Deosil. Yes yes. All that's left, all that re… remains is the final steps and, and, of course, publicizing. Yes. Publicizing. Hehe."

"But what if it doesn't work? What if… people die and the world breaks?"

"Oh Kimberly. Kimberly, the world's… the world's already bra-broken. That's why I'm here, why I'm here doing… this. I am trying to fix a future state that can accom… accomodate… that can support us all. If I break a couple of eggs, well, oops. Oops. Heh. The greater good, and all that."

"And this is all because of me? Because I never came back?"

"No. Na-no, not really. Your Cast… she's wrong. Wrong to tell you… you are the main reason. The main cause. She likes… she likes taun*ting* you. Someone else, someone else was… was *switc*hed before you. Don't feel guilty. Don't feel guilty anymore. You're absol…ved. How's that? Hmmm? How's that? Heh."

Kim didn't answer. The madness inherent in this man's speech terrified her in ways she could hardly understand; it was like finding out God was a mental patient.

"Now, I have… I have business. Business to… business elsewhere. Maybe you two… maybe you two can keep each other company? Hmmm?"

The Architect left through the door by which he had entered, and Kim once again found herself alone with her Cast.

"Guess you screwed up pretty bad, huh?"

"How so?" Kim asked, offended.

"You wanted to be human? I mean, I didn't know what I was missing, but you? You knew you had power. Mr. Cruchetti says it's a sin to throw that away."

"Yeah, well, forgive me for not subscribing to the book of

Cruchetti, but did you even listen to him talk? The man's clearly insane. Fried from whatever it is he's done to his brain creating all this… shit."

"It's not how he says it, it's what he says."

"Whatever Widder-kim."

"Wow. Clever. Doesn't bother me though. Mr. Cruchetti says Widdershins and everyone in it are free from time once their other half is killed. So I'm fine with being Widder-Kim. Least I won't age."

"Of course you will."

"Hell-owa? Are you even listening? You don't really think we're going to let you live, do you? I wanna live forever, that means you get to die."

"Jessie'll come for me."

"And we'll kill him too. If he's not dead already. You really think he loves you, don't you?"

"He does!" Kim screamed, suddenly disappointed that she'd let her Double get to her.

"Wow, you are so naive."

"What do you know about love? Your dad didn't even love you, or he wouldn't have allowed this to happen to you. It was his idea."

"Yeah? Well… whatever!"

They sat in silence, brooding on their hatred for one another. After a while, Kim's Cast started in on her again.

"You're hopeless, you know that? Stopped to wonder how you fell for this boy so quickly?"

The underlying subversiveness of the question spurred Kim's interest; she sat up. It took her a minute, and when she did, she noticed for the first time that her former Cast appeared to have no signs remaining of her previous disability.

"Didn't you have… MS or something?"

"I was really sick, but that didn't give you the right to

strand me here. What's the use of getting better if you can't go home? And no fair avoiding the question."

"But it wasn't me! It was your father!"

"He would have undone it! He wanted me back."

"Now who's naive?"

"Shut up!"

"I don't understand what the problem is. Seems to me, you fit right in here."

"Answer the question!"

"You answer mine! What do you mean, about my feelings for Jessie?"

"Oh come on, isn't it obvious? Feel like you've known him a lot longer than you have?"

"Yeah."

"That's because *I've* known him a lot longer. Pretty much since I got to Widdershins."

"But he just woke his Doppelgänger the other night."

"Stupid, your Jessie *is* the Doppelgänger. He's the one that Mr. Cruchetti was talking about, the one that got switched before you did."

When Sheriff Rash arrived at the door to Dubois's house, he set the cans of gas on the porch and took a moment to catch his breath. He wasn't in the best of shape to begin with, so add to that the injury he'd sustained earlier in the night and Rash knew there was absolutely no chance he was going to make it up and down the route he'd just hiked from his car more than the one time.

The door was open, but the rain and cold air felt as though they were the only things keeping him conscious at the moment, so once under the landing, Rash plopped his back against the smooth, marble wall and concentrated on taking deep breaths. It helped, but it also allowed him the luxury of time, and that meant contemplation and self-awareness followed. Neither of these things were conducive to the Sheriff's plans.

Thus far, those plans had pretty much been held up by their bootstraps; he'd committed to it on the fly and used a head-down, no-turning-back approach that now, under duress and forced self-awareness, began to thin like blood in water. As he waited for his body to catch back up to his mind, the Sheriff was forced to take stock of his situation; things did not look good. How was he going to burn down this house - this monster structure - in the middle of a rainstorm with a paltry two cans of gas?

"Not gunna, unless I can find a hell of a lot of something flammable enough to carry the weight," Rash said, and for the first time in years found himself thinking of his late wife, their home and all the things they'd never gotten to do. Irritated and more than a little morose from the nostalgia, Jim took one last breath, pulled his Knight's Side Sheriff Department hat down over his wet, mottled hair and turned to kick the door the rest of the way open while simultaneously lifting the cans of gas, which seemed to have gotten considerably heavier during his brief respite.

When the Sheriff saw that the first room in Dubois's house was filled with shelf after shelf of books, he began to believe his difficulties had all been repelled by fate.

CHAPTER 56

If the little of Dubois's residence Jessie had seen so far unnerved him, then the path to the center of the house was a slow descent into a world of nightmare paranoia and nausea-inducing non-Euclidian geometry. The endless procession of corridors felt as though they moved at right angles to one another, so that at one point he could have sworn they were walking on the ceiling. Cannon-sized spotlights lit the room from obscured sources, so that their little procession's shadows loomed large across the walls and floor. Jessie couldn't help wondering if those shadows still belonged to them, or if instead, they might be spies for the Architect.

"You have'ta keep your eyes on 'em, or they might hurt us," Patty said, seeing Jessie's concern.

"Keep your mouth shut, freakshow. I've got it under control," Cassie retorted.

Patty's lumbering gait kept her several steps behind Jessie, in front of who Cassie stalked tall, slashing the curved blade of her weapon as she led the way, making a show of practicing her killing strokes. The hatred she directed at Patty was palpable, and Jessie wanted desperately to force an exchange between the two that might bring Cassie around to more tolerant behavior.

"What happened to her?" he whispered to Cassie.

"Just shut up and watch your back."

"Yeah, sure. No problem."

Discreetly, Jessie studied Cassie as they walked. She was beautiful, with cutting cheekbones and creamy brown skin that stood in sharp contrast to bright, blonde hair pulled tightly into a ponytail and tied off with silver ribbons. He found himself wondering if Cassie's hair was dyed, or if her mother had perhaps not been the same ethnicity as her father. Then he found himself wondering what the hell he was doing thinking about Cassie when Kim was still missing.

"Whatever..." Jessie hissed under his breath, angry at himself, his situation and his guide.

"Shutting up means not talking at all, okay? Like, even under your breath. I need to concentrate."

"Why do you have to be such a bitch?"

Cassie turned on him with anger.

"You're something, you know that? I'm trying to make sure nothing's sneaking up on us."

"I think Patty has that covered."

"Oh yeah? Then where is she?"

Jessie turned three-sixty; Patty was nowhere to be seen.

"I guess she didn't appreciate being called Freakshow."

"Who cares? Now shut up and let me focus."

While Jessie was grateful that Cassie had arrived when she did, her aggressive, authoritarian manner made him feel extremely vulnerable. He wasn't sure that he could trust her; she seemed too angry. Still, he found it impossible to let things lie as they were. One of Jessie's social downfalls had always been needing others to like him quickly; it was a survival skill subconsciously developed due to the frequency he had moved from school to school. When you move every semester, you either make friends fast or you're alone all the time.

"Hey. I'm sorry if you think I'm trouble."

"Ah! Didn't I just tell you to shut it? I need you to pay attention too, okay?"

"Yeah, well, I can't pay attention if I think you hate me and might go psycho any second."

"Look, I don't hate you, okay? I don't even know you. I just need you to hold your own, and we'll be fine."

"You know, Kim told me about you."

"Let's get one thing straight kid: Kim didn't tell you anything about me. Her Doppelgänger did."

"I know that's how you see it, but-"

Cassie's eyes told Jessie he was skating on thin ice.

"No buts. They're not like us. They *want* what we *have*."

"I think you have her wrong. Kim's different."

"I'm not the one that has anything wrong. That Doppelgänger stole my friend's life out from under her. That sound fair to you?"

"That's not the way Kim says it happened."

"I was there."

Cassie's words worried Jessie; when they found Kim, would she be safe? Was he?

A rolling fog had moved in, clouding the corners of each successive room, as if they were no longer indoors. This nothing-mist replaced solid reality, and with no reference points, their path began to feel like it was moving. It made Jessie think of the rotating hallway scene in Stanley Kubrick's Sci-Fi opus, a film his mother had insisted they watch once a year for as long as he could remember.

It'd been his father's favorite film.

The space around them had dissolved into some kind of tenuous transmission from another plane; a place where the already peculiar spatial relations that lurked everywhere in Gallows Hill took on a vaguely apocalyptic tone. This was the end result of the mad architect's designs - a home that was no longer a home but an alien shore, a way station on the journey to a bleak and deserted afterlife.

Eventually, actual walls came into view again, the new environment narrowing to a point. Ahead the scene was over stimulating; Jessie could see trees, spires jutting from the tops of buildings, mountains, animals of a decidedly hellish species, all perfectly still.

"Where are we?"

"Don't worry," he heard Cassie say, almost a whisper and realized she was just as scared as he was.

The closer they got to it, the more the image expanded, until Jessie realized it was a painting, a massive piece of unbelievably intricate art that took up the entirety of the space around them, floor to ceiling. He tried to understand it, how the painting created the illusion of narrowing the room, of a three-dimensional place instead of a two-dimensional piece of art. The sidewalk artists he'd seen in New Orleans came to mind as he and Cassie literally folded into the context of the scene before them.

"Let me guess, Cruchetti paints too?"

"Gilbranjo, I think. I've only ever read about his work," Cassie said, noticeably humbled.

A hundred feet from the painting the perspective shifted again, and Jessie realized they had now *entered* it. It wasn't a painting, or it was, or…

"I think I'm going to be sick."

"Don't puke on me, dude."

Flowers grew from the walls, large tree branches bent low over them, and the spires of the town's houses rose toward the opaque, glass-like moon in the distance.

"We must be close. I think this is the battery The Hub

runs on; that's its energy making you feel sick. Massive waves of low-frequency reality, cut and spliced, beamed out and returned in a way that, thanks to all the Doubles running around out there, holds these two worlds together."

A moment later the room around them began to spin. Jessie thought he would vomit for sure this time, but before the nausea could take hold, the scene slipped past them, displaced by a bright white sky that stretched out in all directions. For a moment, he saw a truck, a police cruiser, an older man and... Linda? They were surrounded by an army of people, the man apparently keeping the horde at bay with a gun while Linda screamed wordlessly, splashing her arms through the water that rose up around their ankles.

"What the hell is going on?" Jessie asked, but as soon as he did, the image dissolved in an amorphous swell of crackling energy that, when it rolled back, left only a plain, brown door unconnected to anything else.

"What the hell was that?" Cassie asked, gagging.

"It was that woman who saved me, Linda. And an old guy."

"The Sheriff. He's a buffoon."

"It looked like they were in trouble. What the hell is happening? Where are we?"

"I think we're where we need to be. Look."

Following her prompt, Jessie looked closer and saw the number thirteen stenciled onto the face of the door.

"Well then, let's take a look inside..."

He reached for the handle, but before Jessie's flesh even touched the metal knob, the sky above them ripped open, and one reality forced its way into another as four hectic forms fell upon them, a battle already in progress.

CHAPTER 57

"Cassandra has been here. In fact, I think we just missed her."

Elizabeth spoke from a hunched position, studying a thick, black puddle of sludge that lay bubbling on the faded sienna carpet of the small theatre. Since Cassie had run out on them, things had turned dire, with Dubois' allegiance coming more and more into question, and Encarnación distraction with concern for her nieta.

"La Sombra ha venido por niño."

A noise from behind the screen silenced the two women. Elizabeth raised the umbrella that had not left her side, still closed, and stalked toward the elevated wooden stage that divided the movie screen from the floor. She held the accessory as if it was a sword.

The noise appeared to be driving Dubois into a panic: "Something horrible is in this room with us."

"I'll handle it," Elizabeth said, advancing toward another iteration of the noise.

"My dear Ms. Manhattan, I am quite certain you will need more than an umbrella."

Elizabeth ignored Dubois' unsolicited advice. She mounted the stage and found a small trap door in the center of the thin slats of wood. The small service hatch rumbled with a breeze that whistled in from somewhere beneath; standing above it, she could feel a draft periodically surge up from where the door refused to lay flush with the wood, its hinges old and rusted, its boards warped.

"The wind. I'm assuming there's an opening to the outside somewhere down there?"

"I believe that passage is connected to a short tunnel that comes out near the West garage, but honestly I've never been down there. This room originates in a house in Belize. I think…"

"Belize? So your house is no longer just an amalgam of the houses in Gallows Hill."

"It never was."

Elizabeth shared a look with her Bruja before countering: "Mr. Dubois, I've studied the plans for this structure quite extensively. You are lying."

"Studied? As if at University level? I suppose I should be honored."

"Hardly. You've either been lying to us about what you've been up to, or you're still working with Cruchetti. I'm not sure which is more troubling."

Elizabeth straightened her back, raised her right foot and slammed it down on the trap door, forcing it flush.

"No charge for the repair," she said, and smiled.

Dubois opened his mouth to retort but was cut off when the black puddle beside Encarnación emitted a loud POP, then streaked upward in thick, dark stalks. A second later the goo had completely reformed itself into the shape of a man, a man who now towered over Encarnación.

"Mater Tenorio!" Elizabeth leaped from the stage but was too late to stop the reformed monster from backhanding the old woman, sending her crashing into the wall several feet behind her.

"Now wait just a moment!" Dubois shrieked, the Shadow Shape moving to him next. It studied him for a moment, then moved on, retraining Its focus on Elizabeth.

"You better hope that woman is alive and well."

The monster took one look at her umbrella and laughed.

"Who are you supposed to be? Mary Foppins?"

"I'm the bitch that's going to run you through."

"With your umbrella?"

"That's the plan"

"Bring it."

Elizabeth's umbrella was a gift from her predecessor, the Tenorio's original solicitor, Mitchell Hedgewick. Mitchell had, in turn, received it from a certain stage magician the Tenorio family had a long-standing acquaintance with, technically dating back decades before either Elizabeth or Mitchell were born.

Being that her predecessor had jumped ship as soon as he'd learned the true nature of the Tenorio account, Elizabeth was reasonably sure the older, more desk-savvy man had never had a chance to discover the device's unique characteristics. All the better for his exit. When Elizabeth took over the account, she did so with no illusions about what her duties would consist of. As the child of one of said Magician's descendants, Elizabeth knew exactly what she was getting into. As such, she went into the role as "solicitor" with a considerably more hands-on approach and quickly found that she needed every advantage available to her.

This was, of course, the very reason the magician had given Elizabeth's predecessor the weapon in the first place.

The device itself had a central pole-and-rib construction, made entirely of a steel-like alloy specific to Widdershins. One of the same materials Cruchetti had imported for Freighter to use in the construction of the houses in Gallows Hill. Elizabeth had studied this process of importing natural elements from one side of the mirror to the other. She understood it was a tricky endeavor. As with swapping people, there was a balance to be maintained.

The canopy of the umbrella was leather stitched together with barbed-wire, and the finial - or tip - was a sharpened purple diamond, fused from Tenorio glass. Taken together, the effect this weapon could have on a body that originated in Widdershins was catastrophic. When Doppelgängers came through the glass, they remained partially incorporeal. This made them nearly impossible to wound or kill with conventional weaponry. Not true of Elizabeth's Umbrella; the device penetrated their forms in a considerably more ethereal manner, and being made from the same material as the weapon Encarnación had passed down to Cassie, known in the tribe as the Tenorio Blade of Dispersion, Elizabeth's umbrella could dispel a Doppelgänger in a single strike.

She came in low, jabbing the umbrella full strength but missing as the shadow exploded into a mist. Her charge thwarted, Elizabeth tried to change direction but tripped up and tumbled to the floor. She used her momentum though, and rolled straight up over her back in a full somersault, bouncing to her feet in one fluid motion and flicking the switch at the base of the umbrella's rod to fan the canopy to full width. During her endless hours of training with the device, Elizabeth had developed a technique whereby she could loosen her grip sufficiently enough to spin the handle several full rotations in rapid succession without losing her control over it. This created a kind of wind effect that she now employed to prevent her opponent from re-solidifying.

However, the setback only seemed to focus her target's determination. It was with little challenge that, even dispersed as thinly as It was, the WJ-Thing was able to alter Its density from shadow to solid, dropping back down in pieces before Elizabeth, congealing quickly enough to catch her off guard as It lashed out with Its arms, now two long tendrils moving at blinding speed.

That's when the world turned upside down. Literally.

A gnashing wave of staccato force knocked Elizabeth to the ground, and the walls, floor, and ceiling of the room stuttered and dissolved in every direction. It was like watching someone close a massive set of shutters over reality. When she caught her balance, Elizabeth saw they were no longer in the theatre; around them stretched an infinite white fog, below them the house as though they were viewing it upside down through a glass floor. And they were no longer alone; to Liz's surprise Cassie and a boy she immediately understood was Jessie Roberts stood directly below them.

"What the hell just happened? How did you guys find me?"

"Find you?" Elizabeth said mid-parry, "Cassandra, you're going to need to get over yourself. See to your grandmother, she's hurt!"

Elizabeth dodged the Monster's two attacking appendages, now little more than weaponized rubber bent on hammering her to death, "We all ended up here because we're all looking for the same damn thing. Now, how about some help? Your father might be beyond your ability to punish, but killing this thing'll probably feel pretty good, don't you think?"

Watching the WJ Thing attack, a smile spread across Cassie's face. It was the first Jessie had seen from her, and he recognized immediately the fathomless violence that lay beneath it.

"Alright. Let's end this."

CHAPTER 58

"End it? I was just thinking the same thing!"

The WJ Thing's appendages caught Elizabeth around the throat. She thrashed to get away, but the monster flung her from side to side, slamming her into the floor one, two, three times before Cassie leaped in and, with one clean blow from the Blade of Dispersion, severed the limbs completely. The black stalks disappeared like smoke in the wind before they even had a chance to reach the floor.

"You will regret that," It said, growing two new arms and folding its fingers together to crack Its knuckles, the resulting SNAP so loud Jessie thought it sounded like a branch breaking in two.

"Regret is for the weak," Cassie said, and smiled.

Her arrogance was not unfounded. For a sixteen-year-old, Cassie had the skills of a much older fighter, even if her anger often clouded her battle temperament. This is because her training had, for the most part, taken place inside one of the Vetusta Vitriums. As readily available pocket dimensions, the orbs made excellent prisons, but they could also serve as a handy hideout or discrete living quarters. In the years since her father's defection, many of the members of the Tenorio tribe deserted as well. Those left had succumbed to the rapidly diminishing Rain Forests by finding a safe haven inside a Vitrium specially constructed to hold the entirety of their people. It was here Encarnación had brought her granddaughter five years ago, after her father's disappearance and her mother's murder. Inside, time passed differently, and since that last night in Gallows Hill, Cassie had aged mentally and emotionally no less than fifteen years to the five that had passed in Deosil over the same span.

"Press the advantage, Cassie!" Elizabeth called.

"What advantage?" Cassie retorted, ducking out of the skirmish for a moment to check on Encarnación, who had just regained consciousness.

"Abuela!"

To their left, Elizabeth charged their opponent, her umbrella spinning madly, a blade hungering for Shadow Flesh. For a moment, the monster didn't react, just watched the reunion with disgust.

"Cassandra-" the Bruja began but before she could say anything more, the Monster side-stepped Elizabeth's charge, slamming Its foot into her back and forcing her face-first into Jessie, the two colliding in a tangle of fresh bruises and limbs, Jessie just missing being run through by the deadly umbrella. Re-focused, The Thing fired two projectile appendages across the room, straight at Cassie, but at the last second, broke vector and caught Encarnación. Gripping the old woman by the waist and neck, the Thing plucked her from where she lay and effortlessly pulled the old woman apart at the middle, hurling the resulting disparate pieces against the far wall.

The Bruja died without a sound. The look on her face was anything but that of surprise.

"No!" Cassie's rage exploded; she leaped at the murderer

but missed with her blade by a wide arc, her fury bringing her down so hard on the ground that she nearly collapsed from the force. When she recovered, It was already coming back around for another attack. Cassie's anger drove her into a purified state of attention; she dodged the maneuver, turning the creature's charge into a defensive blunder. Using the advantage, she drew back with both hands and cleaved the Monster straight down the middle. Both halves dissipated entirely before they hit the ground.

With the Monster out of the picture, Cassie turned her anger on Dubois.

"You did this!"

Elizabeth turned to Dubois, "She's right. You've been working with that bastard Architect this whole time, haven't you?"

"Ah, well now, guilty as charged," Dubois smiled and produced a handgun from inside his coat. He leveled the weapon at Elizabeth and pulled the trigger. A dark red hole appeared in her forehead even as Elizabeth Manhattan's brains reached escape velocity through the vaporized back of her skull.

"You bastard!" Cassie charged Dubois. She'd only made it three steps before Dubois fired one off at her. Dodging, she slid to the floor. Dubois tracked her through the weapon's sight, but Jessie intervened and slammed into the old man from behind before he could get another shot off.

"You're dead, old man."

"No. He is not," a voice said from above them.

Cassie and Jessie turned toward the ceiling, in time to see their shadows blossom into three-dimensional space, more giant shadow puppets reaching down for them.

"Don't let them catch you, Jessie!" Cassie screamed. But before either could enact a defensive maneuver, the dark shapes coiled around them, squeezing Cassie until the Blade fell from her grip.

Dubois dusted himself off. He snapped his fingers, and Jessie watched two more shadows swim across the floor toward him. When they reached the treacherous billionaire, the dark shapes blossomed into people: one man, one woman. Jessie recognized the latter immediately. It was Linda Evans.

"No one else is dying until we take this brat to the Architect, capiche, Cuthbert?" Linda said.

"Oh, very well. Tell me, is Paolo mad? At me, I mean?"

"Ask him yourself."

Linda winked at Jessie and he knew right away this was her Doppelgänger. As for the man, Jessie had not seen him before. He was tall, and of Hispanic descent, with the familiar air of an academician, complete with patched elbows and ponytail.

"Very well. Take us to him." Dubois said.

"No problem. Hey kid, wanna do the honors?"

"What?" Jessie asked, confused.

"Not you, stupid. Me."

The voice came from behind him, and when he turned, Jessie once again came face to face with his Doppelgänger.

"I've been with you the entire time, dumb ass. That tickle in your ear? Me."

The world rippled with indeterminacy and anger. The Double still had Richard's blood on his hands.

"I'm here to take you to the Architect."

He was surprised at how fast the flames spread from the books to the walls. It seemed to Jim Rash that Cuthbert Dubois's house *wanted* to burn.

"Lord's work. Amen."

Rash turned and walked out of the house, back down the driveway in the rain. There were more houses to get to, and the Sheriff figured he'd start with the one owned by his second favorite weirdo in town: Bob Freighter.

"Where's Jessie hon?"

"Hmmm? Oh, I don't know. He's around here somewhere."

WJ listened to Talia's distracted answer and knew she was lying. The question was, why?

"Talia, since when are you not concerned about Jessie when he's out at... what time is it, anyway? Why am I so discombobulated?"

WJ raised his arm, but the face of his watch blurred whenever his eyes touched it; same with the one on the microwave and the one on the face of Talia's phone, which lay face up on the table in front of her, beside a small compact mirror she had consulted ceaselessly for the past several hours.

'Hours?' WJ thought to himself, unable to account for how long it had been since he'd come up from the basement. Whenever he thought about time, he found he couldn't put a finger on what day it was, what time it was, or how long any exchange or task took as he moved forward. It was as though he were trapped behind the second hand on a clock.

"Did you say something, Wendall?" Talia looked at him, distracted but smiling. WJ felt himself slide back into the smooth flow of complacency. This is what he wanted: family. People for who he could be dependable. People he could depend on. People who...

There was a knock at the basement door, and Talia's face twisted into a grimace.

"Who's that?"

"Well, um, it would have to be Jessie, wouldn't it?"

Simple, but Talia's face told him she didn't agree. There was a second series of knocks, these considerably more frantic, and to defuse his own unease, WJ went to open the door. Talia's chair made loud, screeching protest as she slammed it backward, the worn-rubber stoppers no hope in silencing her anxiety.

"Wendall, don't open it!"

"Don't be silly," he said, perplexed at her panic. Smiling, WJ turned and opened the basement door, only to find himself face to face with another Talia Roberts, this one covered in crimson gore.

When Chase came to, the pain from his shoulder almost caused him to pass back into unconsciousness. He'd had his share of broken bones in his life, but this... this was crippling. As such, it took him a fair amount of time to gather the strength to stand, let alone start down the corridor in the direction he was pretty sure the party had moved. One hand on the wall for balance, each step made the splinters of bones in his shoulder grind against one another.

The pain was excruciating.

As his body deteriorated, his mind sharpened. Any attempt at keeping events 'chronological' had left the table about the time his head slammed against his dashboard. But chronology felt less important than certain more… ethereal elements that had overtaken him. Slouching against the wall as he moved deeper into Dubois' home, Chase reiterated a number of these elements to himself, all of them bearing more than a passing resemblance to the nightmarish images he had taken away from Arthur Tenorio's house five years ago:

A scream ripped through the halls. Chase ran faster, caught and passed Cuthbert…

…the hall snaked left and then right, then left once more. Sweat stung his eyes…

Chase approached the mirror, unnerved that, in the glass face he saw no reflection…

… He touched the glass and it rippled like the water in a pond…

… The girl appeared before him, slammed into the glass from the other side. Startled, Chase jerked backward, raised his weapon without even thinking about it, then misstepped and landed on his ass. Dazed, he watched the girl open and close her mouth. Wide. She was screaming.

…Chase's reflection had emerged and without realizing, he shot it, once, right through the heart, the bullet passing through the glass like water. His reflection opened its mouth, fell to its knees…

Chase remembered how he and Dubois had argued tooth and nail about the girl. Dubois had been adamantly against the only sane course of action Chase could think to suggest: 911. In the end, Chase relented in light of further unnatural complications. Shortly after rescuing her from the mirror, Kimberly had begun to lose her physical definition, her limbs turning a shadowy black as Chase dragged her past the sconces in the corridor that lead through the misplaced foyer of Arthur's home and out into the night.

"A living shadow," he said out loud now.

That night was the first time Chase ever confronted in

the flesh the ideas that turned his father into the town fool. Leviticus Montgomery believed in and hunted shadowy figures, had outlined several local conspiracy plots that centered around such entities, and swore up and down that Gallows Hill did not exist in the same dimension the rest of the world did. A pocket universe, that was what his Dad had called it. And while everyone in town knew Leviticus as the friendly owner of Gulliver's, they also knew him as a man whose idea of a good time was stalking the woods at night looking for the boogeyman.

As Leviticus's children, Nancy and Chase fought their father's ideas tooth and nail. They had to in order to pull their reputations out from under their father's. When Chase first joined the GHAS and began his association with Cuthbert, he heard the way the group talked and immediately took on the role of skeptic, something everyone welcomed. Everyone except Dubois.

Even Linda, initially another purveyor of healthy if not absolute skepticism, eventually succumbed to the idea that her abuse at the hands of Bob Freighter was something supernatural. Chase refused to acknowledge this, tried to get her to see such ideas as defense mechanisms to cope with the real trauma. Linda, in turn, took this as a slight on Chase's part and this was, he supposed, the reason their relationship remained unacknowledged despite her missing husband and their one night of intimacy. He'd never understood how much his dismissal had hurt her until now. As Chase fought his way down the hallway in Dubois' mansion, he became a believer. What's more, in light of what had happened at the hospital earlier in the night, and in spite of meeting WJ's Doppelgänger, Chase realized everything happening now had its origins in that night, five years before.

Chase figured he had a lot to atone for.

Up ahead he saw Linda lying bloody and broken, her

body slumped against the wall like a sack of potatoes. He turned to gauge how far he had come and noticed the thick cloud of smoke that had filled the hallway behind him. Chase began to cough, and his eyes started to burn. He looked back to Linda, and that was when he spotted the first licks of flame consuming the ceiling above her. Pushing through the pain, Chase headed in her direction and prayed he wasn't too late.

CHAPTER 60

The moment he saw Talia on those stairs leading up from the basement, WJ remembered everything: the message board on eldritchmirrormage.com, Bob Freighter's psychotic attack in the driveway, Dean Stanisberg's tale about the Barker family, and Jessie calling him from the basement. WJ's memories ended with his reflection reaching through the mirror for him...

Before he could say anything, the blood-soaked Talia collided with his center mass, sending them both sprawling to the floor. Eyes open as he fell, WJ watched as the other Talia stumbled over their falling forms in mid-swing with a very large butcher knife. It seemed choreographed: Talia hit him, they hit the floor and tripped the blade yielding Talia, in effect foiling an attempt on her part to turn WJ's head into a sovereign nation. The momentum from her swing and the severity of her stumble sent the homicidal twin face first to the floor, where she writhed in a partially conscious state. WJ stared at his Talia in disbelief.

"Talia... what... what happened? My god, you're covered in blood!"

Jessie's mother breathed a hearty sigh of relief and smiled at him, "Don't worry. It's not mine."

As soon as Sheriff Rash hit Rune Road, he saw the flames in the distance. The night sky in Gallows Hill passed into total darkness as the plume of roiling smoke that spiraled from the burning houses choked the moon from the sky, the orange and yellow flames frolicking at the structure's base and out into the surrounding trees. They were all on fire. Every house in town. How?

A muffled voice crackled indiscernibly over the speaker of his walkie talkie.

"Betty? That you?"

Nothing.

"Goddamnit. Is anyone out there?"

A sound. Faint at first, then growing louder. Bolder. It was laughter. The voice had Betty's high register - she sometimes sounded like a chipmunk - but unlike Betty's voice there was a malevolence present, expressed through an unnerving cadence the Sheriff experienced as pinpricks in his eardrum. The voice sounded… *tainted*, as though multiple people were speaking with the same vocal cords.

"You're not gonna be able to leave, Sheriff. We've taken steps to prevent that. But if you want me to send someone to help you, I can do that no problem."

Rash slammed the walkie down and pulled to the side of the road beside the blazing ruins nestled at the corner of Rune and Derleth. He looked to the sky beyond and saw more smoke. He recognized the voice.

"It can't be. It just goddamned cannot be."

Memories surged, triggering emotions that paralyzed him with cognitive dissonance.

"Gotdamnit Jim. You've really done it this damn time…" the voice said from the other end of the line. Close, but infinitely far away.

Another moment and the top-most spire on the Barker house crumbled like a pack of matches cast into an incinerator. The structure began to fall inward, the flame-engulfed lower floors stealing the majesty of those on top. Seeing the destruction, something new occurred to Jim.

"Jee-zuz!" The Sheriff shifted the cruiser back into gear and jammed his foot down on the gas. The big, L4 threaded tires spun violently for a moment, kicking up rocks in their wake as the Sheriff turned a complete one-eighty and headed back the way he had come. Something about seeing Barker's house come apart made Jim Rash remember passing Chase Montgomery's vehicle on the side of the road when leaving Dubois'. It'd also prompted him to remember that he had ordered Chase to take the eccentric billionaire home after everything went nuts at the hospital, and those two facts combined meant Rash had just set fire to a house that his deputy was still inside.

~

Breathless from the smoke, Chase crawled to where Linda lay unconscious. When he reached her, he tried to speak her name, but all that came from his mouth was a dry, raspy gurgle. The smoke was rapidly depleting their oxygen, and in the condition they were in, it would only be a matter of moments before they slipped from consciousness into whatever blasted abomination waited for them on the other side.

"Luis? Luis, I'm sorry. I don't love you… I love Chase…." Linda said, her eyes unopened, seeing only what her delirium told her to see.

In spite of their situation, Chase smiled. It was all that he had the strength for before he rolled over onto his back beside his love and maneuvered his hand into hers. Linda's eyes opened and Chase saw understanding return to them. They smiled in unison and lay still, all pretense dissolving in the white-hot flames of fate.

Then, a voice.

"Chase Montgomery, get yer gotdamn ass up! We don't have much time!" Despite his pain and exhaustion, Chase's eyes popped wide at the sound. His vision swam at first, only the faintest outline of the man he would have least expected to see moving toward him.

"Sheriff?"

"Who else? Now c'mon, help me get her up and-" that was the last thing Chase heard before he slipped into unconsciousness.

CHAPTER 61

Just as Chase's surprise had failed to overcome his pain and disorientation, Linda's was exactly what she needed to snap back into coherence. Something about the gruff, antagonistic voice of the Sheriff drove a spike of adrenaline into her, and she flopped up and onto her feet before she was even aware of what she was doing.

"Sheriff… we have to get out of here…"

"No shit," Rash had a handkerchief held against his nose and mouth, lowered them long enough to deliver a mission statement.

"Help me get him outta here, then we'll worry about everything else. Whole damned town is on fire!"

They reached down together and lifted Chase. Even unconscious, he howled in pain as Linda hoisted him by the arm with the destroyed shoulder; there was no time for being gentle, this was life or death on the spot.

As soon as they had Chase stabilized, Linda realized she had no idea what part of Dubois' house they were in. The smoke had become too thick, and the building itself had shifted around them. Without Dubois by her side to navigate,

Linda knew they had no hope of retracing their original steps.

"Over there!" the Sheriff yelled through the rag, "There's an open door at the end of this hall. That way."

Knowing there was no guarantee the door would take them to safety, Linda embraced the idea of fate and helped Sheriff Rash carry Chase toward the door.

CHAPTER 62

"You're me."

"No. *You're* me."

Nothing Jessie had experienced since beginning this insane adventure could have prepared him for what it felt like to stand this close to his exact copy. It was life-affirming and horrific at the same time. Looking at his Double, Jessie felt a primal urge to attack it, to kill this imposter. Thinking back to Richard's crash course in the mythology of these beings, he realized this must have been an innate survival instinct. But he thought of his mother, somewhere just ahead of him in the clutches of the Mad Architect Paolo Cruchetti, and he knew he had to play along.

For now.

"The Architect is waiting for you."

Jessie's Doppelgänger led him through the door marked "13", with Cassie, Dubois, Doppel-Linda and her ponytailed friend close behind. Dubois walked with his gun trained on Cassie's back, but Jessie could see she was tense, no doubt waiting for her moment. A look passed between them that told Jessie Cassie would be relying on him when she made her move. He just hoped she understood it would have to be *after* they found Kim and his mom.

Through the door, they emerged into a large room lined with shelves, upon which sat hundreds of glass orbs, no bigger than snow globes. From somewhere nearby, Jessie could hear pounding, like someone was trying to get their attention. He forgot all about this, though, the moment Kim Corduroy stepped from the shadows. She had changed clothes, was now wearing jeans and a forest green sweater, a cheap pair of over-sized, movie star sunglasses pinched tight at the bridge of her nose.

"Kim!" Jessie ran to her. They embraced with a newfound passion; Kim kissed him deeply, uncaring who watched.

"Oh baby, you feel so good! I can't believe we were apart that long."

Something was different. Kim's eagerness had been replaced by a more aggressive tact; she ran her hands over his body, kissed his chin, neck, and ears. Despite the incongruence, Jessie could not pull away.

"I was so worried," was all he could say, knowing it was an exaggeration. He'd been so caught up in everything else, in Freighter, and Linda, and now the revelation his mother was a prisoner, that he'd barely had time to think of Kim. And in truth, there was a pocket of disappointment from her pushing him off Freighter's balcony, not because of his resultant injuries, but because once again, Kim hadn't trusted him to hold his own.

"I've got such plans for you," she said into his ear. Her smile became dark, lascivious.

"Kim, they have my mom."

"I know! That's what I was gonna tell you It's okay. Your mom's okay."

"You saw her?" Jessie's eyes lit up with hope in spite of an uneasy feeling in his gut.

"No, but I know where she is. It's okay. Richard was worried for nothing. Everything the Architect has done has been one hundred percent within the boundaries of their Accord."

"One hundred percent untrue, Doppelgänger," Cassie said, "And Richard's dead."

"Dead? What the hell would you know?"

"Kim," Jessie cut in, taking her hand, "She's right. I saw him die."

The gravity of the situation seemed lost on Kim. Instead, her ire for Cassie took over.

"Jessie, what the hell are you doing with *her*?"

"She saved me, Kim. Me and your… oh."

"What?"

"Your sister. Patty. She saved us both, but then I kind of lost her."

"You lost my sister?"

"That monster is the least of your worries, bitch. There's a body count a mile long littering the trail behind us, and as far as I'm concerned, everyone in this room is going to be held responsible."

"Keep your hands off him!" Kim screamed. She rushed at Cassie, tackled her to the floor. They began to tear at one another like animals. Unable to keep tabs on Cassie in the melee, Dubois lowered his gun, and that was Jessie's cue. He moved to slam into the old man again, but this time his Doppelgänger stopped him with a swift right hook to the side of the head. The room spun for a moment and then Jessie was on his ass, his Double standing over him in triumph.

"No way I'm letting you break up this cat fight, bro."

"I'm not your 'bro.'"

"I'm everything you wish you could be. Charming, cunning, and deadly."

"You got the wrong guy. I'm happy as I am."

"We'll see."

The Double smiled, not seeing that behind them, Cassie had gained the upper hand. She rolled on top of Kim and began battering her with closed fists.

"STOP!" The voice boomed all around them, an echo that ate the sky.

Cassie paused mid-punch, stunned as a man emerged from the wall before her. No door this time, it was as if he simply manifested from the material of the house. As he shimmered into corporeality, Jessie saw that he had a round, tan face, and wore dark pants and a collared shirt with faded white-and-blue strips. On his head, a green banker's visor obscured a receding hairline. Smiling, he approached Jessie with a smile and offered him his hand.

"Jessie Roberts, I am Paolo. Paolo Cruchetti. Yes, that is me."

CHAPTER 63

As Sheriff Rash struggled to fit Chase into his police cruiser, Linda watched Dubois's house burn. The fire crawled so high into the sky that it appeared to cast shadows on the moon, and it looked to Linda like what was left of the rain was bending around those flames, avoiding them altogether. It was as if some Prime Mover watching over the scene *wanted* Dubois' house to burn. And for the first time, she felt as though she agreed wholeheartedly with whatever force might be controlling the Universe.

"Did you say the entire town is on fire?"

"Yes! Now buckle up. Roads'r gonna be bad, don't need you smacking your head, you already look like you've been in a fist fight with a bulldozer."

Linda smiled and stepped up into the vehicle. How was a safety belt a concern after all she'd been through?

"You're one to talk."

The Sheriff popped the truck into drive and cut a slow half-circle, then headed back out onto Bauble. A quarter mile and they'd be on Eeryx, and soon after, the Turnpike.

As they drove, Linda stared out the window unseeing,

dozens of images washing through her mind. Images that made no sense here, in the cold light of the moon.

A voice warbled in over the static on the radio and surprised both of them.

"Sheriff Rash? This is Ted Parsons at Woodsville Sheriff's station, you copy?"

"Parsons? Thank the lord. Tried to contact you earlier but there was interference. Over."

"It's the storm. There's some nasty lookin' smoke coming from your direction, wanted to be sure everything's okay. Couldn't reach Betty at the station, and there's reports that, well, huh, not sure how to say this or even if I should. Sounds kinda crazy."

"Been a crazy night, Ted."

"Well, people calling sayin' they can't get into Knight's Side, that there's some kinda invisible wall around the whole thing. I was gonna send an officer out to look, but thought I should check with you first. Over."

Rash and Linda looked at one another, chills turning their healing moment of camaraderie to terror.

"Ted! Lissen, you gotta get me back-up. I can't explain what's happenin', but I need ambulances, fire trucks, and cops! State if you can get 'em."

"Jim! You're cutting out. Look, my stations getting calls from people about disappearances. A lot of them. Do you need -"

Parson's concern disappeared in an electronic hiss, and the Sheriff was left on the precipice of an internal apocalypse. An invisible wall around Knight's Side? Disappearances? He clicked over and tried the hospital switchboard, received the same pops and squarks he'd heard as a kid, when he used to play with his father's Marine Band radio.

"This is Sheriff Rash. Is anyone reading me?"

Nothing.

"Jim, this is insane. What the hell do we do? If Chase doesn't get medical attention soon-"

"Hold on tight, that's what you do. I'm going to get us to the hospital, then I'm going to find out just what the hell's going on."

The rain had stopped, but a thick white fog had rolled in, obscuring everything but the small patch of road directly in front of them. Rash squinted with concentration as he brought the truck up to eighty miles-an-hour, taking the roads by pure intuition. When they exited onto the Turnpike, things got a little better, but Parson's words echoed in Jim's head. He tried to remember what Terry had said to him earlier, about a construction crew burying boxes on the outskirts of town.

"Shit," Rash said, remembering Terry's disappearance, juxtaposing it with the voice on the walkie earlier.

"Can't be. Just can't," he said out loud, not meaning to.

"Huh?" Linda asked, watching Chase over the back of her seat.

"How's our guy?"

"He looks stable, but for how long I wouldn't want to say. Oh, Chase…"

"Love him, dont'cha?"

Linda's initial outrage at Rash's question died the moment she saw the smile on his face: it was heartfelt and sincere, and it told her what she should have already known. Namely, that everyone else already knew how she felt about Chase, so why hadn't she?

"Chase is tough," she said, wiping a tear from her eye.

"Stubborn as all hell, too-"

"STOP!!!" Linda screamed suddenly, instinctively reaching for the wheel. They'd both been too rapt in the moment to see the people in the road until it was too late.

Rash slammed on the brakes and the cruiser careened off the road and into a thicket of trees.

The scene went dark, for how long neither of them knew. Then things began to flicker. At first, Linda thought it was lightning, but when her vision returned enough for her to take in their position, she saw Rash, winded but unharmed. Same for her; the Sheriff's insistence on her safety belt had seemed asinine earlier, but turns out it had saved her life.

"What the gotdamn hell?" Rash said, staring at the dozens of figures spilling from the trees that surrounded the road, coming directly for them, their inhuman eyes glowing with darkness.

He turned the key. Nothing.

"Sheriff?"

He turned the key again. Still nothing.

"Sheriff, you have to get this truck moving now."

"I'm trying, case you hadn't noticed."

He turned the key again. Nothing.

"Sheriff…"

"Gotdamnit, I know! What difference's it gonna make, anyway? 'Case you hadn't noticed, they're blocking the road."

Rash turned the key one final time. Nothing.

"Oh my god… is that Abel Crosse? And Frank Keith?"

"I think we just found our missing persons."

The Sheriff didn't respond. His face was bleached white, his mouth open wide with shock.

Directly in front of them, leading the mass of ghostly Knight Siders, was Declan O'Rourke.

CHAPTER 64

"Paolo!"

From Dubois's mouth, the name sounded angelic. The billionaire ran to his erstwhile lover and the two men embraced, exchanged a passionate kiss of reunion and renewal.

"I'm sorry I backed out on you. I just... I just couldn't..."

"Bertie, you don't have to explain. You don't have to. You know me. You know me and that everything I've done, everything I've done... has been for us. Yes. Heh."

Cruchetti turned to address the rest of the room, "Now. Hello. A big hello. It's always nice to... it's always nice to meet new people. Yes. Hmmm. But can we, can we maybe, maybe we can all just sit down and talk to one another... talk to *each other*... before anyone else is killed. Please? Yes. I mean... you people think I'm the... you think I'm the bad guy, but together... you've killed more people in one night than I have in... well, more than I have in my entire life. And I've had a long life! Yes, a long life."

"You've gotta be kidding me?" Cassie said, "Look Cuckoo

Clock, I killed one Doppelgänger, you've taken both my Great-Grandmother and Elizabeth from me, kidnapped Jessie's mom, who knows what else."

"Not me. No. Uh-ah. No mam. I can't be held responsible for the actions of… the actions of the Pall."

"You make it sound like you're *not* the one pulling their strings, organizing them."

Cruchetti chuckled, a sound of pure madness.

"My dear… my dear Cassandra. I may have been the man who set the more… the more indus*trious* inhabitants of Widdershins… I set them on their path. I most certainly do not, no, not at all, I do not condone or participate in their more… radi*cal*ized activities. No. Uh-ah. I am simply a… simply a businessman… a businessman trying to launch the greatest invention in human history. Yes. In human history. And the Pall… the Pall are my most passionate investors."

"Investors?"

"Time. Energy. Resource. Capital… capital is overrated when your soul mate… when your soul *mate* is a…" Cruchetti turned his head to defer to Dubois, "Cuthbert? Millionaire? Or… have you… have you finally crossed the line to B-billionaire? Hmmm?"

"Paolo! You know I do not like to brag."

"Wow. You two are something else. Talk about your privileged Western male. Everyone holds the 'Mad Architect' in this mystical regard, like you're some legend. But really you're just another bullshit conman with tourettes, or whatever."

"My dear, there is no need to be crude. Business such as ours takes its toll on the body *and* the mind. You would do well to remember that," Dubois hissed.

"Oh shut up. You're inconsequential; it's your money that's important, not you."

Cruchetti winced at this, put his arm around Dubois as if to shield him from the comment. Jessie noticed he gave an almost imperceptible nod to Linda's Double and without warning, she stepped forward and caught Cassie by the ponytail, pulled on it hard enough to bring her to her knees. But something unexpected happened as Cassie hit the floor; the Double cried out, violently recoiling. It took a moment for Jessie to put the pieces together, but watching the blood pour from Doppel-Linda's hands he got it.

The ribbons he'd noticed earlier in Cassie's hair. They weren't ribbons at all. They were razors.

"You bitch!" the Double shrieked in pain, dropping Cassie's weapon and focusing all her energy on containing the bleeding. Amidst her screams, the room fell into confusion, and beneath its cover, Cassie threw Jessie a wink: she was making her move now, ready or not.

And then all hell broke loose.

Cassie ran head-on at Pony Tail, snatching her blade from the floor as she went, then driving it straight through the man's chest. Luis' Double dissipated in a cloud of black particles before he even had a chance to scream.

Across the room, Dubois fired his weapon at Cassie but missed. Seeing this, Jessie pushed away from Kim and leaped into the fray. He smacked the gun from Dubois' grip just in time to send his second shot wide. There was a moment where they stood face to face, young man and old man, and then Jessie surprised himself by popping Dubois in the mouth, knocking him backwards into the wall. Another bullet disappeared with a ricochet as Cuthbert stumbled and fell, sending the gun sliding away only to stop in front of Jessie. Battering back his uncertainty, Jessie stooped to grab the weapon, but at that moment someone caught him around the neck in a stranglehold.

"No!" he screamed, thrashing against his attacker. Their grip was strong, but Jessie managed to twist loose enough that, from the corner of his eye, he saw it was Kim who had him by the throat.

"What the hell are you doing?" Jessie asked through gasps for air, unable to comprehend her actions. His thrashing grew more violent, until he loosened her grip enough that his elbow came up and caught Kim in the side of the head, knocking the sunglasses from her face. As soon as Jessie saw her eyes, he understood how he'd been fooled. Her eyes were normal. This wasn't his Kim; it was her Cast. The one that was supposed to be dead.

~

As it happened, Patty had not abandoned Jessie, after all. Kept in captivity for five years, her newfound freedom had taught Patty that, despite the cumbersome size of her new body, she was capable of wondrous things because of it. So when she realized Cassie didn't like her anymore, Patty loosed her thoughts and let her body fade. No more than an outline, she stayed behind the other two, undetectable as part of the shadows. Cassie and Jessie weren't paying any attention to her anyway, so Patty decided to be very quiet and simply watch.

Alone in the shadows, she thought of that faraway day in Cassie's house. All Patty had wanted to do was play with her dolls. When she'd gone into the kitchen and found the door to the basement open, that was the beginning of the bad time.

Terrible flat, black hands snared her, pulling her down the stairs like a strong wind, through the mirror to the place where the floor moved like snakes.

"Now Patagonia, I want you to be a brave little girl," a voice said from the shadows.

Before her, Kim lay unconscious, another Kim standing over her, frightened. The Kim on the floor shook, and white foam dribbled from the side of her mouth.

"Your sister is very sick, but we can fix her, Patty. Only we'll need your help. Will you stay here to help her?"

Patty could see a man in the shadows now, no more than a dark shape amid a darker background; she couldn't see his face, but she recognized his voice.

"She's not deaded, is she?"

"No. But she needs your help. Will you help your sister? So she can get well again?"

"Y...yes," Patty answered, so scared she wet her pants.

"Then right this way, young lady. And may I commend you on your bravery. Kimberly could not have asked for a better sister."

The man stepped from the shadows; it was Cassie's father. As soon as Patty saw him, a voice in her head screamed:

"RUN!"

She turned to do just that, but something caught her, dragged her kicking and screaming into a round room made entirely of glass.

That was the last time Patagonia Barker saw the outside world until her sister's Double freed her several hours earlier.

In the here and now, Patty kept up with Jessie and Cassie, watching how they acted toward one another. She wasn't used to seeing people or the way they interacted. She was afraid she would do or say something to make them mad. She felt very self-conscious, and even if Jessie was Kim's boyfriend now, she knew he was scared of her. Because Patty knew she wasn't like him anymore. She was a monster.

When they arrived at the room with the glass spheres, Patty recognized it immediately. It was the place where she'd been held prisoner, where Kim had freed her only to be captured in return. So while everyone else was distracted, Patty followed the path she remembered, hoping to find and release Kim.

But there were so many of the orbs, and all of them had people inside. How could she know which one held Kim?

CHAPTER 65

"You're not Kim!" Jessie shrieked and finally broke free of her hold.

"Don't be ridiculous. The other one's not Kim. *I'm* the original."

"Richard said you were dead."

"A lie he used to absolve himself of guilt. Richard could have come after me; instead, he took *her* side, decided he'd try and see what would happen if he let her stay and grow up in Deosil."

"No way! Richard would never do that."

"You really are an easy one to fool, you know that? You think there's any 'good guys' here?"

"Don't listen to her, Jessie!" Cassie yelled as she took Doppel-Linda's head off with one smooth arc of her blade. Both the head and the body dissipated before they hit the ground. All subordinates exorcized, Cassie squared up to take on the Big Boss.

"Paolo Cruchetti! I have come to exact revenge for the Tenorio tribe. Prepare to meet your maker, little man. My vengeance will be free of mercy!"

"Teenagers," Cruchetti quipped, "always so dramatic. Yes. Dramatic. Ha!"

"How's this for dramatic, nutbag?" Cassie said and lunged forward, letting her blade fly. Both Cruchetti and Dubois flinched violently, but to their surprise, they were not Cassie's target.

That was Kim.

The blade pierced her chest with a loud CRUNCH, and Kim's body went limp. However, now it was Cassie's turn to be surprised, as Kim didn't disintegrate like the others. Instead, a thin stream of blood ran from her mouth, down her chin as she stood slack-jawed in awe.

"You… idiot. I'm not… the Double…" she said before she fell to the floor, dead.

Shocked by the image of Kim's death, it took Jessie a moment to compartmentalize the scene for what it was. When he did, he knew he had precious little time to save Cruchetti's life, or he may never see *his* Kim again. With this in mind, Jessie snatched Cassie's blade from Kim's lifeless body. The sound it made as it slid free of her ribcage caused him to gag.

"Don't touch that!" Cassie screamed.

"Where's my Kim?" Jessie demanded of Cruchetti, waving the blade back and forth between him and Cassie, trying to sell the idea he would use it on anyone who got in his way, "And where the hell is my mom?"

"Well well. Now, if you… if you kill *us*, you'll never know. You'll never find your mom, will you? Hmmm? No. I think not. Hahaha." Cruchetti gloated, well aware he retained the upper hand.

"Jessie! Give me my blade. Now!" Cassie screamed from behind him. Chaos seemed very close, and Jessie felt like it might be the manifestation of the Architect's mind, made palpable by their surroundings.

"No! Not until my mom and Kim are safe. Don't think I won't kill you, too. You knew they were in danger and you didn't even care. Now I'm calling the shots!"

"Well played. Yes. Well played, Jessie. Yes. I will do… I will do as you *ask*."

"You will?"

"I will. Yes. Uh-huh. If you follow me… if you follow me into my office, Yes. If you do, I can produce your mother, and her friend… her friend the professor. And Kimberly… I can produce them all within only a few minute's time. Yes, a few minutes. Really. They are all… inside my Double V's, the Pall's Double V's. Housed inside Vetusta Vitriums. I need only send my… I need only send my most trusted man. Yes. Uh-huh."

"You're not really really going to trust Humper-doo here, are you?" Cassie asked.

"Does it look like I have a choice?" Jessie retorted, still poised as though he might strike any one of them dead at a moment's notice. Around them, the tension grew thicker, made everyone's actions and reactions more pronounced. Madness filled the air; Jessie thought he could taste it on his tongue, a bitter, metallic flavor that made his head swim.

"Oh please, Cassandra! You are worse than your father," Dubois said, reclaiming his pistol and aiming it once again at Cassie, a smile slipping over him as he leveled the weapon at her head.

"Bang. Just like your friend."

Cassie seethed with hatred, but there was nothing she could do.

"Okay then. Right. We're ready? Yes? Then all of us, let's go. Yes. This way, to the other side. Yes. Heh-heh."

One by one, they followed the Architect through the final door, their minds swimming in the wake of his madness.

CHAPTER 66

They stood in a simple office. The walls were wood panels mostly obscured by bookshelves lined with dusty tomes. Between these, a system of exposed copper piping ran vertically up the wall and then crisscrossed the ceiling. Similarly, the floor was revealed as long, thin slats of dark paneling where it peeked out from beneath a series of colored, uneven rugs. In the exact center of the room was a modest drawing table on top of which balanced several precarious stacks of paper, beside that a tall, brass lamp and its red shade created an eerie glow that reminded Jessie of Richard's living room. As a whole, it was not difficult for Jessie to picture this environment as the lair of an architect from the forties or fifties, before computer-aided drafting made sketching archaic. As Cruchetti spoke to them, he situated himself on the stool behind the table, picked up a sharpened number two pencil and began to work.

"I know. I know what you're thinking. What you're thinking. Outdated. Curmudgeon. Yes. Well, I am guilty. Guilty on both counts. Yes. I confess. In my designing, I prefer to do things… the old fashioned way. It helps me to… fudge the edges. Yes. Fudge the edges, so to speak. Uh-huh."

Seeing him in this environment, Jessie thought Cruchetti had the air of a Norman Rockwell painting. His hair was thinning, a sandy blonde that made him look washed out, unreal. The flesh of his face was etched and wrinkled where hours of heavy thought had left their mark. He seemed physically fragile but still managed to exude a sense of authority. As he spoke, Cruchetti adjusted the green eyeshade he wore on the front of his head; the stereotypical accouterment of one who spends hours studying tiny figures by incandescent lights. Behind the desk, the lamp popped and futzed once and then dimmed briefly, only to return at a stronger wattage. In the far corner, a small round table stood about three feet from the ground. On it, a tray of steaming mugs brought the delightful aroma of Earl Grey tea into the room.

"I can bend time and space. Yes. I can do that, but I can't seem to access… I can't seem to get pure 120-volt Alternating Current. Nope. Not in this new world of mine. But, uh-huh, don't worry my boy. No. I'm not stalling. Not stalling at all. Someone is fetching your mother and your girl as we speak. As. We. Speak. In the meantime… in the meantime… help yourself to some… have some refreshments. Yes. Please?"

"Refreshments?" Dubois parroted, practically drooling. He motioned with the pistol and Jessie's Doppelgänger produced a pair of handcuffs and shackled Cassie to the pipes furthest from them.

"Jessie!" she practically pleaded. Jessie looked away, unwilling to stop Cassie's restraint.

"Yes, Cuthbert. Yes. Tea. Oh, and… and I happen to have those tasty little biscuits… the ones you love so much. I have those, too. Yes."

"The ones shaped like trumpets?" Dubois sounded like a

child. With Cassie now subdued, Jessie noted the billionaire set his gun on the table before falling on the refreshments.

Cruchetti nodded.

"You always think of everything, Paolo!" Dubois complimented through a mouthful of biscuits. Watching Dubois eat, Jessie realized for the first time in what felt like days that he was famished. Uneasy but necessary, he approached the table and helped himself to the Architect's hospitality, his good hand still brandishing Cassie's blade.

Once he began eating, Jessie found it nearly impossible to stop.

"Before we begin… before we start, Jessie, I would like to assure you… I assure you that your mother and her friend are both unharmed. Unharmed. Yes. Also, might I add… might I add, they are very much looking forward to seeing you. Yes. Just as soon as we close the door on all this… as soon as we finish up with all the Doppelgänger business."

"No changing the deal! You said you were bringing them!"

"Yes. Yes, I am. I am, but think about it. How safe do you think Kimberly will be… how safe is she around this one? Hmmm?" Cruchetti indicated Cassie with a nod of his head.

He knew Cruchetti was right. What's more, based on Cassie's strength and behavior, Jessie entertained no illusions that a simple pair of handcuffs would prevent her from avenging her tribal honor.

"What about my mom?"

"Just outside that door. Yes. Just outside."

"In the room we were just in?"

"I thought it best to keep her… best to keep your mother and her friend… together. Yes. Together inside a Vestusta Vitrium, one of the pocket dimensions. The Double V's."

"He's lying to you, Jessie! How can't you see that? He's twisting my actions so -"

"Ach! *Twist*ing your actions, Cassandra. Please! I'm sure…

I'm sure that after witnessing your display of... your uncon*troll*able blood lust, Jessie doesn't need my two cents... doesn't need me to see how dangerous *you* are."

Cruchetti was right.

"Jessie, when things... when things began to go a bit... when things went crazy... with Robert, and... yes, well, I wanted to make sure you and your family... I wanted to make sure you were all safe. I wanted to do the same for you and Kim... *your* Kim - that is. Safe. But you proved... well, you proved very adept at thwarting... at undermining me at every turn. Yes. Every. Turn. So I... so I had to bring your Cast into the mix. Yes."

"My Cast?'"

Cruchetti blushed, sipped from his mug as if for strength.

"Oh my. Oh my oh my oh my. In all this time, in all this time, has no one managed to tell you? Hmmm? No one?"

"Tell me what?"

Cruchetti looked to Dubois.

"Do not look at me! Paolo, I have had my hands full, you made sure of that!"

"Well well. There's really only one way... only one way to say this, Jessie. One way and that's to come right out with it. Directly. Yes."

"What the hell are you talking about?" Jessie asked, and saw Dubois suck in a breath and hold it, as if waiting for a bomb to go off.

"Jessie, you aren't the origi*nal*. Not the first Jessie. No. You're... well, you *are* the Doppelgänger. Yes. Hmmm-huh. *You* are."

CHAPTER 67

"Sheriff. Long time no see."

Rash didn't know how to respond to the man standing before him. His former boss and friend, Declan was a man whose absence Jim had learned to accept. For years the story had sat wrong with Rash, the idea that when hit by the train, there had been nothing left of Declan O'Rourke, not even the tiniest scrap of flesh or bone. Now he understood why.

"Maybe you can help me understand this, Declan. Where've you been? I mean, who the hell did we bury in your plot at Morningrise?"

"Jim. Do you really want the answer to that?"

"Damned right I do. And I want to know why the hell you're here now, with all these people."

"Don't worry yourself thinking about whys and wherefores, Jim. The simple truth of it is, I'm here now to help fix a world that's been dead and rotting on the cosmic vine for decades. You find an injured dog on the side of the road, do you pass it by or stop and help it?"

"You mean like putting a round in its head to ease its suffering?"

"I don't know. Is that what you'd do?"

"Stop listening to this bullshit, Jim," Linda cut in, "That's not Declan."

"I've been away too long, but yeah, now I remember how paranoid your kind are. I was one of the first to be taken from Knight's Side. I've been helping replace people almost ever since. Most of the town's our's now."

"The missing people? Then what, these are all Doppelgängers?" Linda asked, afraid from having experienced the malevolence of her own Double and assuming the predilection was a trait of the species. Then:

'Jesus,' she thought, 'is that what we're talking about here? A new species?'

"Declan, how can you be involved in any of this… this nonsense."

"C'mon Jim. Let go of this innate need to call anything you don't understand 'nonsense.' You have to admit, anyone who considers the Big Tree's menu world-class cuisine must have a pretty limited worldview. Nonsense is what people always called the strange shit we knew was here, dormant but festering. The 'Weird,' Jim. Do you remember? That's how I thought of it, back when Leviticus ran his mouth twenty-four/seven. You know what it was like having that man as a Father-in-Law? Not easy, I can tell you that."

Chase stirred in the backseat; Linda turned and saw his eyes were open. They made eye contact, and he raised a finger to his lips. His mangled arm lay across his chest at an unnatural angle, and blood spatters decorated the entirety of the uniform beneath his bomber.

"Yeah? Well boo hoo. Now cut the shit and get out of our way, Declan or… whoever the hell you are. We have ta get Chase to a doctor."

"Afraid I can't do that, Jim. The door's about to open, we wouldn't want you all to miss the party."

Rash turned to Linda, "You're right. That ain't Dec. He'd never risk the life of an officer, let alone his brother-in-law."

"Jim, ya ain't listening to me. None of this is going to matter in five minutes."

While the Sheriff argued, Linda took stock of the dozens of faces around them. She recognized many of them, but even those were different somehow. They all looked hungry for whatever was about to happen.

All around them the rain had been steadily increasing again, runoff pooling in the drainage ditches at the side of the road, the sewer systems clogging, repelling the water back up into the trees that surrounded them, where it soaked the ground and in turn began to flood the road. Linda looked from the peoples' faces to their feet, saw the water had risen to cover their ankles. Behind them too, where the road should stretch back to the horizon, there was nothing but the world as it was reflected in that water. She could see inverted images of the sky, the trees, their crowns touching the water, their trunks reaching into the clouds, disappearing into the storm that continued to rage, the sound of hammering rain perforating the conversation to her left.

"Why?" Rash asked.

"Well Jim, the truth is, you people had your chance. Meanwhile, Widdershins is tied up in this fog of a reality, half-formed bits and pieces of places, things, people. It's depressing, you know? You have so much and waste it. We have so little, and see what we've done? We can organize in a way you can't. We don't hate, we don't kill."

"You seem to hate us."

"Declan? What the hell's happening here?" Chase said, sitting up, tears in his eyes at the sight of his former brother-in-law. Chase had loved this man; in some ways, Declan had served as a surrogate father to Chase, and when he'd disappeared, the loss had taken a lot from him. Chase remembered Declan's eyes, so patient and wise. He remembered how they had leaked salty tears when Nancy had first been diagnosed with Lymphoma, how wide with surprise they had grown when the chemo actually worked. The eyes on the man before him were not the same. Instead, they were jet black; pupil-less.

"Chase Montgomery! Good to see you, son. How the hell are ya?"

"Not too good, Dec. What the hell's going on here? How are you… alive?"

"Chase, that ain't Declan O'Rourke," Rash said.

"Long story me boyo, and we don't have time for that now, as the song goes."

Chase smiled at the partial quote and remembered fondly that Declan's favorite band was Talking Heads.

"Nancy'll be so happy to see you."

"Chase…" Rash intoned his name as a warning.

"She's doing really good. Cancer never came back; her hair's normal now, too."

"Chase! Gotdamnit! That's not your brother-in-law!" Rash screamed.

"Chase, I need your help, okay buddy?" Declan, even keel.

The Sheriff stepped from the cruiser, pulled his revolver from his hip.

"Stop talkin'!"

Declan O'Rourke continued to ignore the Sheriff, even as Rash leveled the revolver at him.

"Jim, hold on…" Linda said, trying to curb the escalation. Chase saw Rash's gun, attempted to sit up further to grab the door handle. Careful not to touch his bad arm, Linda caught him by his other one.

"Jim, what're you doing?"

"Chase…" Declan practically cooed, smoothing these new wrinkles in reality with the calm, friendly demeanor that had defined him in life.

"Tired of this shit. Only one way to fix it, kill all of you… you… whatever the hell you are."

"JIM!"

Declan's calm facade broke. His face became one sharp leer as he took two quick steps toward Rash, arms outstretched to attack. Rash's reaction was instant: the Sheriff fired at point-blank range, and the bullet hit Declan square in the chest. There was a single moment of agony that appeared on his face, and then O'Rourke dropped face-first into the water that was now up to their knees. He disappeared with a splash and did not resurface.

"No!" Chase screamed and shrugged Linda's grip from his good arm, kicked the door to the truck open and dove into the water after Declan.

"Chase! Jim, you asshole! What have you done?"

Hysterical, Linda leaped from the truck and began splashing through the water, falling onto her knees, her arms launching great swathes of water in her wake as she tried to locate Chase.

No dice; he was gone.

CHAPTER 68

"I… I don't understand."

"I wouldn't imagine you could. No. Jessie, let me tell you a story. A story. Yes. I knew your father. He was a good man… a good man who wanted the best for his son, yes. His son… who was sick. Yes. I convinced your father to bring his son to me… yes, convinced him to bring me his son. When he did… when he did, together we brought the boy… we brought him to Widdershins. Widdershins, yes, where that boy has lived… he's lived a life that would not have been possible… would never have been poss*ible* if he'd stayed in Deosil. No. Not possible."

"I don't understand. How did my father know about Widdershins?"

"Here. Yes. Look… look at this," Cruchetti rifled through the stack of papers before him and produced an old photograph taped to a sheet of notebook paper. He held it out to Jessie, who took it with no hesitation. In the picture was the face he had known all his life through photographs.

"That's you," Jessie said, recognizing the other faces in the picture, "And… Richard. Who's the fourth man?"

"James Barrie, the novelist."

"James Barrie? Like, Peter Pan?"

The Architect nodded.

"Richard… he introduced me to James. Yes. And James, in turn… he introduced me to your father."

"My father couldn't have. How? He wasn't that old. No one's that old."

"Except for those who know about Widdershins. Those who kill their Doubles. Like your father," Dubois said, and Jessie's head reeled.

"I liked your father… liked him very much. Yes. I liked Nicholas *and* his brothers, the original 'Lost Boys.' Their fates… their fates were regrettable. Richard's too. Yes. Surely regrettable. But this mirror business… this is really just the most delicate thing, you see?"

"I thought you hadn't killed anybody," Cassie said.

"Semantics. *I* haven't. No."

"Don't worry, the fat man died quickly," Jessie's Cast said, smiling.

"Can we get back to my father, please? I don't understand."

"Your father was born in 1903 as Nicholas Llewelyn Davies, the youngest of five brothers," Dubois cut in, "They were Barrie's wards and his inspiration. But when we began to unearth the truth, about Barrie's novel, things eventually got out of hand. Nicholas was the last to survive. In 1960 he killed his Doppelgänger; twenty years later he faked his death and moved to America, changing his name to Nico Roberts. Later, he met your mother, and they were married. Two years later he was dead, for real this time."

Jessie had no idea how to process anything he was hearing.

"When a Doppelgänger is born, part of the Cast's life essence is siphoned off. But if the Cast kills the Double - or if the Double kills the Cast - the remaining version of that person will live forever, if left to natural devices. Murder is still a show stopper. That is what this is all about, realigning the boundaries. I am afraid all of Paolo's early experimentation ended up creating something of a rift and we have to clean things up a bit."

"Is that what all those people you kidnapped are doing trapped in those orbs?"

"Yes, Cassandra. An unfortunate… a regrettable necessity at this point. We're trying… trying to balance things. Again. Yes."

"You wouldn't have to do any of this if you had just listened to my grandmother."

"Your Great-Grandmother… bisabuela… she considered anything… *any*thing outside of a campfire and pissing on leaves… evil. Yes. She did."

"Listen to you. Earlier tonight, your boyfriend here begged us to protect him from the big bad Architect."

"Things changed the moment I looked into Paolo's eyes again."

"Whatever. I'm sure you'll flip flop on him again when it comes time for him to answer for his crimes."

"Progress is not a crime."

"Progress? Is that what you call seducing my father into stealing our people's secrets? Secrets no Westerner should have?" Cassie's words dripped with venom.

"Listen to yourself. Do you even know what you are saying, or are you just regurgitating everything Encarnación told you? Did you ever stop to think that for as powerful and well-meaning as your great-grandmother was, she simply could not overcome her crippling fear of the future? News-flash: People do not like change. It scares them. Brujas are no different."

"Widdershins is a sacred place you've corrupted with

ideas of profit and dominance."

"Corrupted? Hmmm? Have you… have you ever wondered about our Prime Mover? Hmmm? Do you think… do you believe this world is sup*posed* to have plateaued? Or should it… should it continue to evolve, until we accomplish our cosmic goal? Yes? Maybe?"

"Some things were not meant to be known."

"Poppycock," Dubois said loudly, frustration setting in.

"So what? We're all supposed to just let you switch our world with Widdershins? Give everyone a Doppelgänger to replace them?"

Cruchetti burst out laughing.

"Cuthbert, what have you… what have you told people to make them think… to make them think I have such grand designs? No, Cassie, I don't… I don't want to rule the world. No. I simply want to change it. Yes. Change it; bring The Hub… yes, bring The Hub to its *full* potential."

"Points of departure and arrival across the entire globe," Dubois cut in again, clearly growing tired of his lover's difficulty expressing himself, "And to do that, we need a main knot where the two worlds are intertwined. There's already one at your tribal grounds. Knight's Side will serve as the second leg, and eventually…"

"I have… I have *my* sights set. Set on Scotland. Yes."

"Scotland?" Dubois asked, "Well, that is not until the next phase of development."

"And what about your foot soldiers? What about The Pall? Grandmother had someone stationed in their organization for the better part of a decade. They think you're helping them bring in a complete apocalyptic scenario."

"My dear, a fifth of the way into this new century and everyone is preoccupied with the Apocalypse. The Pall is not an issue. Most of them want what this lad wants - a place to belong and people to care about him. This is why they will come around. Anyone who does not, well, they may need to be… convinced."

"What about the people in those glass prisons?"

"They… those people are only restrained… they're only in the Double V's because things aren't finished. They're not… complete. No. Not finished, and I didn't want to have… I didn't want people killing their friends and neighbors. I didn't want panic. No."

"Once all this is situated," Cuthbert said, slipping his hand into Cruchetti's, "no one will even remember any of this. No one is even going to know the bloody difference in five years, whether they are from here or there. For Christ's sake, Jessie, you didn't even know what you are."

"He didn't have a choice! That's the point."

"No, the point is Encarnación raised you as a self-right-eous brat indoctrinated with her prejudices, and as heir to her empire, she made sure you would die before bringing the tribe into the twenty-first century. There is that nasty little word again: Change. Booooo!"

"My grandmother knew that if balance ever shifted in the Universe, everything would come apart."

"Cassandra, the balance… the balance has already… it's shifted. Look at the world; the world… it's practically doubled over in its… in its death grips. Yes. What I'm proposing… what I want is to *fix* all that. I don't understand why you can't see that. No. Why you are so blinded by your great-grandmother's indoctrinations, hmmm-hmm?"

"Okay. Maybe you *are* right. Maybe you do just want to fix things. That's fine. That's what *you* want. What I want? What I want is to kill you."

"Alright. Alright then, little girl. Yes. So much like her father, isn't she Cuthbert? Yes. So much."

"Oh yes."

"Don't say that."

"Why not? Why not… say it when it's *true*. True! You want to kill me? Hmmm? You want… to kill me? Then… go ahead and try. Yes. Go ahead."

Cassie smiled, raising her arms to show she had freed herself from her restraints.

"Gladly."

CHAPTER 69

Kim had all but given up hope when the sound of a distant explosion stirred her. She opened her eyes, and there was Patagonia, lumbering toward the small, glass prison that held her.

"Patty! Patty, over here! I knew you'd come back for me!"

"Everything's on fire, Kim! I'm scared!"

"Don't be scared. Did you find Jessie? Where is he?"

"I did! I did! And I found Cassie too! Only she doesn't like me."

"Shit," Kim said, realizing a reunion with Cassie might very well prove to be fatal to both of them. She would have to be careful; too many people wanted her dead."

"You want me to try and break the glass?"

"Yeah. Quickly, Patty!"

"Okay. Hold on."

Patty picked the orb up off the shelf and whipped it against the ground. The impact was so loud Patty covered her eyes with her right arm; when she looked again, the orb had grown to full-size. Inside, Kim wretched.

"Oh god, that was awful…"

"Sorry," Patagonia said, turning away in shame.

"No! Patty, do whatever you have to! Just get me out of here!"

Patty stepped into her next blow, delivering a force wave to the glass that sent it rolling backward. Inside, Kim flopped and floundered as she turned end over end, the loud sound of thick glass on wood floors echoing like a bowling ball down a gutter.

"Oh gawd…"

"Sorry, Kim."

"Here, try pushing me against the wall, so I don't roll again."

Patty did as asked, and this time when she hit the orb, the combined force of her attack and the immovable resilience of the wall sent a series of large cracks across its sparkling circumference.

"Hit it again! Hit it again!"

Patty began to pound on Kim's prison, each blow carrying the momentum of the last, her spiked fists digging into the glass, widening the cracks until it was nothing but spiderwebs piled atop one another.

"That's it, Patty! Just a few more hits!"

Patty reared back and unleashed another massive blow. The prison exploded, sending glass in all directions, hundreds of pieces raining across Kim's arms and face, catching in her hair and clothes. When the cacophony settled, Kim stepped free, only to see that a shard of glass the size of a window had impaled Patty through her midsection and another, smaller one protruded from the side of her neck.

"Patty!"

Kim kneeled at her sister's side, trying to find a way to remove the glass. Blood was everywhere, frothing and pumping from the wounds, both massive, the one in Patty's neck having no doubt pierced a major artery. Kim wanted to remove it, but she knew if she did, she might kill her sister. They needed time - the one thing they didn't have.

"Kim, I don't feel so good. I think… I think… I'm gonna go to sleep now."

"No! Patagonia, you stay with me, you hear?"

"Everything feels like its turning inside out…"

Kim had an idea.

"Patty, hold on."

"What are you doing?"

Kim thought about the wounds she'd had when she'd first been captured and placed inside the prison; nothing major, but her fight with the Shape in Freighter's home had left her pretty badly bruised, dozens of shallows cuts covering her arms, hands, etc. And looking at herself now, only a few short hours later, Kim realized all those wounds had healed. If she could get Patty inside another one of the Vetusta Vitriums, Kim might just save her sister's life.

Cassie tossed the handcuffs to the floor before the Architect and smiled.

"I so can*not* wait to kill you two!"

Cassie charged Cruchetti, but before she could engage him, Jessie's Doppelgänger threw himself across the path between them, catching Cassie mid-run with a collision that sent them both tumbling to the floor. An instant later, they were locked in vicious combat, pummeling one another with their fists.

"Jessie! My blade!" Cassie ordered, but Jessie didn't move. He was paralyzed by the situation. If he helped Cassie, she would kill everyone in the room, and he might never find Kim or his mom again. If he didn't help her, Cassie might die.

As luck would have it, fate intervened at that exact moment when the ceiling came down on top of everyone in the room.

The fire had finally done its damage.

All around Gallows Hill, the houses that had once comprised the points on a higher dimensional dodecagon crumbled, the flames finally eating through their structures. And because all those houses were linked, the destruction compounded exponentially. As Jessie's house, and Kim's house, and Freighter's house all fell in on themselves, finally too, Dubois' mansion let out an enormous, unearthly groan and buckled inward. The flames shot through the dozens of conjoined arteries the buildings shared until the resulting fireball was hurled down that final corridor and directly into the room at the heart of the mansion. The room marked '13.'

Chase dove headfirst into the dark water, eyes wide open, the cold a shot to the chest that rivaled the blow that had broken his shoulder. The pain lit his nervous system like an electrical charge, waked him from his stupor to a world of nonsense and ghosts. He was off the map but had to face Declan no matter what.

With his good arm, Chase paddled downward, burrowing through the cold depths, the weight of the water unnatural enough to make him wonder if it was water at all, or the same liquid-like, magical glass he'd seen five years ago...

... He touched the glass, and it rippled like the water in a pond...

Regardless of the liquid's origin or physical make-up, the added friction wracked his shoulder with fresh torture. But Chase continued downward, into a bottomless depth that defied all logic. Where had the street gone? The grass? The trees?

Down. Down. Down he went.

Something shimmered before him, a fragmented rectangle, a nonsensical apparition haunted by a vague sense of the familiar. A door, the outline behind which, light shone through. His lungs on the verge of exploding with his last, stale breath, Chase kicked his way through the portal hoping for respite. The world spiraled once, and then black became the brightest of lights and Chase expelled his breath and immediately drew another. He didn't choke; the water was gone.

He hit the floor on two feet, barely able to salvage his balance until, magically, Chase realized his pain was gone, his shoulder... mended?

"You're inside the body of your Double. Don't get too used to it - all that damage is still going to have to be taken care of when you go back. For the next few minutes though, you'll be right as rain."

Declan O'Rourke stood just the way Chase remembered him: smiling, his arms folded across his chest.

"Declan?"

This was not the same Declan that Jim had shot in the chest a few moments before.

"So good to see you, boyo."

The two men cleared their distance and met in a boisterous hug.

"I know you have questions, but we don't have time for explanations. Chase, you have to stop what's about to happen."

"Give me something, man. I mean, we're way off the map here."

"Everything your father used to talk about, all of it is real. I know that's probably hard for you to accept, but it's the truth, sure as I'm standing here talking to you now."

"After the last couple of days? I'm buying whatever you're selling. But Declan, what do I tell Linda?"

"The day of my accident, they took me. Cruchetti used me as a guinea pig. Hopefully, one day we'll be able to raise a glass, and I'll tell you the entire story. For now, though, I need you to save my town."

"How?"

"There's a wall Cruchetti had put up around Knight's Side. It's invisible, but not without physical properties."

Chase thought about Reggie Lark and the rich guy he'd said had hired them to bury those boxes. Had Dubois been in on this all along?

"I don't understand. A wall? For what?"

"With all the water from the storm collecting inside these walls, the barrier has turned the entire area surrounding Knight's Side and Gallows Hill into one giant mirror; a kind of reflecting pool. Once it's complete, our town will switch places with *their* town."

"Whose town, Dec?"

"Some nasty characters that call themselves The Pall. Doubles angry at living on their side of the glass."

"Their side?" A stunted understanding dawned on Chase, and for the first time, he surveyed his surroundings. At first, all he saw was the limitations of the room, then he realized they weren't in a room at all, or at least not a complete one. It looked like a bombed out building, three walls standing, the other absent, and in the distance, lightning illuminated their surroundings like staccato images on a website's carousel. A building here, some trees there. A house, a street light, and a bit of avenue. Things he recognized and some he did not, robbed of their context, singular and seemingly unconnected.

"Places don't switch the same as people. Widdershins is littered with the bits of rooms, streets, locations within which the Doubles of a few hundred people were activated. If Cruchetti is successful, the storm itself will transmute the rest, fill in all the gaps. You'll be left with a town that looks the same, like the guy you just spoke to who had my face. But it won't be Knight's Side anymore than he was me."

"And how the hell do I stop that?"

"You break that barrier, Chase. That's what you do. But time's a'wastin'. Go, and know that I always loved you like the son I never had."

CHAPTER 71

I t happened so quickly, no one in the room had a chance to prepare or react. The wall with the door erupted first, exploding inward, burying everything in rubble. Meanwhile, the flames had already spread through most of the structure, and because Cruchetti had built Gallows Hill utilizing multiple dimensions, the fire traveled not only along physical pathways, but through more existential avenues as well. Thus, by the time the door came down, the Architect's office was surrounded by flames.

Engulfed in a wave of panic and confusion, Kim arrived just in time to follow the destruction into the room. The debris had knocked Cassie unconscious, and as she entered, the first thing Kim saw was the two Jessies locked in combat. Luckily, the blood stains on the Cruchetti's Jessie made it easy to tell the two apart.

Bounding over piles of rubble, Kim collided with her target, catching Jessie Two unaware and knocking the wind from him as they hit the ground.

"I'll kill you!" he choked, black tears staining his cheeks as Kim beat him into a fugue state, her frustration and fear lending her a frenzied strength unlike anything she'd ever experienced before. A final blow to the back of her enemy's head stunned him into silence; Kim let Jessie fall to the floor and turned her strength on the rubble that lay atop the boy she loved, too dazed to help himself.

"Kim…" Jessie choked, his face covered with bruises and dirt, "You came back."

"I wouldn't leave you for the world."

"I love you."

"I love you, too. Now, we gotta get out of here."

She grabbed him by the forearm and with one clean lurch, pulled Jessie to his feet and toward the mangled doorway, the only visible egress from what was otherwise a room now choked with smoke.

They were almost out when, inches from escape, something pulled them hard in the other direction, and the reverse momentum brought them both to the floor. From there, the flames surrounded them quickly, and as Kim scanned for another way out, she saw a sludge-black figure now stood between them and the door.

It was the other Jessie again. He'd shed his flesh in favor of a nice, shiny suit of Shadow Skin.

"Not so fast bitch," he said, his vocal cords a chorus of down-tuned hatred, "We have unfinished business."

No sooner had Chase disappeared from sight than Linda followed him into the water. Whatever door he'd been granted access to, however, was denied to her. The Sheriff watched as she stalked back and forth, swinging great fistfuls of water from left to right, crying and screaming. Rash couldn't take his eyes from the reflections on that water; inversions of the world around them, the trees and road and sky, everything slipping through the surface layer. Reality became a massive decal slowly pulled from the wax paper backing that conveyed it.

The world around them stuttered as a new world slipped over the top of it, an unbearable affront that pushed the Sheriff's terror into the red. His shooting became frenzied. He emptied his revolver, then leaned into the cruiser for his shotgun, removing it from the safety mount between the front seats just in time to blow a hole in a person he would have recognized as Franklin Keith only yesterday. Today though, it wasn't Franklin Keith. Rash had to keep telling himself that.

Before she even realized what was happening, the other Jessie's left arm shot out and ensnared Kim's face in a thick, black web that sent the world of flame and smoke around her spiraling away. In its place came a dark tide; an ocean of nothing. It washed over her and left only a bottomless abyss, like sleep but without the unconsciousness. No light, no sound, no smell, nothing but void in this new space she occupied.

Kim screamed into this abyss, a silent, airless rattle that tapered off unheard, even by her own ears. She fought and kicked, swung her arms violently in all directions but never made contact with her target. She was alone and extinguished, except for a distant awareness of her own form. The idea that the Doppelgänger had somehow transported her to another place entirely stole over her; perhaps some back alley world Cruchetti had discovered in the armpit of the Universe. This idea inspired another burst of fight, but before long fatigue stole over her and with hope draining away, Kim succumbed.

Almost defeated, she had one gambit left. Kim didn't know what would happen if she released Patty from the sphere that was currently sustaining her life, but she really didn't have any other choice. There was a chance it might kill her. But after as panic forced her to weigh her sister's life against Jessie's, Kim stopped swinging and ran her hands down her body until she located the tiny glass orb containing Patty.

"I'm sorry," she said, and whipped the orb at the ground, hoping it would be enough to shatter it.

CHAPTER 72

When the Sheriff began to shoot, Linda's panic broke like a fever. Chase was gone, the water continued to rise, and an army of Doppelgängers descended on them from all sides. She heard Rash's revolver click empty three times and then saw him go to the truck. As he pulled the shotgun free and turned to fire, lightning flashed across the sky and for the first time Linda saw how the burning image of light was duplicated when it reflected against something no more than a quarter mile to the West.

"What the hell was that?"

"Never mind the weather! Re-load this for me!"

Rash tossed her the revolver and Linda just barely caught it.

"Bullets in the truck," he called, pumping the beast again and blowing a hole in someone who looked like his receptionist Betty, imitation flesh melted by gunpowder and hot lead.

Linda barely had a chance to load the gun before she had to use it to break up an advancing throng of Doubles. One.

Two. Three people exploded into liquid pitch right in front of her, the gun's hammer sticking on the fourth. Before she could fix it, Chase burst through the water to her right, his good arm flailing wildly for purchase on something, anything.

"Sheriff!" she screamed and tossed the gun at Rash, who caught it but dropped the shotgun to do so. SPLASH the weapon went, now out of service for the remainder of the night.

Linda high-kneed it to Chase, pulled him from the water and dragged him gasping to a large stone several feet to the right of where the road used to be.

"Where the hell were you?"

"Get me to the truck. NOW! I have to… I have to…"

"Calm down, I got you," Linda reassured him. Mustering all her strength, she hoisted Chase onto her shoulder and carried him to the cruiser. Behind them, Rash's shots slowed; he was picking his targets now, his panic ebbing as his wartime training finally kicked in.

"Here," she opened the back door for Chase, but he fought her attempts to help him inside.

"What the hell are you doing?"

"It's a wall! Linda, the men on the side of the road, the storm… they're going to switch the whole town!"

Another flash of lightning tore the night in half. Linda's eyes were quick, caught the strange doubling effect again in the distance. And that's when she understood. She remembered the anonymous gift that Cuthbert had received recently: a scale model of the entire town displayed beneath a glass dome. He'd told her it was a dedication, but now Linda understood she'd been a fool to ever trust the bastard in the first place. The model wasn't a gift, it was a diagram; a schematic of how, using nothing more than rain and an invisible border, Cruchetti had made the world's biggest piece of Tenorio Glass, a virtual black hole set to swallow the entire town.

Linda knew what she had to do.

She smacked Chase on his bad arm, and the pain brought him to his knees. Stepping over him, Linda took her position in the driver's seat.

"What are you doing?"

"I love you, Chase Montgomery!" Linda screamed as she slammed the door of the truck.

"Linda! Wait!"

Keys still in the ignition, Linda revved the engine and popped the cruiser into drive. The gears slipped at first, and the tires spun, showering Rash and Chase with water. But then the submerged tires caught traction and sent the truck speeding through a nearby group of insurgents. The bodies ricocheted off the truck, the front end bucking once as she hit higher ground and came out of the water, cleaving through grass and small trees, catching the turnpike at forty, revving it still, fifty, sixty, seventy-five. At Seventy-seven miles per hour, Linda Evans drove the cruiser straight into the invisible wall. There was an explosion, a burst of Halloween orange and cacophonous disaster as the meta-physical superstructure succumbed to the feedback of Magick turned in on itself.

"Linda!" Chase screamed at the top of his lungs, clawing desperately to stand but failing. He fell to his knees, the water rushing from around him as the town drained, the backward reflection that had almost entirely taken the place of the world around them evaporating like smoke, leaving nothing but a barren haze. Chase watched as the cloud dissi-pated, waited to see if like in the movies, the hero would come walking from the wreckage.

She did not.

J essie would later describe what he saw when he opened his eyes as a terrifying hiccup in reality, something he would long maintain no human was supposed to see. A corridor sped by him, obliterating the room as it went. Reality bent and something overtook him, a sensation that began with a fierce tickle in the back of his throat. The last thing he saw before the world became one giant, shining room of mirrors was the encroaching front grill of a large truck and a mangled perversion he immediately recognized as Kim's sister Patty.

T he hiccup ended, and Jessie found himself laying next to Kim, both on soft grass far from Dubois's mansion. "Where?"

"It's over," an older man in a Sheriff's jacket said. It was the man Jessie had seen in his vision, just before meeting the Architect. He offered Jessie a hand, and Jessie accepted.

Once vertical, Jessie saw Kim was already up. He stood and ran to her, and the two embraced fiercely.

"Patty?" Jessie asked, and immediately regretted doing so when Kim began to cry. He hugged her tighter, and whispered in Kim's ear, "I'm so sorry."

"Don't be. It... It's not your fault. You're... Jessie, you're the only good thing that's happened to me in a long time. I can take the bad, as long as it's with you. I love you."

"I think I've loved you from the moment I met you. Kim..." Jessie's seriousness turned to laughter, and Kim looked at him with mock outrage.

Smiling, she threw a flirty elbow at him.

"What's so funny?"

"Don't worry - they're contacts."

A smile cracked Kim's face. They embraced, then turned their attention to the scene around them.

And what a scene it was.

Dark smoke choked the sky. The rain had stopped, but the fires still burned. Had all the places inside Dubois's mansion been destroyed? What about Jessie's house, or the entire town of Gallows Hill for that matter? As the first cracks of dawn broke the stormy sky, Jessie found himself hoping none of it had survived.

There were several other people around them, but none who actually seemed like people at all. Jessie was too exhausted to be concerned. Besides, they were off in the distance, receding, fog rolling in reverse back into the lake from which it had lifted. They were shadows, spirits. Ghosts. The ghosts of other people's lives.

No mom, no sister, no WJ, no home, no town; they were all ghosts now, too. Even Cassie, it seemed, had perished in whatever catastrophe had brought the confrontation between worlds to an end.

Jessie kissed Kim. Their hands intertwined; fingertips shared secrets across palms that, through the commingling of sweat, renewed their dedication to one another. They had killed their Casts, and according to lore, could never die a natural death. But they were alone; lost children, eternal, the fitting inheritance passed down from J.M. Barrie to Jessie's father, to him.

CHAPTER 73

Sheriff Rash stood perfectly still, cataloging the many ways reality had betrayed him. Not just reality, but everyone who had ever taught him *about* reality. Rash found himself at a crossroads. He'd worked long and hard to develop the crusty, unapproachable exterior that shielded the scared kid who'd been thrown into the jungles and fought his way out stained by the blood of his buddies. Those shields were what had helped him through the war and every day since, and if they were going to fall apart now, well, Rash knew he was in some damn serious trouble.

The Sheriff thought about how Declan - the real Declan - had considered it his duty to watch over the neighboring town of Gallows Hill, and shamefully juxtaposed that ideal with his own approach to the job. The first thing Jim had done when he replaced Declan was to say to hell with that place. Jim Rash had always told himself it was his staunch pragmatism that had made that decision, but now he was forced to see his actions for what they truly were.

Fear.

Wallowing in the undeniable revelation of his own

cowardice, Rash lowered his head and tried to imagine what came next. He didn't have any answers, which was fine, because it was only a moment before Chase Montgomery began to scream.

~

It wasn't the pain that finally shattered Chase Montgomery, it was the image of the woman he loved slamming into an invisible barrier at top speed, instantly incinerated in the resulting metaphysical explosion. Unable to prevent this tragedy, unable to do anything at all in his present condition, all Chase could do was scream.

"Chase!" Unsure, Sheriff Rash did the only thing he could think. He did what he'd done to more than one wounded buddy in the war, the only way to quiet them so the medic could patch them up with crazy glue and gauze: Jim hauled off and punched his Deputy as hard as he could. It hurt like hell, and would only add to Chase's injuries, but once he fell backward into unconsciousness, the silence that followed was the loudest thing Rash had ever heard. In its grip, the kids helped him load Chase into the cruiser, and they took off at top speed, Rash praying to a god he didn't believe in that they would be able to make it to Woodsville's hospital in time.

"What happened here?" Jessie asked, his voice brittle over the sound of the cruiser's tires on the wet blacktop.

"Don't exactly know. What happened to you two?"

"I don't know," Jessie answered, haunted. He and Kim sat sideways in the passenger seat, Jessie in her lap, her arms around him, clasped before his heart.

They drove in silence, until they saw the first sign for Woodsville, and the Sheriff sighed in relief. When they hit the exit to Route 2, Woodsville General Hospital's outline in the distance, he spoke.

"One question. Dubois's house?"

"I don't know. There were flames. An explosion. I think… I think everyone but us is dead."

There was a pause. Jessie held Kim's hand and stared out the window as they approached the emergency entrance.

The Sheriff got out and spoke to the two paramedics that rushed from inside with a stretcher and all the fixings. They unloaded Chase from the cruiser and wheeled him inside. The Sheriff watched them go, the automatic doors whooshing closed behind the excitement. He turned back to Kim and Jessie.

"You're her sister, right? That little girl."

"Yeah."

"What about you, kid?"

"Jessie Roberts."

"You'n your mom moved into the old Tenorio place last week, didn'tja?

Jessie's eyes popped as a new horror descended on him.

"My mom! My mom and her boyfriend WJ, they're missing."

"Missing? How long?"

"I don't know, but Cruchetti said he had them somewhere, he said…"

"Cruchetti? As in Paolo Cruchetti?"

"Yeah. It was him. Cruchetti and Dubois and… oh my god."

"Okay, look. How about you kids tell me everything that happened and I'll make it my first order of business to find your mom and her friend, okay?"

"But we need help! We need…"

"Kid, I am the help. I'm the Sheriff."

EPILOGUE 1

THE ARCHITECT

Before he opened his eyes, he made sure the sounds had stopped. The sounds he would hear for the rest of his life, his long, interminable life. When he was confident the Thing that had once been Patagonia Barker was no longer there, he braced himself and took in the state of the room.

It was a nightmare.

Everything was burned. The fire had left nothing but destruction in its wake. He knew without having to venture any further that the entire mansion and most likely all of Gallows Hill would similarly lay in ashes. A life's work undone. But that wasn't the worst of it.

Previously unimaginable amounts of blood and gore saturated every surface in sight. The splintered wood of cross beams and exposed cement foundation were soaked in thick chunks of flesh, hair, and streams of what looked like entrails. A thick, black ichor nested in clumps along what was left of the walls - really just pockets of drywall and shattered metal joists. Similar atrocities formed insanely intricate geometric patterns that ran back and forth across the floor. The word FOREVER had been scrawled in dark brown blood across the face of his table, which somehow still stood, the only thing in the room besides himself that remained intact. The skin from the face of his lover lay draped across Paolo Cruchetti's lap, a message well received in blood.

Why had she left him alive? She was, after all, right to hate him. Patty and her sister had both been experiments, the eggs cracked to make something new, to bring both worlds together instead of tearing them apart. It had all worked so well at first, only to backfire at the penultimate moment. He'd made his monsters, and his monsters had turned around and destroyed him.

Maybe it was time to make new monsters.

From the top drawer of the table, the Architect retrieved a small glass mirror. It looked like a woman's compact. Beginning with a deep breath, he gripped the gray metal frame with both hands and stretched it as though it were made of putty, elongating it to either side until it was a little wider than he was. He turned it on its side, and the glass quaked once and re-solidified into the shape of a door. A blood-red handle slid through the glass's black surface; when the ripples on the obsidian face ceased, he grasped the handle and pulled. The portal opened, and a stairway unrolled before him. It lead down.

Sixteen steps to the bottom. A small pile of sawdust sat in the center of a forest of mirrors. To the left lay Arthur Tenorio's body, the throat tore out, the eyes wide open, a testament to the eternal shock that had ushered him from this world. The Architect shrugged and kicked the corpse once before turning toward the stairway on the other side of the mirrors. Slowly he climbed, a single exposed bulb illuminating the door at the top, his destination. When the Architect reached that door, he rapped lightly on its surface. After a moment it opened.

"Hello," he said to WJ.

"Uh, hello?"

"Please… please excuse the intrusion. Yes. But I'm afraid… I'm afraid I have some… I have some terrible news. Yes. Terrible."

A sharp thwack followed by a stifled gurgle interrupted the exchange. WJ stepped briefly away from the door, and the Architect slid past him into a kitchen decorated in blood. What he saw made him start, but only for a moment.

On the floor before him, Talia Roberts knelt over the body of her Doppelgänger; her left hand wrapped around the Double's throat, while the right bludgeoned Its head with a steak tenderizing mallet. The course-cut face of the implement was clotted with the malleable black putty that had once composed the top of the Doppelgänger's head. Midswing, Talia looked up at them and smiled an uncomfortable, guilty smile.

"Hee..llp…" the dying clone choked, only to receive one final blow that splattered what was left of Its face across the tile. Victorious, Talia stood and regarded the man before her.

"Professor… my dear Professor Roberts. Yes. You… you are in a pocket dimension. Something we call a Vetusta Vitrium - a Double V. Yes. Hmmm. A place made to trap… to trap or protect. Yes."

"And which are we?" Talia asked.

The Architect's unease showed in his delayed response. Still, there was no doubt that he held all the cards.

"You… you were in danger. Yes. You were. Wendall was, at any rate. Yes. Very much so. And that… that is why I kept him here while we… while we sorted things out. Yes. Much the same as you are… sorting things out. Hmmm?"

"And you?"

"Pardon? Oh! Apologies, I've just… I've been through something of a trauma myself. Yes. Horrible, nasty business. Horrible. I… I am Paolo Cruchetti. Yes. The Architect. And I have come… I am here both to retrieve you, yes, and to offer my condolences."

"Condolences?" Talia stood, kitchen hammer still in hand. He knew he had her.

"Yes. Please. Please, if you would both… if you would follow me."

Cruchetti led them at an intentional distance through a new doorway and down the corridor. When they emerged from the out of place foyer, they did so into the smoking rubble of his former office. And it was there that Talia saw the unthinkable.

"Oh my god no. Jessie! NO!"

Talia ran to the corpse of her son's Doppelgänger, in reality his Cast, oblivious to the distinction from her own flesh and blood. She howled as she pulled her son's pulped head from where it had partially melted to the floor. The Architect winced at the sound of her grief, but his own pain lessened as he passed it first to Talia and then to WJ, who attempted to console Talia but fell backward when she thrashed at him angrily, screamed terrible things to his face. Shaken by the sight of Jessie's corpse and Talia's pain, when WJ regained his composure, he stood next to the Architect and watched the woman he loved convulse with primordial grief.

"How did this happen? Who… who could do this?"

"That is… that is exactly what I intend to show you. Yes."

EPILOGUE 2

FRIENDS

When Cassie opened her eyes, she had no idea where she was. For a moment, she thought she might be dead, and that her years of disbelief in an afterlife had been wrong.

Then she saw who was sitting across from her, and Cassie understood how things had played out.

"Hi, Cassie."

"Patty, you saved me. I was horrible to you, but still, you saved me."

"Yeah. I didn't want you to get killed. Too many people get killed, so I saved you and now, can we please please please be friends? Please?"

Cassie tried to get a handle on the bloody images that ran through her head. She remembered fire, and screaming, and... horror. That was the only word for it; horror unlike anything her training had prepared her for. She thought about her abuela, about how she had seen her ripped in two, right before her eyes. Torn to shreds by... a thing not unlike Patty. This thing that looked like a monster but had the heart and mind of a little girl. A combination Cassie thought she might just be able to use to her advantage.

"Patty, do you really want to be my friend? I mean, I was pretty crappy to you."

"I know, but we used to be friends, Cassie! And you're not like my sister. She's not really my sister. And her and Jessie are afraid of me. That makes me sad."

Cassie couldn't quite process any of this at the moment, but one thing she knew for sure, in the lottery of friends, she'd hit the jackpot. Whatever it was Cruchetti had done to Patty, he'd made her a weapon to be reckoned with.

"Patty, are the bad men still alive?"

"I don't know. I don't want to think about that, okay? Can we just be friends now?"

In spite of herself, Cassie laughed at this. Her own childhood had been truncated, given over as sacrifice for the mission. Robbed of the chance to kill her father, or Kim's Doppelgänger, or Cruchetti, it occurred to Cassie that she still had a lot of work to do if she was ever going to make things right.

"Of course we can be friends, Patty. How about we make a new game together? Would you like that?"

"Oh boy would I! I'm glad you're not ascared of me, Cassie."

"Me too, Patty. Now, let's find some place to go where we can talk, okay?"

EPILOGUE 3

TERRY QUINN

Terry must have made it out of Gallows Hill just before the barrier's activation. The storm still raged as he made his first stop, somewhere far enough East of both Gallows Hill and Knight's Side to see the lights of another, bigger city in the distance. He didn't know how he knew where he was going, but he did. He was going to see Professor Grymes, a friend of Bob Freighter's and someone who could hopefully help him, help all of them.

Afraid in a way he didn't understand, Terry's thoughts were as scattered and plentiful as the raindrops that assailed him. He thought about everything he'd been through, about Freighter, about the awful things happening in Knight's Side, and tears welled in his eyes. But they were black tears now, and they shared the same substance as his flesh, an obscurity where there was once something he could rely on. Seized by the severity of his transformation, Terry wanted to cry for his lost humanity. But lightning in the distance reminded him of the illumination yet to come, and picking up speed, Terry began using the shadows and in-between places to slip over long distances in seconds, miles transformed to moments. It was incredible, and the realization of his newfound power made Terry realize that maybe, just maybe, humanity was overrated.

www.ingramcontent.com/pod-product-compliance
Lightning Source LLC
Chambersburg PA
CBHW071745110726
47908CB00006B/1702